The Best of Funny, You Don't Look Like One

Drew Hayden Taylor

THEYTUS BOOKS

© 2015 Drew Hayden Taylor

Library and Archives Canada Cataloguing in Publication

Taylor, Drew Hayden, 1962-
[Funny, you don't look like one. Selections]
The best of Funny, you don't look like one / Drew Hayden
Taylor.

ISBN 978-1-926886-33-6 (pbk.)

1. Indians of North America--Canada--Humor. I. Title.

PS8589.A885B473 2015   C814'.54   C2013-907130-X

Printed in Canada

Cover Photo: Dan David

THEYTUS BOOKS

Published by Theytus Books
www.theytus.com

We acknowledge the financial support of The Government of Canada through the Department of Canadian heritage for our publishing activities. We acknowledge the support of the Canada Council for the Arts, which last year invested $154 million to bring the arts to Canadians throughout the country. *Nous remercions le Conseil des arts du Canada de son soutien. L'an dernier, le Conseil a investi 154 millions de dollars pour mettre de l'art dans la vie des Canadiennes et des Canadiens de tout le pays.* We acknowledge the support of the Province of British Columbia through the British Columbia Arts Council

The Best of Funny, You Don't Look Like One

Funny, You Don't Look Like One: Observations from a Blue-Eyed Ojibway

Funny, You Don't Look Like ~~One~~ Two: Further Adventures of a Blue-Eyed Ojibway

Funny, You Don't Look Like One, Two, Three:
Furious Observations of a Blue-Eyed Ojibway

Funny, You Don't Look Like ~~One, Two, Three,~~ Four: Futile Observations of a Blue-Eyed Ojibway

Introduction

I'll be honest with you. Years ago when I started writing these personal slices of creative non-fiction, I had no idea what I was doing or what I was starting. Occasionally I would have an idea or a concept that I wanted to investigate or discuss, but had no real way to explore it. I mean, seriously, who sits down and says "I think I will write a small humourous essay about 1) being mixed blood 2) being Native 3) trying to understand the world around you or 4) all of the above".

At that time I was writing a little for television and beginning my playwriting career, and the thought of writing a two hour play, or convincing the producers at *The Beachcombers* to invest several hundred thousand dollars into an idea that really could be deconstructed in less than a thousand words of prose, seemed like too much effort for what I wanted to say. So one day, I thought I would approach my *topic-du-jour* from a commentary perspective. Basically an essay of sorts. Since these were topics and issues that intrigued and perplexed me, perhaps that was the best way to present them, explaining matter-of-factly why these thoughts were interesting enough to travel all the way from my brain to my finger tips, while adding some humour to spice things up.

I started sending them to venerable institutions like *The Globe and Mail, The Toronto Star, This Magazine* and others. This is where things get really weird. These newspapers and magazines bought them. Even weirder, people read them and responded, both in letters to the editor, and personally to me whenever I would bump into them. Especially one of my first sizable essays, *Pretty Like a White Boy* which dealt with being blue-eyed in a Native community. I cannot tell you how many people over the years have come up to me and said when they first read my autobiographical angst, they realized they weren't the only ones to ponder these same thoughts. Wondering who you are and where you fit in your society is a universal query, and my little kick at the can highlighted the issues for a small demographic of the Indigenous community.

By then, the flood gates had been opened and I started writing my slices of life, and the rest, as they say, is history. After I had pumped out a few dozen, I was approached by Theytus Books who suggested they would make for interesting reading in an anthology form. Four volumes later, I've lost track of all the adventures I've had, all the problems I have explored, and all the jokes I've attempted to tell. In the end, this is all storytelling. That's how I see it: From my unique perspective on the world, I just wanted to share the stories I have come across, and the ramifications they have had. In the end, not a bad way to make a living I suppose.

Here, in your hands, are what I consider the best of the four *Funny, You Don't Look Like One* series. You may agree, you may not. There may be some old favourites and some new ones you had missed (if you are a fan of my rants). Keep in mind these cover a lot of time, I started writing these in the early '90s and a lot has changed in Canada and the Aboriginal community since then. That's why I keep finding new things to write about.

Ponder. Laugh. Get angry. Question. Act. My five states of being.

Drew Hayden Taylor
Curve Lake, Ontario

FUNNY, YOU DON'T LOOK LIKE ONE:
Observations from a Blue-Eyed Ojibway

Pretty Like a White Boy

In this big, huge world, with all its billions and billions of people, it's safe to say that everybody will eventually come across personalities and individuals who will touch them in some peculiar yet poignant way. Characters that in some way represent and help define who you are. I'm no different—mine is Kermit the Frog. Not just because Natives have a long tradition of savouring frogs' legs, but because of this particular frog's music. You all may remember Kermit is quite famous for his rendition of *It's Not Easy Being Green*. I can relate. If I could sing, my song would be *It's Not Easy Having Blue Eyes in a Brown-Eyed Village*.

Yes, I'm afraid it's true. The author happens to be a card-carrying Indian. Once you get past the aforementioned eyes, the fair skin, light brown hair and noticeable lack of cheek bones, there lies the heart and spirit of an Ojibway storyteller. "Honest Injun," or as the more politically correct term may be, "Honest Aboriginal."

You see, I'm the product of a White father I never knew and an Ojibway woman who evidently couldn't run fast enough. As a kid I knew I looked a bit different but, then again, all kids are paranoid when it comes to their peers. I had a fairly happy childhood, frolicking through the bulrushes. But there were certain things that even then made me notice my unusual appearance. Whenever we played cowboys and Indians, guess who had to be the bad guy (the cowboy)?

It wasn't until I left the reserve for the big bad city that I became more aware of the role people expected me to play, and the fact that physically, I didn't fit in. Everybody seemed to have this preconceived idea of how every Indian looked and acted. One guy, on my first day of college, asked me what kind of horse I preferred. I didn't have the heart to tell him "hobby."

I've often tried to be philosophical about the whole thing. I have both White and Red blood in me. I guess that makes me pink. I am a "Pink Man." Try to imagine this: I'm walking around on any typical reserve in Canada, my head held high, proudly announcing to everyone, "I am a Pink Man." It's a good thing I ran track in school.

My pinkness is constantly being pointed out to me over and over and over again. "You don't look Indian!" "You're not Indian, are you?" "Really?!?!" I got questions like that from both White and Native people. For a while I debated having my status card tattooed on my forehead.

And like most insecure people, and especially a blue-eyed Native writer, I went through a particularly severe identity crisis at one point. In fact, I admit it, one depressing spring evening I dyed my hair black. Pitch black.

The reason for such a dramatic act, you ask? Show business. You see, for the last eight years or so, I've worked in various capacities in the performing arts, and as a result I often get calls to be an extra or even try out for an important role in some Native-oriented movie. This anonymous voice would phone, having been given my number, and ask if I would be interested in trying out for a movie. Being a naturally ambitious, curious and greedy young man, I would always readily agree, stardom flashing in my eyes and hunger pains calling from my wallet.

A few days later I would show up for the audition, and that was always an experience. What kind of experience you ask? Picture this: the movie calls for the casting of seventeenth century Mohawk warriors living in a traditional longhouse. The casting director calls the name Drew Hayden Taylor, and I enter. The casting director, the producer and the film's director look up and see my face, blue eyes shining in anticipation. I once was described as a slightly chubby beach boy. But even beach boys have tans. Anyway, there would be a quick flush of confusion, a recheck of the papers and a hesitant "Mr. Taylor?"

Then they would ask if I was at the right audition. It was always the same. By the way, I never got any of the parts I tried for, except for a few anonymous crowd shots. Politics tell me it's because of the way I look, reality tells me it's probably because I can't act. I'm not sure which is better.

It's not just film people either. Recently I've become quite involved in theatre—Native theatre to be exact. And one cold October day I was happily attending the Toronto leg of a province-wide tour of my first play, *Toronto at Dreamer's Rock*. The place was sold out, the audience very receptive, and the performance was wonderful. Ironically one of the actors was also half-white. The director later told me he had been talking with that actor's father, an older non-Native chap. Evidently he asked a few questions about me, and how I did my research. This made the director curious and he asked about the man's interest. He replied, "He's got an amazing grasp of the Native situation for a White person."

Not all these incidents are work-related either. One time a friend and I were coming out of a rather upscale bar (we were out yuppie-watching) and managed to catch a cab. We thanked the cab driver for being so comfortably close on such a cold night. He shrugged and nonchalantly talked about knowing what bars to drive around. "If you're not careful, all you'll get is drunk Indians." I hiccupped.

Another time, the cab driver droned on and on about the government. He started out by criticizing Mulroney himself, and then eventually, his handling of the Oka crisis. This perked up my ears, until he said, "If it were me, I'd have tear-gassed the place by the second day. No more problems." He got a dime tip. A few incidents like this and I'm convinced I'd make a great undercover agent for Native political organizations.

But then again, even Native people have been known to look at me with a fair amount of suspicion. Many years ago when I was a young man, I was working on a documentary on Native culture up in the wilds of northern Ontario. We were at an isolated cabin filming a trapper woman and her kids. This one particular nine-year-old girl seemed to take a shine to me. She followed me around for two days, both annoying me and endearing herself to me. But she absolutely refused to believe that I was Indian. The whole film crew tried to tell her but to no avail. She was certain I was white. Then one day as I was loading up the car with film equipment, she asked me if I wanted some tea. Being in a hurry, I declined the tea. She immediately smiled with victory, crying out, "See, you're not Indian. All Indians drink tea!"

Frustrated and a little hurt, I whipped out my status card and showed it to her. Now there I was, standing in a northern Ontario winter, showing my status card to a nine-year-old, non-status, Indian girl who had no idea what it was. Looking back, this may not have been one of my brighter moves.

But I must admit, it was a Native woman that boiled everything down to one simple sentence. You may know that woman—Marianne Jones from *The Beachcombers* television series. We were working on a film together out west and we got to gossiping. Eventually we got around to talking about our respective villages. Her village is on the Queen Charlotte Islands, or Haida Gwaii as the Haida call them, and mine is in central Ontario.

Eventually, childhood on the reserve was being discussed and I made a comment about the way I look. She studied me for a moment, smiled and said, "Do you know what the old women in my village would call you?" Hesitant but curious, I shook my head. "They'd say you were pretty like a White boy." To this day I'm still not sure if I like that.

Now some may argue that I am simply a Métis with a status card. I disagree—I failed French in grade eleven. And the Métis, as everyone knows, have their own separate and honourable culture, particularly in western Canada. And, of course, I am well aware that I am not the only person with my physical characteristics.

I remember once looking at a video tape of a drum group, shot on a reserve up near Manitoulin Island. I noticed one of the drummers seemed quite fair-haired, almost blond. I mentioned this to my girlfriend of the time and she shrugged, saying, "Well, that's to be expected. The highway runs right through that reserve."

Perhaps I'm being too critical. There's a lot to be said for both cultures. For example, on the one hand, you have the Native respect for Elders. They understand the concept of wisdom and insight coming with age.

On the White hand, there's Italian food. I mean I really love my mother and family but seriously, does anything really beat good Veal Scallopini? Most of my Aboriginal friends share my fondness for this particular type of food. Wasn't there a warrior at Oka named Lasagna? I found it ironic, though curiously logical, that Columbus was Italian. A connection, I wonder?

Also, Native people have this wonderful respect and love for the land. They believe they are part of it, a mere link in the cycle of existence. Now as many of you know, this clashes with the accepted Judeo-Christian (i.e. Western) view of land management. I even believe somewhere in the first chapters of the Bible it says something about God giving man dominion over nature. Check it out, Genesis 1:? "Thou shalt clear cut." But I grew up understanding that everything around me is important and alive. My Native heritage gave me that.

And again, on the White hand, there are breast implants. Darn clever them White people. That's something Indians would never have invented, seriously. We're not ambitious enough. We just take what the Creator decides to give us; but no, not the White man. Just imagine it, some serious looking White doctor (and let's face it people, we know it was a man who invented them) sitting around in his laboratory muttering to himself, "Big tits, big tits, hmm, how do I make big tits?" If it was an Indian, it would be, "Big tits, big tits, White women sure got big tits," and leave it at that.

So where does that leave me on the big philosophical scoreboard? What exactly are my choices again? Indians: respect for Elders, love of the land. White people: food and big tits. In order to live in both cultures I guess I'd have to find an Indian woman with big tits who lives with her grandmother in a cabin out in the woods and can make Fettuccine Alfredo on a wood stove.

Now let me make myself clear—I'm not writing this for sympathy, or out of anger, or even some need for self-glorification. I am just setting the facts straight. For, as you read this, a new Nation is born. This is a declaration of independence, my declaration of independence.

I've spent too many years explaining who and what I am repeatedly, so, as of this moment, I officially secede from both races. I plan to start my own separate nation. Because I am half-Ojibway and half-Caucasian, we will be called the Occasions. And of course, since I'm founding the new nation, I will be a Special Occasion.

WHY THE NATIVES ARE RESTLESS

The Erotic Indian

A contradiction in terms?

Native sexuality. Now there's something you don't hear much about. Sensuality within the Native community seems to be oddly non-existent if you observe much of the pop culture that surrounds us. Culturally speaking, Native people do not automatically spring to mind when it comes to affairs of the heart, or other organs. Unlike other cultures—Latins, Italians and the French, to name just a few—Indians do not share a reputation for romance and love. Now this in itself is odd when you take into account that fifty percent of the over one million people in Canada who claim some form of Native ancestry, are under twenty-five years old. Once tragically thought of as "the vanishing Indian," there has been an amazing population explosion in Native communities across the country. Either Aboriginal scientists have mastered the difficult science of cloning more than just sheep and cows, or somebody out there is doing something a hell of a lot more interesting than hunting deer. Perhaps a game one Elder referred to as "hiding the pickerel."

Whoever is generating this fifty percent population explosion is obviously not paying attention to pop culture. Or as one mother of four on the reserve put it, "See what happens when the Internet goes down?" Historically, Native people were not generally viewed as potential love partners, except in the voluminous amount of historical romances with characters like Iron Horse or White Wolf, and their bulging muscles (among other things). Pocahontas, the first and ultimate Indian Princess, was perhaps one of the only symbols of love to break this barrier. But keep in mind that, in reality, she was only thirteen years old while her beau, John Smith, was actually around thirty. There's a word for that kind of love.

The term "Indian Princess" is in itself an odd phrase, since most Native cultures never had an established royalty or nobility. The only possible exception might be in the Two-Spirited community (also known as gay and lesbians) where "God save the Queen" takes on a whole new meaning.

This brings up an interesting question. We as Native people are aware of our own sensuality. Is it important to make the dominant culture aware of it too, to further enlighten them as to the wonderful and myriad aspects of Aboriginal culture, or should we be content to keep our little amorous secrets amongst ourselves and revel in them, and by doing this, maintain a reputation for stoicism while being perceived as sexually uninteresting?

And of course in North American culture there is a fine line between expressing sensuality and exploiting it.

Several years ago I went to Hawaii and saw, to my amazement, in almost every tourist and souvenir store, a calendar titled "The Girls of Hawaii." Inside the calendar, every month had a topless Polynesian girl smiling benevolently out at the viewer.

At first I was stunned. And then I realized I was stunned, and I couldn't figure out why I was stunned. After all, I had seen photographs of nude women before. I'm a man of the world. Then it hit me, it was the cultural representation I perceived or, moreover, the presentation of the culture as well as the women that were being used to sell the calendar. No different perhaps than "Bushwomen of the Kalahari" wet t-shirt contests. I found myself being offended.

And, no doubt, part of the shock was also trying to imagine some poor soul trying to develop and promote this same type of calendar here in Canada. "Indian Princesses of Canada" with page after page of scantily clad Aboriginal women, in buckskin bikinis, holding a newborn fawn or frolicking about on some glacier, freezing their you-know-whats off. But I could not help thinking how unlikely this seemed. For one thing, I cannot foresee the Aboriginal women of Canada allowing such a thing to be developed and marketed, as well as most Native men with a traditional background. Politically, spiritually and ethically, there would be too much to overcome and I believe the repercussions would be formidable, to say the least. Besides, it would be a very "American" thing to do.

Oddly enough, though I did not know it, my concerns were a foreshadowing of things to come. "The Girls of Hawaii" was an early example of the dubious development of the sensual Indian as it began to evolve, albeit in a different and questionable fashion. American pop culture, and its erotica machinery, seems to have discovered and is currently exploring, the untrodden land of the Erotic Aboriginal.

During the last half-decade or so, there have been two popular actresses carving a career out of the American porn industry. They have gone by the names of Jeannette Littledove and Hyapatia Lee. Both have used their Native heritage to market themselves extensively. "Hyapatia" is supposedly a Cherokee word and she is quoted as saying, in reference to her Native heritage and beliefs,—"Why tear down a tree to build a church when you can simply worship the tree?" As a Native person, I don't remember ever worshipping a tree. Not even a bush. But then again, I don't get out much. In fact, if my memory is correct, didn't the Druids of ancient Europe have a thing for Oak trees and mistletoe?

On the cover of a recent issue of *Blueboy*, a skin magazine for gay men, was a tall, good-looking, obviously Native man, complete with the prerequisite bone choker. The caption beneath this almost naked Aboriginal: "Indian Summer-Hung Like Crazy Horse." He obviously must have been Ojibway.

In the December issue of *Playboy*, two of the women "featured" claim and display their Aboriginal heritage to the public. Coincidently, the cover girl of this particular magazine, Danielle House, is the former Miss Canada International that lost her crown the year before for punching out her ex-boyfriend's new girlfriend. Inside the magazine she proudly asserts her Inuit—"do not call her Eskimo"—background and her ambition to be the spokesmodel for the Canadian Fur Association. "It's my heritage and I'm proud of it," she says. Oddly enough, she wasn't wearing any fur in the layout. I know, I looked.

The other "naked Native" is Playmate of the Month Karen McDougal, who proudly handles a dog team and sleigh stark naked, except for the fur boots and hat. Evidently the Inuit have been doing it wrong all this time. She credits her Cherokee grandfather for her high cheekbones. She had cheekbones?

While *Playboy* and porn are not the best examples of Native sexuality, they do illustrate the point: being the Erotic Indian seems to be a marketable product now. Something as private and personal as a person's, and a culture's, own passionate practices is fast becoming part of the monster known as pop culture.

Just one thing, please, no Pocahontas blow-up doll.

Ich Bin ein Ojibway

The phone call came on a lazy Thursday afternoon, which wasn't that unusual since those are the only type of Thursday afternoons I practice. The voice on the other end was from some sort of international institute for Canadian studies and she wanted to know what I was doing the following Thursday. I checked my anemic calender and replied "Nothing. Why?"

"Would you like to come to Germany for eight days?" Quickly my mind raced over everything I had heard about Germany: beer, schnapps, frauleins and something I'd vaguely heard about some wall coming down. That was enough for me, and it wasn't long before I was hunting down my under-used passport and practicing my "Ich bin ein Ojibway."

It seems there was going to be a conference at some university in Marburg, Germany about "Canada's Indigenous People," and I guess they wanted a real live Indian to attend. It seems their first choices, Daniel David Moses and Maria Campbell, for one reason or another, couldn't make it, so I was third on the list (always the bridesmaid, never the bride).

I should have known it was going to be a strange trip right from the beginning. There I was, waiting to board my plane at Pearson Airport when I happened to glance in the duty free shop. There, piled high, calling to my Aboriginal background, was a display advertising "A Traditional Native Canadian Meal." I could feel the heartbeat of countless generations pounding in my chest as I read what was contained in the genuine wood box: Indian bannock, wilderness tea (apple/cranberry), smoked trout, wild rice. It was enough to inspire me to send a care package home. My poor mother doesn't drink nearly enough apple/cranberry wilderness tea, let alone bread all the way from India.

Once on the plane I ended up having what started out to be a pleasant conversation with a teenager on his way to Israel by way of Germany. His parents had bought him a new CD Walkman and he was proudly showing it off. His parents had also thoughtfully provided him with some CDs to listen to on the way there, until he had the chance to buy his own in Israel. At one point during the seven-hour flight, he asked me if I wanted to listen to his Walkman. I innocently asked what kind of music he had that I could listen to. He then rummaged around in his bag and brought out a new CD with the plastic still on it.

"This one is Ray Charles. You look old. You should like him." It was a longer flight than I had expected, but thoughts of stuffing him, his Walkman, and Ray Charles in the overhead luggage bin made me pass the time merrily.

Germany itself was a wonderful time, once I got over the porno shop in the airport lobby and seeing people walk around happily stuffing their faces with french fries covered in mayonnaise—both of which I neglected to experience. My tastes are a little too conservative in both areas.

But soon it was time to pay my bill, so to speak. I was immediately whisked away to the conference in Marburg, a cute and adorable hamlet somewhere in the northwestern part of the country. I was asked to sit in on the almost two dozen lectures being given on Native people. They ranged from topics as diverse as "The Subversive Humour in Maria Campbell's *Halfbreed,*" to "Feminism in Canadian First Nation's Poetry," to the always exciting "Selected Problems of the Canadian Micmac."

I say "always exciting" sarcastically because most of the lectures were given in German. I felt like I was trapped in a continuous rerun of *Das Boot.* One of the students was provided as an ad-hoc interpreter, but having somebody whisper in your ears for two and a half days can give you a headache. I never did learn how to say, "Do you have any aspirin?" in German.

But by far the high point of the conference was a particular paper given (luckily in English) called "Environmental Conflicts: Hydro-projects at James Bay." Basically it was about the Crees' successful efforts to cancel the electrical contract between Hydro-Quebec and New York State.

After delivering her paper (quite well I might add), the speaker opened the floor up for discussion of the work. Immediately, a man off to the left of the room put up his hand and instantly proceeded to point out little inaccuracies in her paper and criticize her method of research.

Someone whispered into my ear that this gentleman was a representative of the Quebec government, stationed in Germany, sort of like the equivalent of a provincial ambassador. The man then started to talk about how, unlike any of the other provinces, Quebec is quite proud of the relationship and dialogue it has set up with its Aboriginal people, and the unique bond they have forged together!

I began thinking, is this the same Quebec that is in Canada? The same one containing the community known as Kanehsatake, often incorrectly referred to as Oka? What about Restigouche? Feeling that I had to say something or turn in my status card, I brought that up for discussion. No sooner had I sat down then a woman behind me stood up and said, in an obvious French accent, that I "Shouldn't bring Oka into this—half the people there weren't even Canadians."

I debated going into the whole concept of the Iroquois Confederacy not recognizing the border, but I noticed the poor presenter standing at the front of the room. Evidently the discussion planned for her paper was going slightly off topic so I decided not to pursue the subject. I still occasionally bleed from where I bit my lip.

The rest of the trip was fantastic and incredible. People were wonderful, the beer was tasty and there were sausages galore. It was interesting seeing buildings that were older than when what's-his-name stumbled on Turtle Island (there went the neighbourhood).

But I had an interesting thought as I stood there, looking around at what is often called the Old World. If what's-his-name could "discover" a continent with an estimated one hundred million people already living there, why couldn't I?

Unfortunately the Dusseldorf authorities don't take kindly to flags being planted in their city square. So much for the short term rise and fall of the empire of Drewland.

Missionary Positions
and Vegetarian Warriors

Recently a friend of mine, who works for a Native theatre company, was walking down a street to meet me for lunch. She was wearing the fur hat a family friend had given her. As she reached an intersection, a total stranger came up to her and snarled, "Do you realize you have a dead animal carcass on your head?" Surprised and a little frightened by this sudden and unwarranted antagonistic approach, my friend avoided a confrontation and went on her way. Later on during the meal, I suggested she should have responded with, "You have a dead animal carcass for a head."

The more I live in the city, and the more I watch and read the media, the more I become amazingly aware of a disturbing fact of the dominant Caucasian world. That is, very little in the philosophical practices of these people has changed over the centuries. The philosophies and goals have merely become different, become more "politically correct," but the method of achieving them still remains the same.

As the saying goes, "The more things change, the more they stay the same." I never really understood it—what it meant, the philosophical implications, the truth of it all. But as the years have gone by and I have observed more and more of the world around me, I have grown to understand the saying. At least a small part of it, and it scares me.

I refer to the dominant mentality that exists within Western society. The overwhelming belief that what "they" believe is correct, and what everybody else believes is wrong. I say "they" instead of "we" because in some ways I and my people are products of the implementation of these philosophies.

Most Canadians, hopefully, are aware of some of the tragic history of Native people. How we were forced to give up our land, forced into various Christian religions, forced into residential schools, forced onto reserves and forced by the government to give up children for adoption, and a hundred other "forced to's" all because the White race, in most cases (there are always exceptions I realize), has a firm belief that its way of doing things is the best and only way; everybody should be forced to do or believe things that way, or they are not salvageable or welcome members of society. And in most cases, it is the White people's duty to its "cause," be it political or religious or whatever, to enforce White beliefs, regardless of the consequences to other people.

A big charge, I know, but easily proven: the Crusades, the Spanish Inquisition, the conquest of the Americas, missionary work, Manifest Destiny, Nazism, white supremacy movements. Need I go on?

And as I stated, the beliefs that fueled the passion exist today in many of the more socially conscious causes.

Case in point: vegetarians. Now, I have nothing against vegetarians: some of my best friends are vegetarians. I've been known to eat the odd vegetable myself. But some of these vegetarians have, I think, certain attitude problems. Some, when they see me eating a chicken leg or chomping on a roast beef sandwich, have this peculiar look that seems to be a combination of moral superiority and disgust. I know one person, who as a political protest to her meat-eating boyfriend, refuses to even walk down the meat aisle at the grocery store. But it goes way beyond that.

Several years ago I was working on a documentary series with a vegetarian producer. Late one night, on our way back from a difficult day of shooting, the crew stopped off at a roadside diner for dinner. Two of us sat at the counter with the producer. The crew member ordered fried chicken, and no sooner had the words gotten out of her mouth when the producer proceeded, in graphic detail, to tell her about chicken farms. I listened with a smile, having spent years being lectured to by well-meaning missionaries that came to our reserves with their own particular brand of truth.

As he finished, he caught me smiling and turned to me saying, "Not so fast. Now it's your turn." I got the ten-minute lecture on the evils of eating veal sandwiches. At least I learned one thing: never order veal in front of a vegetarian unless you want to piss him or her off. As I sat there, I was wondering if he actually thought he was making converts by doing this?

Regardless, it just made me relish the sandwich all the more, out of spite. I hate it when people inform me that eating a simple sandwich is a political statement. If this keeps up, pretty soon I won't be allowed to have an English muffin until things change in Northern Ireland.

As a relatively well-read individual, I was already aware of what he was saying, but I happened to have made the choice to eat meat, partly because I enjoy the taste, partly because it is part of my cultural heritage. But evidently a meat eater's choice isn't as well respected or logical as a vegetarian's choice. We are the enemy. How about those commercials done out west by k.d. lang urging people not to eat beef? A paid advertisement urging people to switch to a different philosophy because it's better.

I know there are beef and pork commercials on T.V. too, but they are not suggesting vegetarians change their lifestyle to accommodate them. They are just urging meat eaters, as is the way with advertising, to try Ontario beef, or whatever. Two different standards, because vegetarians think their lifestyle is morally and spiritually better.

A few months ago, my partner, a lapsed but struggling vegetarian, asked me to attend a lecture by a well-known vegetarian dietician, and being open-minded, I went. Many of the things he had to say were accurate, health-conscious and made a lot of sense, but I still noticed a bit of mania in him. Something said to me, "This guy thinks he's right, and everybody else is wrong."

"The human body isn't made to eat meat. It destroys the body rather than builds it up. Nature has not made us carnivores." Tell that to all the Aboriginal tribes of North America, especially the northern nations, whose diet consists mostly of meat. I'd like to see a vegetarian try and dig up a potato in three feet of snow. The Plains Indians survived almost totally on a diet of buffalo meat, and they were amongst the strongest, healthiest people on the continent.

Another comment he made was about how the digestive tract has to draw calcium from bones in order to process the meat. He then went on to say that the "Eskimos" (which made me more suspicious of how accurate he was) have an incredibly high rate of osteoporosis. I know many people who have worked in the north, and Inuit themselves, and after asking some questions, nobody seems to know anything about this high rate of osteoporosis. I wonder why?

In fact, these people eat an amazing amount of animal flesh, some of it pure fat, yet for those that follow these traditional diets, they have a surprisingly low level of cholesterol and heart disease. Maybe nature did mean for them to eat meat. Could it be possible that this particular vegetarian was wrong?

And often, these same people belong to the animal rights organizations. Worthwhile organizations, within their own rights, yes. Nobody wants to see animals suffer, but the problem starts when the organizations set out to destroy the ways of a people who have lived peacefully with and harvested the bounty of the land longer than the immigrant culture has been on this continent. I think not.

Just recently I saw a character on *Saturday Night Live* throw a bucket of paint on an image of someone wearing a fur coat, actively promoting his belief that fur is wrong. Throwing paint on someone you disagree with? Now there's a sophisticated political act of protest I'd like to follow. Surely evidence of a superior civilization. No doubt members of the Church of the Divine Spray Can.

Several years ago, when the boycott against seal fur came into effect, it wasn't just coats from Newfoundland seal pups that were affected, but all seal products from all over the Arctic. People that had nothing to do with that whole mess suffered as a result. But certain people were convinced that if one branch of the tree is bad, you should cut the whole tree down. As a result, Inuit communities in the North were devastated. It was no longer economically viable to hunt seals, even for food. The bullets and the gas for their outboard motors cost too much to make the hunt worth it.

Instead, many communities experienced a horrendous increase in criticism about the Aboriginal way of life. A modern example of non-Native people making sure everybody follows their rules.

Another example of moral superiority is found in certain aspects of the philosophy behind feminism. When I started seeing my partner, Marie, who describes herself as a "woman who advocates feminism" she was asked by her friend, someone she describes as a "radical feminist," if I was "conscious." By whose standards? Hers? Evidently this is a term used to characterize someone who believes the radical feminists' particular sociopolitical agenda.

As someone who was raised by a hard-working, single mother and brought up in a culture that has a traditional respect and reverence for women, I find the term "conscious" a little presumptuous. And from what I understand, this radical feminist looked a little disappointed when Marie, answering her question, told her no, not in the Western sense. I refuse to be a card-carrying anything. But when her friend found out I was Native, she sighed a breath of relief, uttering, "At least you're both oppressed." Marie happens to be Filipino. Am I to assume the only saving grace she could find in me was the fact I was "oppressed?" Nothing else about me mattered, only that?

If I understand all this correctly, only certain people, an incredibly small fraction of the world's population that believes in western feminism, can be classified as "conscious." What are the rest of us who truly embrace these beliefs that for the most part are created and followed by middle-class white women of privilege? Are the rest of us perhaps unconscious, or maybe subconscious?

Somebody once asked me if I, because I was dating Marie, was going to become a feminist? I said sure, when Marie becomes a Native person. We respect each other's beliefs and convictions—Marie is now quite well known in Native artistic circles, and I have often accompanied her to and supported many of her feminist causes.

And does the term "consciousness" only refer to feminism? If so, that's awfully bold of them to appropriate that word. I'm tempted to go up to these people and ask "Are you conscious? Do you know about Native beliefs or Native issues?" Is that allowed?

But to me, the most obvious example of "my way of life is better than your way of life" is Sunday morning television. There you see wall-to-wall television evangelism. People screaming at you to believe only in their way of worshipping God, and nobody else's. To me this exemplifies this whole attitude.

These people have made a career out of telling others to follow their way of doing things, or risk going to hell. Their creed, their dogma is the better way. Sound familiar?

You never see Native people on television preaching about the benefits of their religion. As you're eating your scrambled eggs on Sunday morning, you don't see an Ojibway Elder shouting out to pray to the Four Directions, and to send in fifty dollars for some traditional sweetgrass so you too can have your own cleansing ceremony. When's the last time you saw a Native person going door-to-door, trying to convince you to come to a sweat lodge?

It's not our way. The Native way, the Native belief, is to basically say, "You're more than welcome to join us in what we do, but you don't have to if you don't want to. You have your way, we have ours." I don't see that often outside of Native circles. Take the abortion issue for example—both sides screaming at each other, actually coming to physical blows because each thinks they are morally right, and the other side is morally wrong. Again, sound familiar?

Now this is not to say people are not entitled to their opinions. Everybody has them, and everybody should. But I, as an individual and a Native person, don't appreciate having other people tell me 1) my lifestyle or beliefs are wrong, or 2) they have a better way for me to live, or that their opinions are better than mine.

And I am well aware that not every single person in today's society may have this driven state of mind, but enough do to make life for the rest of us difficult.

I, like everyone else, have my own political and philosophical agenda I live by, but who the hell am I to say that my viewpoint, my lifestyle choices, are better than anybody else's? That would be very arrogant of me. So, please, feel free to ignore everything I've just said. Heaven forbid, I wouldn't want to possibly influence anybody.

MIRROR, MIRROR ON THE WALL

An Aboriginal Name Claim

Recently I was innocently and harmlessly strolling through the newly reopened Art Gallery of Ontario when I looked up. Looked waaaayyy up. There, towering at least twenty-five feet or so above me was a huge word carved into immutable stone. The word, Ojibway, is the name of the Aboriginal nation I'm lucky enough to be a member of. And around that incredible noble tribe, inscribed forever upon that wall, were a half dozen other words, naming various Native tribes throughout Ontario. So I thought to myself on that unusual day, "Now this is something you don't see every day."

By unusual I mean that you don't see the name Ojibway printed in public that noticeably unless it's on the front page of a newspaper with phrases like "land claim" or "mass suicide" attached somewhere. Growing up, I used to think phrases like that were all one word. For instance, "Ojibway Land Claim." That's usually the only time you would see that word unless you were an anthropologist, archeologist, government official or lacrosse player.

So we kids would run around the reserve yelling out to our friends, "Hey, how's your Ojibway Land Claim?" and "I hear Running Arrow (his real name was Bill) has got a new Ojibway Land Claim. Cool!" and "I bet my Ojibway Land Claim is bigger than yours!" Ah, the wonders of youth.

So, there I stood, in the Art Gallery of Ontario, looking up at that majestic looking word hovering high above me, thinking, "Sure is nice. Clean looking too. Even spelled it right. Pity the word's wrong." Perhaps the word "wrong" is a little too harsh, because I know that is the term that most Canadians are familiar with. Let's just say it's become… antiquated. With Native culture flourishing in its renaissance, more Native words are actually being used to describe Native things. What an interesting concept.

This is a fascinating reversal of history since for the longest time, Native names were used to describe things that weren't very Native.

"Canada" for instance, or the word "Toronto." How many "Canadians" think of Native people when they hear the word "Toronto?" Probably about as many people as think of our Wisconsin Native brothers when they hear the word "Winnebago."

And Frobisher Bay is now called Iqaluit and so on. Nowadays, no self-respecting Ojibway-type supporter of the Cultural Rebirth would use that term. Most Ojibways prefer to be known as Anishnawbe. Say it with me—the Anishnawbe.

This is because Ojibway is not really what we call ourselves. This is a name that has been foisted upon us poor, unsuspecting Anishnawbe. The origins of that questionable word are kind of hazy, but there are several schools of thoughts on Ojibway and how we came to be called that.

According to the all-knowing and all-curious anthropologists who are so fascinated with us, "Ojibway" translates into something to do with the word "puckered." Now, while the majority of Ojibways are fantastic kissers (and I can attest to that), I mean puckered in a different context. The first theory has to do with moccasins. Now supposedly the Anishnawbe had a very distinctive way of sewing the seams on their moccasins that give it a certain "puckered" appearance. If this is true, the entire contemporary Anishnawbe Nation may have to change its name to the noble Reebok First Nation.

The other, somewhat more grisly explanation has to do with the way human skin puckers up when it's being burned alive. Now, scholars who claim this don't seem to be sure if we were the burners or the burnees, and frankly, I'm not sure which is worse. But that would explain my mother's fondness for barbeques. So there you go. Scientists believe we were named after shoes or burning human skin. That's a proud choice.

Obviously, certain Native academics disagree with this interpretation of history (now there's a surprise). According to Ojibway writer and cultural historian Basil Johnston, the word "Ojibway" is actually a bastardization of a Cree word describing the Anishnawbe people as "those who stutter." It seems, evidently, the Cree are a very proud nation who consider themselves to be elegant speakers of the language and enunciate their words perfectly. But, in their opinion, the Anishnawbe mangle the language and mumble their words. Thus we were labeled "those who stutter." Thanks a lot, guys.

The Iroquois, on the other hand, deemed it necessary to refer to us as the "Adirondacks," or so I've been told. Not because we were big and strong like the same-named mountain range, but because, as the name translates, we were bark eaters. Historically, the Anishnawbe used to peel certain types of bark and stuff it into rabbits and ducks as they cooked. This bark was loaded with vitamin C and helped prevent scurvy. And in times of winter hardship, all that would be available to eat would be mosses and bark brewed into teas.

None of these names coined by other nations are exactly flattering. That's why I prefer the name we call ourselves. Anishnawbe means "the good beings" or "the people." And not burning ones. Just regular pass-the-tea-what's-for-dinner-who-are-the-Leafs-playing-tonight type people.

And to tell you the truth, that works out just wonderfully for me. I'd rather be known as a good being than a bark-eating-mumbling-human-burning-puckered-shoe any day. Unless the shoe is a Bata. Then we're talking serious money.

An Indian By Any Other Name

Last week I, a reasonably well educated man of the ever increasingly more complex '90s, made a tremendous political and social faux pas. I made the terrible mistake of referring to myself, and other people of my ethnic background, as "Indians." Oh the shame of it all. You could hear the gasp echo across the room. It was done, I assure you, in the most innocent of intentions, but nevertheless, I was soon castigated by both my brethren and, in my humble opinion, the overly politically sensitive members of other Native groups. And the white people! Needless to say, in these politically correct times, I was inundated, by these people, with criticisms about my use of such an outdated term. "We're/You're no longer called Indians!" was told to me over and over again.

Evidently I am in severe error for responding to that term for the last thirty-one years. No doubt an oversight on my part, and the part of my entire family, and reserve, not to mention the vast majority of the country. Growing up in school, all of us were proud to be "Indians." It had a certain power to it that set us aside from all the white kids (or should I say "Children of Occidental Descent"). Somehow the cry of "Proud to be of the Indigenous Population" just doesn't have the same ring. Or picture this: you arrive thirsty in some new town, and you ask the first skin you see, "Yo, neechee, where's the nearest First Nations' bar?" Sorry, just doesn't work for me.

I guess I'm out of date? Oh I understand the reasoning behind all the hubbub. Columbus, a member of the "European/Caucasian Nations," thought he had found India and all that. That's cool, but there's also another school of thought that says that Columbus was so impressed by the generosity and gentleness of the Native population of the Caribbean, he wrote back to Spain that they were "of the body of God," or in Spanish, *corpus in deo.* In deo—Indian. A pretty thin link, but who knows? I have known some Indians with God-given bodies.

But a person in my position doesn't have to defend himself with theoretical history. I was too busy handling the deluge. By deluge I mean the flood of politically correct terms I was permitted and urged to use following my *faux pas*.

It must be obvious to most people that in the last couple of years Native people in Canada have gone through an enormous political metamorphosis, similar to what people of African descent went through in the United States. Years ago they used to be called Niggers, then Negro, then Coloured, then Black, and finally today, I believe the correct term is African-American or African-Canadian.

That's nothing compared to the choice selection of current names and categories available to the original inhabitants of this country. And these names or classifications have nothing to do with any tribal affiliations either. These are just generic terms used to describe us "Indians." Grab some aspirin and let me give you some examples.

First of all, let's start with the basics. Status, non-Status, Métis. So far painless. I guess next would come the already mentioned Indian, followed by Native, Aboriginal, Amerindian, Indigenous and First Nations. Pay attention, there's going to be an exam later. From there we can go to on-reserve, off-reserve, urban, treaty. Got a headache yet? How about the enfranchised Indians, the Bill C-31 or re-instated people, the traditional Indians, the assimilated Indian? I'm not finished yet. There are the wannabe's (the white variety), the apples (the red variety), the half-breeds, mixed bloods and of course, the ever popular full-bloods. My personal favourites are what I call the Descartes Indians, "I think Indian, therefore, I am Indian."

Get the picture? Right, there are two dozen separate names for our people. Where does it all stop? I wanna know who keeps changing all the rules? Even I get confused sometimes. That's why I usually use the term "Indian." I'm just too busy or too lazy to find out which way the political wind is blowing or to delve deeply into the cultural/governmental background of who I'm talking to or writing about. By the time I go through all the above-mentioned categories, I've missed my deadline. Then I become an unemployed Indian.

But I know what you're thinking. Why should I listen to this guy? What the hell does he know? He's just probably some Status, off-reserve, urban, Native, Aboriginal, treaty, half-breed Indian. This week anyway.

What Colour is a Rose?

As a Native writer there are always three questions I get asked, *ad nauseam,* whenever I give a lecture or a reading for a non-Native audience. Question one: "What do you feel about cultural appropriation?" My answer: "About the same as I feel about land appropriation." Question two: "When you write your plays or stories, do you write for a specifically Native audience or a White audience?" My answer: "I'm usually alone in my room when I write, except for my dying cactus. So I guess that means I write for my dying cactus." The final, and in my opinion, most annoying question I often get asked is: "Are you a writer that happens to be Native, or a Native that happens to be a writer?"

I was not aware there had to be a difference. I was always under the impression that the two could be and often were, synonymous. But evidently I am in error. Over the past few years of working as a professional writer, I have slowly begun to understand the rules of participation in the television and prose industry in terms of this difference. It seems there is a double standard. Surprise, surprise.

It is not uncommon, though deemed politically incorrect, for White writers to write satires about Native people quite freely, particularly on television. Notice many of the "people of pallor" script credits on such shows as *North of Sixty* (which, granted, does have one talented Native writer), *Northern Exposure* (I guess I'll have to move to the North since it seems that's where all the Native people live), and movies like *Where the Spirit Lives* or *Dance Me Outside*. All these shows have strong, identifiable Native characters created by non-Natives.

However, should a Native writer want to explore the untrodden world outside the Aboriginal literary ghetto, immediately the fences appear, and opportunities dry up. Evidently, the powers that be out there in the big cruel world have very specific ideas of what a Native writer can and can't do. Only recently, a friend of mine submitted a story to a new CBC anthology series in development, about Native people, called *The Four Directions*.

His story outline was soon returned with an explanation that the producers thought the story wasn't "Native enough" for their purposes. I myself submitted a story to the producers, and during our first story meeting, I received a stirring and heartfelt lecture about how they, the producers, were determined to present the Native voice as authentically and accurately as possible, and how committed they were to allowing us Native-types the chance to tell our stories our way. I was then asked if I could cut the first eight pages of my twenty seven page script. Oddly enough, they seemed puzzled by my sudden burst of laughter.

I once wrote an episode of *Street Legal* and accidently caught a glimpse of a memo from the producer to a story editor asking him to rewrite the dialogue of my Native Elder to "make him more Indian." I guess as a Native person, I don't know how "real Indians" talk. Bummer. These are just a few examples of the battle Native writers often face.

I hereby pose a question to these people who judge our stories. I personally would like to know by what set of qualifications these people examine Native stories. Is there an Aboriginal suitability quotient posted somewhere? If there is, I would love the opportunity to learn more about how I should write as a Native person.

For a story to be "Native enough," must there be a birch bark or buckskin quota? Perhaps there are supposed to be vast roaming herds of moose running past the screen. Oh geez, I guess I'm not Native enough. I momentarily forgot, moose don't herd, they just hang out with flying squirrels that have their own cartoon show.

Or maybe I's got be good writer like dem Indians whats W.P. Kinsella writes about. It no sound like any Indian I ever hears, but what the hell, I maybe win bunch of awards. On second thought, you never mind. I get head ache trying write like this.

So what's a writer to do? Damned if he does, damned if he doesn't. And what if I want to write stories about non-Native people? It's possible, but will I be given a chance? I'm sure I could do it. I've learned enough about how white people really live from watching all those episodes of *Married With Children* and *Baywatch*.

This all brings us back to the original question. Am I a writer who happens to be Native, or a Native that happens to be a writer? Do I have a choice? I think that the next time I get asked that, I'll ask the equally deep and important question: "Is a zebra black with white stripes, or white with black stripes?" Just watch. They'll make that into a racial question.

Call of the Weird

When I first read the job description for the position of Artistic Director of Native Earth Performing Arts, Toronto's only professional Native theatre company, I don't remember coming across any paragraph or subsection anywhere on the page requiring me to become the "oracle of Aboriginal trivia."

On any given day, questions of unusual and frequently surreal nature are posed to me and the other intelligent, though often puzzled, members of the office. The number of times I've seen heads, with telephones attached, shaking in amazement, makes me wonder about the logical processes of people's minds.

We are a theatre company. That is what we do. We produce plays by and about Native people. Check it out, it's in our mandate. We'll fax it to you if you don't believe us. The majority of questions that Bell Canada sends our way are not within our realm of expertise. Although one of our functions as a theatre company is to educate the public that does not mean informing one person at a time about obscure issues, while our other work waits. We have lives too, you know.

Our beleaguered office staff has put together a collection of some of the more ... interesting... inquiries to come through our office in recent months.

I'm trying to find Sam Ke-something-or-other. I really don't know how to pronounce his last name. Do you know where I can find him? Or: I'm trying to locate a Bob Whitecloud of the Sioux Tribe in the States. I heard he might be in Canada. Can you tell me how to get in touch with him?

It's a little known fact that Native Earth Performing Arts is the focal point for all Native people in North America. The one million or so people claiming some sort of Aboriginal ancestry all pass through our doors at one point or another. That's why we have to replace our carpets at least four times a year.

Do all the seats face the stage?

I guess you can call us slaves to conformity. We did try having the seats face the back of the theatre but audience reaction, shall we say, was not that favourable.

Hi, I'm wondering if you can help me. I'm trying to locate an Apache wedding prayer.

I checked. Sorry, no Apaches in our office, married or not. I did, however, manage to find a Mohawk secret handshake.

I'm with a casting company for a movie. I'm looking for a Native man, tall and lean with long, dark hair and presence. Preferably he should be in his early 30s. And yes, he has to look very striking.

Yeah, most of the women in my office are looking for him too. What do you want me to do about it? The line starts behind them.

I'm phoning from Edinburgh, Scotland. I'm doing research on Native people in the 1930s. Can you send me information?

There were none. I have it on good authority all Native people were killed off in the late 1800s. But in the latter part of this century, due to an over-abundance of bureaucrats in Ottawa, the Federal Government decided to create a new department to employ these people. So the Department of Indian Affairs was created with no Indians. Through secret DNA experiments, a new race of Native people was created at a clandestine location known as … Algonquin Park.

I'm Herman ---------- from Germany. I'm looking for people of the Bear clan. My last name means bear in German. Do you know any or can you help me find the Bear clan?

Sorry, we have yet to update our data base and cross reference our membership, actors, directors, stage managers and others by clan affiliation. We're awaiting the software to come out for Windows.

We're an organization of men against men who commit violence against women. We want to know if you guys could provide any ceremonies or spiritual things of that nature that would help us with healing and matters like that.

While that is a noble cause, we are not "Ceremonies 'R' Us," or "have medicine pouch, will travel."

Do you know where I can get my hands on some Inuit throat singers?

As a Native organization, we do not condone violence against the Inuit.

In all fairness and honesty, we do try to be as polite and helpful as possible, and pass callers on to the appropriate organizations. But we are in the business of making art, not a Native trivial pursuit game. But it makes me wonder if the Mirvishes ever get calls asking, "*There's this Jewish song I keep hearing. Hava-something. You wouldn't happen to know the full title and who sang it would you?*"

Pocahontas: Beauty and the Belief

I must and will confess. I saw the Disney film *Pocahontas*. I was curious to see how the Land of Mickey would treat this all-American Native legend. Briefly: the music was, naturally, marketable; the animation was, of course, fabulous; the animals of the forest were, predictably, cute (though subconsciously you couldn't help thinking that Pocahontas's people made a regular habit of eating Bambi and Thumper); and it sort of confirmed the old adage, "Never let facts get in the way of a good story."

When John Smith first gets a good look at her, standing in the mist of a waterfall, her long, black hair blowing and flowing sensuously in the wind (I wanna know what kind of hair conditioner she uses) and her little off-the-shoulder buckskin dress hugging her body tightly (which is noticeably more curvaceous than Snow White; only goes to show you what a steady diet of Bambi and Thumper will do for you), you can't help but be a little uncomfortable knowing that the real Pocahontas wasn't much older than eleven or twelve years old when the whole thing came down with the colonists.

Evidently, according to some historical reports, she also "amused" the Englishman by doing nude cartwheels through the colony. And from what I understand, there may even be some doubt as to whether John Smith and Pocahontas ever really met, let alone had any serious romantic relationship. But other than that, it was a good movie.

The whole Pocahontas legend can be looked at from several different levels. First of all, it became the stuff great romances were made of. Check out any bookstore that has a sizable stock of historical romances. Count how many of them involve a forbidden romance between a Native person and a White person, and the fiery savage passion that smolders and threatens to break free from beneath the taut leather. You get the picture.

When you look at the story objectively, it's about a romance between, at best, a twelve-year-old Indian girl and a thirty-year-old sailor who was captured by Pocahontas' father. According to Smith, and only Smith's word, Pocahontas laid her head on his, openly defying her father, the Chief of the tribe, as Smith's head was about to be clubbed and crushed.

To quote the Native actress and playwright Monique Mojica's play, *Princess Pocahontas and the Blue Spots,* "Where was this girl's mother?" To the best of my knowledge, this is not behaviour most mothers would condone in a twelve-year-old.

In the movie her mother is dead. But as we've already seen, this movie is not exactly big on historical accuracy.

If Pocahontas' mother had been around, no doubt she would have also warned her against falling for someone who says his name is John Smith. How many women have heard that before? And how many hotel rooms have this name scrawled on the register? Could it be that this man is four hundred years old and still out there?

Both legend and Disney portray Smith as a handsome, strapping blond-haired, blue-eyed man. This would explain why Pocahontas would fall for him, according to a theory of a Mohawk friend of mine. Over the years, he has come to believe that, for some reason, most Natives are attracted to shiny objects and like to collect them. This includes turquoise, silver and blondes. That's something for a sociologist or anthropologist to ponder.

When all's said and done, Pocahontas (her real name, by the way, was actually Matoaka; Pocahontas was a nickname her father called her, meaning "playful one") will make Disney a lot of wampum (which again, in reality, is not actually a form of Aboriginal currency), and that at Christmas (it's basically an accepted fact that Christ was not born on December 25), kids all over North America could expect a little American Indian princess doll (no doubt made somewhere in Asia). Sometimes you just don't know what to believe.

Note: Pocahontas later converted to Christianity, married a colonist named John Rolfe, went to England, saw the original production of *The Tempest* just a few weeks after the author died, and was consumed by smallpox at the age of twenty-two.

Waiting for Kinsella

It was the showdown that never happened, the case of the missing confrontation. Even though it seemed, at least to me, like the media built it up to be something potentially and politically volatile, I must confess that it died with a whimper, not a bang. I am, of course, talking about my appearance at Toronto's International Festival of Authors with the most notable of alleged Aboriginal cultural appropriators, W.P. Kinsella. Speaking as an Ojibway playwright and Artistic Director of Native Earth Performing Arts, Toronto's only professional Native theatre company, it seemed it was expected of me to face the man from the West, armed with only baseball bats (his advantage) or lacrosse sticks (my advantage). But showdown at the W.P. Corral it wasn't.

The day I saw my name on the brochure of invited writers, a dozen or so authors after Kinsella, I knew this festival wasn't going to be as much fun as I had anticipated. I felt the potential cultural storm beginning to blow in. Already, many of my Native friends were attempting to generate within me a murderous literary froth and an Indigenous intellectual rage; they were urging an Aboriginal *Jihad* for lack of a better term. I was getting the impression that this festival wasn't big enough for the two of us.

The media were no help. I did three interviews concerning the festival. First question: "So Drew, excited about the festival?" Second question: "Tell me about Native theatre/literature in Canada." Third question: "Cultural appropriation. Kinsella's gonna be there. Comments?"

When asked a question, I always try to be polite and answer it. Yes, I do have opinions on the whole Kinsella thing. Yes, I have read his stories and, while I consider him a gifted storyteller, he obviously doesn't write his Native stories with the same kind of love he puts into his baseball tales. Anybody who's read both and compared them can tell. And if there's no love involved in the stories you tell, why tell them? But I repeat, I am NOT gunning for Kinsella.

So there I am, being polite and answering these searing journalistic questions (must have been a slow day at the O.J. trial), and this stuff starts popping up in print, on radio and television. MuchMusic even did some sort of head-to-head debate between me and Kinsella by interviewing us at different times, asking us the same questions, and intercutting between the two of us. I haven't seen it but I'm told it looked like an interesting debate.

It all came to a not-so-spectacular head one night at one of the social functions for the festival. I arrived somewhat late for the festivities. I had no sooner walked in the door when two publicists, within a dozen seconds of each other, came racing over to me and quickly but quietly whispered in my ear, "Kinsella's here!" My first reaction was, "So what?" I looked across the crowded room at where they were pointing and saw him—a tall, thin chap with long blondish hair, mustache, beard, cowboy hat, and striped shirt with a western bolo tie. He looked vaguely familiar. I couldn't place the memory but something about it seemed tinged with irony.

If, by some chance, we were placed in a conversational position, I had no idea what I would say to him. One Native writer friend suggested that I tell him he can't write. Not only would that have been rude, but in my opinion, inaccurate. The man can write, but it's his choice and treatment of subject matter that I would question. Another person, urging I remain neutral and non-confrontational, suggested I talk to him about baseball.

However, there was no baseball to talk about and the game is about as important to me as Native self-government probably is to him. But these are now trivial points.

To this day, even with all the press, I have absolutely no idea if he knows who I am. But during the entire festival (and I'm sure it was completely by accident), we never ended up sitting at the same table for dinner, or perchance talking together. My entire contact with him consisted of squeezing by him in a crowded room on my way to the bathroom. Our conversation involved a grand total of two scintillating words: "Excuse me." Instead, the week passed and the man has long since left. I'm sure he's a nice man. And I'm sure he's as sick and tired of this whole damn thing as I am. So contrary to rumours you may have heard, I have not put a contract out on him or placed an ancient Ojibway curse on him. I figure anybody who looks and dresses like George Armstrong Custer (I remembered) is a marked man anyways.

Whatever Happened to Billy Jack?

I don't know about all people, but to me, political revelation is often inspired by the strangest places. As usual, it was another lonely Friday night, the kind I've been seeing much too regularly. And in those wee morning hours I sat on my couch in front of the television. I was munching on a bowl of popcorn, lightly dressed with low-fat margarine, when an image I remembered from my childhood flashed across the screen. There, sandwiched between phone-sex commercials and offers for self-improvement videos and cassettes (interesting combination), stood Tom Laughlin, the famous Billy Jack to the common folk, the hero of my childhood.

You have to understand that in the early '70s there were precious few cinematic characters for young impressionable Native kids to relate to. It was either him or Jesse Jim on *The Beachcombers*.

So there he was at the climax of the film, an Indian barricaded with his rifle, surrounded by a multitude of cops wanting to shoot him full of sizeable holes, yet Billy Jack was managing to hold them off with superior skill and moral fibre. I understand they used to screen this movie every night at Oka.

Billy Jack's girlfriend enters the church and notices he's been shot. Stoic as all us Indians are in the movies, he ignores his bleeding side, saying quite melodramatically, "An Indian isn't afraid to die."

As I sat there munching on my popcorn, I thought "Obviously we don't know the same Indians."

That's not, of course, to say that Native people are cowards or aren't willing to stand up for what they believe. As a Native person I know how quickly the Aboriginal people in this country are willing to take a stand, no matter what the consequences. What I am referring to, instead, is the stereotypical impression characters like Billy Jack give to the world; like we all appear mystically in the nick of time on our motorcycle/horse/jeep and strut around in our black T-shirts and black hats karate kicking white people in the side of head. Well … there may be a few, but generally you don't see too much of this on your average reserve.

As a Native person living in today's world, I am only too aware of the false impressions a lot of people have of our Aboriginal society. I have yet to find one of these stereotypes that I fit into properly. I don't know, maybe my white blood throws the bell curve off or something. But I do know dying isn't on my list of favourite things to do in the near future. Hopefully.

In my experience, I've noticed four specific stereotypes that the majority of Native people are lumped into by the media. And because four is a special number in Native beliefs (i.e. the Four Directions) I like to call these the Four Sacred Stereotypes.

The first consists of the ever-popular sidekick syndrome. It seems it was impossible to get anything done without your trustworthy Indian companion like the Lone Ranger's Tonto, Nick's Jesse Jim, or Hawkeye's last two Mohicans. No wonder they were the last two Mohicans—they kept hanging around with a white guy instead of women.

The second is the fiery young Aboriginal radical, dedicated to saving his people whether they like it or not. Give him a soap box, a court room or a barricade and his spirit cries out against the injustices forced upon his people by the oppressive and dominant white society that for the centuries has been systematically draining the life blood out of ... Well, you get the picture. Again, Billy Jack kicks into action (literally). The third is my personal favourite: the borderline psychotic, often drunk, out-of-control Indian who, given a chance, wouldn't hesitate to separate your spirit from reality quicker than you could dodge a bullet. Witness Arthur from *A Dream Like Mine, Clearcut,* Injun Joe from *Tom Sawyer* or the Indian from *Predator* or *48 Hours.* I like to call these people IWABA (Indians With A Bad Attitude).

Finally, we have the fourth stereotype, the mystical all-knowing Indian with one foot in the astral plane, the other in a canoe. You know the type: they melt in and out of the bush almost as effortlessly as they speak metaphorical wisdoms about humanity and the world in poor English—without cracking a smile. You couldn't swing a dead cat without hitting that type of Indian on shows like *Little House on the Prairie, Grizzly Adams,* and so on.

Or if the writer/director is feeling particularly adventurous, how about a psychotic, radical Elder sidekick!

But like I said before, none of these descriptions really fit me. My best friend is Native, so that sort of eliminates the sidekick syndrome. Perhaps we're two Indians in search of a white man? Now there's a scary thought.

I'm fairly certain I'm not the fiery radical type. While it is true being born Native in this country is a political act in itself, that's about the extent of it for me. I find radicals don't get paid nearly enough.

And as for the psychotic, angry drunk, being a writer is about as psychotic and angry as I can handle. As for me being out of control ... talk to my mother.

Unfortunately I have some difficulty melting in and out of the bush magically. I've been told I have the unusual talent of being able to trip over footprints.

I sometimes wonder if there's a heaven for outdated stereotypes, a place they all hang out when no longer in vogue. Somewhere out there is a card table with Tonto, Billy Jack, Uncle Remus, Shylock and the rest, playing cards to pass the time. I wonder if Billy's still wearing that black t-shirt and hat.

Academia Mania

Once upon a time, many years past, there was a man who told a story from his wayward youth. As he so bravely put it, it was a long time ago on a reserve far, far away, when he was but a young and innocent Aboriginal living with his family in the serene outdoors known today as Northern Ontario. Then one day, as often happens in tales such as this, a wandering group of archaeologists/anthropologists/sociologists (so grouped for they all looked and acted alike) appeared in his peaceful community.

It seems these intrepid academics were there in search of knowledge. They were fearless story hunters, wanting to document the legends and myths of these proud, oral people. Legends they wanted, and legends they were determined to get, for the annals of history and their publishers. First in their quest they went to the Elders of the village saying, "Tell us your stories so that we may document them."

The Elders, believing stories are meant to be shared with good friends and caring people, refused, saying to the puzzled academics, "Strangers do not demand a story, they ask politely." Thus the academics were chastised. With no stories to bring back, and no victory to print, the academics pondered and prodded until they found willing confidants for their earnest, though ill-conceived, purpose.

The children of that community boldly approached these white warriors of writing declaring, "We know the legends and stories of our people and we will gladly share them with you if you will honour us with gifts. Financial ones," spoke their young leader.

Eager and anxious, the academics gladly brought forth their small change in exchange for the fables and myths of these proud people. Every morning for many days, the children would entice these eager men with a legend of these proud forest people, often about the trickster Nanabush and his mischievous adventures, or about the animals that abound in this primeval forest, or occasionally about the people themselves.

And later, after the tale was told, the children of the community would retire to the woods from whence they sprang and spend the afternoon enjoying the spoils of their barter. Down went the potato chips and pop they gladly consumed, all the while pondering and creating fresh new tales they would tell these pale strangers. They kept close to their hearts the real stories of their people, and instead offered only the imagination and creativity of a child's mind. For what they traded were new legends, barely days old. Many decades later, one of these children-turned-adults happened upon a bookstore. There, in a book of Native legends published many years before by a non-Native researcher, but used frequently as source material, he came upon a story that was ... oddly familiar.

Then it dawned upon him. In the pages he held in his hand were those same spirited stories commissioned all those years past. Childhood memories flooded his mind as he recalled those fun-filled days of free junk food and gullible academics. "Ah," he thought, "the brilliant, mischievous days of youth." Seldom in his later years had he achieved such heights of roguish achievement.

The smile stayed upon his impish face as he replaced the book. The trickster of legend was alive and well and living in the glorious halls of academia.

The Story Real: Some are tall, some aren't. Some are fat, while others have a lean and hungry look about them. Most wear glasses or contacts, but not all. And believe it or not, some could be your next door neighbour. I am referring to academics.

There's an old joke in the Native community. What's the definition of a Native family? Two parents, a grandparent, five kids and an anthropologist (or academic). Get the picture?

Not a week goes by in the offices of Native Earth Performing Arts, that we don't get a call from some student or professor from a university/college doing research on Native theatre in Canada. And each time I put the phone down I struggle to suppress a shudder. I can't help but wonder: what wonderful images are they getting from our work?

When is a door not a door? When it's ajar. When is a symbolic metaphor describing the Native individual's relationship with the Earth, or Turtle Island as the Natives call it, and the spiritual and physical sustenance that it provides, as well as the water being an allusion to the blood of said Turtle Island, or perhaps in this reference, the term Mother Earth would be more accurate, not a symbolic metaphor?

Sometimes you just wanna yell, "He's just fishing, for Christ's sake!" This is a strange race of people who spend their entire life fulfilling some need to constantly study and analyse other people's writings and work (in this case Native works), but seldom attempt the same work themselves. It's sort of like people who watch pornographic movies but never have sex.

I remember reading an article written by British playwright Willy Russell, author of such plays as *Educating Rita* and *Shirley Valentine*. He was relating a story of a lecture he secretly attended, a lecture about his work.

At one point, the academic brought up for discussion the final scene of *Educating Rita*, where as a going-away gift, the former hairstylist Rita cuts the professor's hair. "This," said the man with letters behind his name, "was a direct metaphor to the Samson and Delilah legend where she is taking his strength by cutting his hair. The author obviously … " At this moment, Willy Russell stood up and said, "Uh sorry, you're wrong. I just wanted to end the play on a funny and touching note. It has nothing to do with Samson." They proceeded to get into a rather intense argument over the interpretation of that scene. The academic refused to believe that Russell hadn't intended that final image to be a metaphor.

As a writer I recognize the fact that all stories, in whatever form they're written, are the equivalent of literary Rorschach tests, all open to interpretation and understanding. Often that's the fun of taking a literature class, dissecting the piece for the underlying imagery. And adding subtextual elements in the stories I write lends a certain amount of fun to the writing process.

However, as Freud used to say, sometimes a cigar is just a good smoke.

Case in point—a non-Native friend of mine wrote his master's thesis on Native theatre in Canada. In one of the chapters he examined some of my work. One night in a drunken celebration after successfully defending his thesis, he let me read his dissertation. As he celebrated his new found academic status, I sat there reading some new and interesting theories about the symbolism in my plays.

To put it bluntly, they were wrong, completely way off, not correct, inaccurate, barking up the proverbial wrong tree. Especially the section where he thought a crow in the text was a manifestation of Nanabush, the Ojibway trickster figure. I sat there for a while, on that bar stool, quietly debating if I should tell him of the error. But looking at the sheer joy in his face after all those years of university finally completed, I held my tongue. I'd rather have him drinking happily than in a fit of depression. If he thinks a crow is Nanabush, let him. There's a whole flock of Nanabushes living around my mother's house. He'd have a field day.

That seems to be the latest fad with academics. Subscribing all actions and at least one character in a written piece to the trickster figure. As playwright/poet Daniel David Moses describes it, "They all like to play 'Spot The Trickster'."

But then again, these same people, the academics of this world, are responsible for introducing my books and other writings to the curriculum of various high schools, colleges and universities. The very computer I'm writing on I owe to their influences. So I guess I mustn't bite the hand that feeds me.

So perhaps, just for clarity's sake, I should take the time to make sure these no doubt intelligent people understand that it's just the inherent trickster tendencies that exist on a subconscious level in all literary works penned by Aboriginal writers and are representative of our culture. In other words, I'm not responsible for these views or criticisms; the trickster is at fault here. The trickster made me do it.

Yeah, they'll buy that.

A View From a Cafe

Recently, I was sitting at an outdoor cafe enjoying some coffee and good conversation when I couldn't help noticing two men approaching the patio.

Still on the sidewalks, they came along the railing that enclosed the patio, stopping at each table, asking for money. They looked quite ragged, drunk, and had obviously seen better times. Both were Native. I am Native.

As I watched these two men of the street hustling money from a captive audience, I felt something. I wasn't sure what it was. Embarrassment, shame, pity? I had never felt these emotions toward fellow Natives before, and it troubled me.

As I sat there feeling ashamed, something occurred to me—what right do I have to feel ashamed of these men? It's their lives, it's a free world. Then I began to feel ashamed of myself for taking such a high moral ground.

Over the past thirteen years, I have been involved in various capacities with the media. During this time I have worked on approximately seventeen documentaries about Native culture, arts and substance abuse. I have done enough research, been to enough communities, talked to enough of these people to know that in the vast majority of cases, it's not their fault that they live this existence.

I know all the stories and all the reasons.

Such factors as improper adoptions, the aftereffects of residential schools, coming to the city seeking work and finding an environment totally alien and unwelcoming, despair over a disappearing culture, language and way of life—I could fill up the rest of this column with a steady stream of contributing factors. But the result would be the same, tragic stories leading to a tragic existence.

But still, in the back of my mind, were these two men panhandling from middle class white people, perpetuating stereotypes and giving credence to an image most Native people have spent their life fighting.

There was the case of one prominent Native artist in the city who, when approached for money, got into a terse discussion on the street with such a person, perhaps one of these very gentlemen, about the image they were presenting to the public. The discussion quickly deteriorated into an argument about attitude and rights, and the artist walked away frustrated.

In this city, I have seen and constantly recognized approximately one to two dozen hard-core street dwellers in my daily travels who pursue the same practice as these two foraging men. On the other hand, there is an estimated Aboriginal population in Toronto of around seventy thousand people. Not a bad ratio, all things considered.

But because of this preconceived alcohol-oriented luggage and the fact that visually, these Native people tend to stand out in one's memory more than say, a white street person, their image will stay with a passerby more readily.

I can see people at those patio tables saying when they get home, "A drunk Indian hit us up for money." And again, I shudder.

Perhaps the fault is within myself. There is a term used in Ontario, most often in Toronto, that is an offshoot of Anishnawbe—the word Ojibway people used to describe themselves and their people. Basically it translates as the "original" or "first" people.

The term has been modified to accommodate the growing Aboriginal middle class that has appeared in Toronto and other major cities. They are sometimes referred to as "Anish-snobs."

I see these men, I know their story, I feel anger for what has happened to them, yet seeing them at the corner of Queen and Bathurst or at this patio, harassing people for money—against my will, I get embarrassed.

Does this make me a bad person?

FOR THE TIMES
THEY ARE A-CHANGIN'

Grey Owl is Dead
but His Spirit Lives On

Sometime during that ancient age known collectively as the '60s, there lived in the United States a black activist and writer named Eldridge Cleaver. And during those tempestuous times this man noticed an unusual trend developing in the mating rituals of that period. It had become very apparent to him that more and more white women, specifically blondish types, seemed to be dating an awful lot of black men, and vice versa.

He chalked it up to these women wanting to rebel against the restrictive social norms of middle class life, to upset their parents and the status quo of the day. This rebellious practice seemed to be in vogue back in those days. He also reasoned that the black men, wanting to sample the privileged world that had been denied to them by the dominant white society, thought this was great. Who were they to argue?

And because this new cross-cultural dating trend was first discussed in Cleaver's book, *Soul On Ice*, it has been referred to, in some circles, as the Soul-On-Ice Syndrome. The name says it all.

That was in the '60s. This is the '90s, and as they say, the more things change, the more they stay the same. Except this time, the trendy thing happens to involve Native people. Finding an Aboriginal companion seems to be all the rage these days. So, in the name of social commentary, I would like to rename the particular courting phenomenon: the Spirit-On-Ice Syndrome.

But in this case, we're not just talking about dating, we're talking about the whole enchilada (if I may appropriate that cultural metaphor). It seems that ever since *Dances with Wolves* and *Dry Lips Oughta Move to Kapuskasing* hit the public, the white world is beating a path to the reserve door seeking spiritual fulfillment, Elders' wisdom, and discount cigarettes.

Recently an Elder from my community told me about a visit by two white women to his house. These were the most recent in a regular influx of what he calls "wannabes, groupies, and do-gooders" who, and

I paraphrase their words, "I really-respect-and-honour-your-culture-and-want-to-be-a-part-of-it-so-please-let-me-participate-and-learn-from-your-sacred-and-ancient-ceremonies-so-I-can-understand-your-ways-this-isn't-just-a-phase-I'm-going-through-I-really-mean-it-so-can-I-huh?"

My Elder friend and I sat around for a good forty-five minutes trying to figure out what, specifically, they wanted to "understand?" Why we eat so much macaroni and tomatoes; why seventy-five percent of the Native population doesn't vote? And why we wear buckskin on hot summer days? (I haven't figured that one out yet myself.)

This one blonde woman who was visiting my friend had recently divorced a black gentleman. (I wonder if they met during the '60s?) Now she was becoming fascinated with Native culture and I guess Native men. At one point, according to her, her parents had asked her if she was ever going to date a white man, to which she replied, "I doubt it. They have no mystery."

Mystery? That was good for another forty-five minute conversation with my Elder friend.

What mystery? We get up in the morning, put our clothes on, have coffee (usually fully or extra-caffinated), go to the bathroom … yes, Indians do go to the bathroom but in a secret Indian way that can't be revealed. Maybe that's what she was talking about.

There are many more of these mystery-drawn people than you would expect. A friend of mine went out last summer to attend a Sun Dance. When she arrived, she was one of the few Native people there. Eighty percent of the people setting up camp were non-Native. She was somewhat peeved.

There's also the story of this woman who went to Mexico, and became enamoured with this Mexican Indian who took her into one of the Aztec ruins. There he told her about an ancient Aztec ceremony that involved making love on the steps of the pyramid. She believed him and they did.

Stories like that remind me I'm only half an hour from the Peterborough Petroglyphs. Hmmm …

And there was this time I met this woman, quite casually, who was opening a Native art gallery. She introduced herself as being from the Six Nations Reserve in Southern Ontario. Several weeks later I asked her from which of the Six Nations she was—Mohawk, Cayuga, etc. She looked at me for a moment then confessed that she was actually white, she had married into the reserve (she was now divorced), and she was quite proud of the fact that she still had her status card.

Some weeks later she started dating an Alaskan Native painter, went to visit him, received an Indian name, and refused to be called by her own English name. She had her brand-spanking-new Indian name put on her business cards.

Is it any wonder my Elder friend and I are a little cynical? After five hundred and one years of oppression, destruction and general annoyance we are now, overnight, chic. Irony can be painful.

But I should be fair. Not all white people who come into our communities can be classified in this way. I have one aunt (who's French) who speaks better Ojibway than I do and has a thicker accent than me. And she didn't show up on our reserve all those years ago to "understand." She just fell in love and couldn't have cared less if my uncle was Indian. Many other family members and friends fit into this category. They accept us as who we are, but they don't want to be us. Who can argue with that?

We also mustn't forget that there are some Native people out there that for one reason or another, want to be white. So we're willing to make you a deal. Ship ours back, and we'll ship yours back too.

Pow Wows, They Are A-Changin'

When I was growing up, my mother used to talk about how much things had changed on the reserve from when she was a kid. I heard the countless stories of hauling innumerable pails of water from the pump, chopping wood, fighting swarms of Indian-loving mosquitoes without the protection of OFF!, wading through armpit-high snow to get to the outhouse as you battled hungry wolves, and so on. You know, the usual stories.

But when you're young and stupid, you don't listen, let alone think of things having changed all that much. And, as with the nature of the heavens, words like my mother's eventually come back. I can't believe how much things have changed since I was a kid. Specifically, pow wows.

Growing up on the Curve Lake First Nations Reserve in Central Ontario, I remember the social event of the season was our annual pow wow held at (where else?) the baseball diamond. While some of my cousins and other relations danced their buckskinned little hearts out, I'd run around on those hot dusty days, competing with all the other local kids to collect all the returnable pop bottles thrown away by the tourists. Hey, it was a living.

Nowadays, everybody drinks from cans. Non-returnable cans. It's quite tragic when the end of an era is symbolized by an empty Coke can being tossed into a garbage container.

Twenty years ago we used to think it was quite exotic when dancers from Akwesasne (a Mohawk community near Cornwall, Ontario) would come to dance at our pow wow. We'd all stand around oohing and ahhing, pointing and whispering, "Wow. Look, real live Mohawks." I was at a pow wow recently, where Native people from Central America, not to mention others from all over Canada and the United States, danced and sold things. People just a little more exotic than your average Mohawk to this now jaded eye.

In my day, the majority of dancers wore straight buckskin with the occasional colourful trappings attached. But if they were feeling adventurous and daring, it might be solid white buckskin.

In this day and age, the colours and designs of the dancers' regalia can dazzle your eyes and puff up your pride. Fancy dancers, shawl dancers, grass dancers, jingle dress dancers, and traditional dancers (both male and female) have their own particular clothing style. You're lucky if you can find one in eight or nine dancers wearing a sizeable amount of buckskin. Dictates of fashion have moved on.

The spectre of commercialism has also reared its head at today's pow wow. At some of the larger gatherings, it's not uncommon to see tens of thousands of dollars of prize money up for grabs. A few weeks ago I witnessed a group of tourists approach two young boys who were dressed in their dancing outfits. They marvelled over the boys for a moment and then asked them if they could take their picture. Immediately both boys, in stereo, stuck up two fingers saying in well-used, practiced tones, "Two bucks." That's a long way from collecting pop bottles.

Food and craft booths have changed over the years. Eons ago, all the money I made on the pop bottles (after cashing them in) went directly back into the pow wow through the purchase of god-awful amounts of traditional Native junk food like hamburgers, fried bread, corn soup and pop.

Today the list of traditional "Native foods" being offered at pow wows has grown to include pizza, candy floss, tacos, baloney on a scone, lemonade, etc. My favourite were these two stands side by side, one selling buffalo burgers (made from real buffalo), the other peddling something called an Indian burger (I can only hope it was made by real Indians, not from real Indians).

And I've given up trying to keep track of all the things for sale at these events. The gambit runs from your basic tacky tourist stuff to very expensive leather works, sculptures and paintings. Several dozen booths (some with inventive names like Imagin-Nations and Creative Native) hawk your standard Aboriginal paraphernalia like dream catchers, medicine wheels, glass beads, braids of sweetgrass, gobs and gobs of silver and turquoise, etc.

Then there were the more … interesting things for sale. Playing cards designed in the style of your favourite Canadian tribe (I've got a full house; three Haida chiefs and two Cree medicine men—beat that!). Another booth was offering Tarot card readings; evidently a traditional

Native activity I'm not familiar with. At one pow wow I saw a booth selling a large selection of New Age books. One particular publication caught my eye—*How to be a Shaman In Ten Easy Steps*. Geez, all these years we've been doing it the hard way!

So, as I stood there in line waiting to use the portable Royal Bank Instabank conveniently located beside the port-a-pots, I couldn't help but marvel at all the changes over the years. Pow wows have gone high tech and modern. Then, off in the distance I saw a man draining a bottle of pop (one of the large, still returnable sizes) and tossing it away. Feeling a twinge of nostalgia, I left the line, picked it up and put it in my bag. Some traditions never die.

Aboriginal Lexicon

Linguistic terms often used in relation to Canada's Indigenous people are fast becoming words of everyday use. But sometimes these words have a specific and contextual meaning, above and beyond their accepted use. To help cut down on potential misuse and misunderstandings, I have put together a list of contemporary Aboriginal buzzwords to help facilitate their proper usage in dialogue. Please use them with care.

Assembly of First Nations: Political organization claiming to represent all Status and Reserve Natives except for those who have opted out, like the Iroquois Confederacy and certain western tribes. Sort of like the situation in the former Soviet Union.

Blockades: Preordained trump card, or why else would the Creator have placed a large portion of necessary and needed roads on Native territory.

Dream catchers: Aboriginal merchandising at its best. They are everywhere.

Government (1): Source of all evil.

Government (2): Source of all funding, allowing various Native organizations to criticize government as defined above.

Indian giver: A case of saying one thing but reversing it and doing the opposite. Like treaties.

Kashtin: Simon and Garfunkel with a tan.

W.P. Kinsella: Aboriginal enemy #1, or the second coming of Shakespeare if you have anything to do with the new television series based on *Dance Me Outside* called *The Rez.*

Land claims: Native equivalent of karma.

Minister of the Department of Indian Affairs: Person who has no real grasp of what's going on out there but acts like he or she does. Like the U.N.

Native / Quebec relations: An oxymoron.

Oka: Where past treatment meets current reality. See Malcolm

X's comment concerning the assassination of JFK, "A case of the chickens coming home to roost."

Pocahontas: In film, Tonto in drag, or in reality, a twelve-year-old with a fabulous publicist.

Quebec: Province wanting sovereignty from Canada but unwilling to allow Native communities the same right within Quebec. A case of "do as I say, not as I do."

Self-government: Self-determination or the right to have our own Trudeau or Mulroney.

Tobacco: Sacred ceremonial herb or cursed addictive plant, depending on how long your family has been in this country.

Treaty Rights: Not to be confused with hunters and anglers, logging, mining or government wrongs.

Wannabe: Elements of mainstream society suffering from culture-envy. The Anti-apple.

White people: Politically incorrect term for those of European descent. More currently acceptable terms are People of Pallor, Colour-Challenged or Pigment-denied.

Wine / Beer / Liquor: Tasty recreational beverages or cursed addictive intoxicant, depending on how long your family has been in this country.

FUNNY, YOU DON'T LOOK LIKE ~~ONE~~ TWO:

Further Adventures of a Blue-Eyed Ojibway

OPINIONS!
(Who Gives a Flying ... !)

Indian Givers

My birthday is approaching quickly and I am beginning to dread it already. Not because Father Time seems to be eating a bigger slice of my birthday cake every year, but because of the presents I might receive from well-meaning friends. At the risk of sounding ungrateful, it's an interesting comment on society when, as a Native (Ojibway) person, I often receive gifts from my non-Native friends that run the gambit of every possible Native-influenced present that could be bought in a store.

For some unexplained reason, there seems to be this subconscious belief amongst many white acquaintances that since I am Native, I must therefore be given a Native-flavoured present at every possible occasion, like a tin logo of the Indian Motorcycle Company that currently hangs on my bedroom wall, for example. It seems to be mandatory. To do anything else would be rude and possibly precipitate a blockade of some sort. Thus, the clay pottery that I have received over the years that dots my mother's house back home.

In birthdays past, as well as house-warmings, Christmases and a variety of other well-known seasonal celebrations, there always seems to be a tendency to give me, as well as many of my Native friends, a confusing collection of Aboriginal giftware. Over the years I alone have received art prints, dream catchers galore, medicine pouches, videotapes of Native movies, and enough T-shirts for a dozen wet T-shirt contests. For instance, on my last birthday, a good friend of obvious Caucasian ancestry gave me *Where White Men Fear To Tread*, the autobiography of Russell Means, famed American Indian Movement activist. I appreciated the gesture but it was a rather long book about a man I wasn't particularly interested in knowing better. Being Native doesn't automatically make you interesting. But don't tell him that.

Thus the conundrum. You appreciate the social and financial support for your culture and all its many artists, but sometimes you just want a pair of black loafers with no feathers attached. I thanked my Caucasian buddy for the gesture anyway.

My former girlfriend took part in the wedding of a longtime friend; she was the only Native participant, and all the bridesmaids and ushers received presents for their efforts. Everybody else in the wedding party received *faux* diamond jewelry. Instead, my former girlfriend received something called an Answer Feather that consisted of the three staples of First Nations gift giving: a leather strap, a small obliquely carved piece of bone, and a lone feather, quail I believe. According to the tag, it was a "traditional healing tool for those seeking answers," like "Why didn't I get any real jewelry?"

Yet on the other hand, my Native friends often give me (and I should add that I often give them) culturally vague clothes, books, appliances, music etc. On many long drives, a CD of Shaggy is just as enjoyable as Kashtin. As I'm writing this, I am wearing a straight black T-shirt with no identifiable Native logo anywhere on it, given to me by a Mohawk family.

If you go to my mother's house on the Reserve, you will notice very little of a representational Aboriginal content in her house. Other than what I give her from the seasonal celebratory overflow that I frequently encounter. In fact, she does have a decidedly non-Aboriginal barbeque I gave her for Mother's Day a few years back. And she's as Native as they come. I will confess however, I did give her moccasin slippers one year for Christmas, but only because they were a lot prettier than those worn paisley ones she had. But please don't hate me for that.

It makes me wonder if Native people are not the only recipients of culturally-appropriate tributes. Do Caucasian people feel the urge to give the Japanese chopsticks as a wedding gift? Or maybe Mexicans get sombreros for graduation? Do the Swedish get their national flag at a baby shower? On Arbor Day, do you present your favourite American with an assault rifle? These are difficult questions.

I realize that one shouldn't look a gift horse in the mouth; in fact, some may consider it rude and if so I apologize. But I would just like to point out that it is possible to give a gift with no cultural baggage attached. We do manage to exist in other areas of reality besides the Indigenous one. As one friend put it, "there is no particular Native way to boil an egg." The same goes with gift giving.

I look up on my wall, to my Native Images calendar, with a good looking Indian guy in a leather vest representing the month of May, and see my birthday not too far distant. I could really use some new dress pants but I better clear a shelf for all the Jack Weatherford and Tony Hillerman novels I know I'll get.

Some of My Best Friends Are Vegetables

There's an old joke in the Native community that goes something like "What's another term for an Indian vegetarian?" The appropriate answer: "A very bad hunter."

Finding a Native vegetarian is something akin to finding a non-bingo going, non-hockey watching/playing, non-denim wearing, non-dream catcher/feather-hanging-from-the-rear-view mirror type Indigenous person. But for some reason, there seems to be whole masses of non-Native ones out there, in Canadian society, drinking their carrot juices and eating muffins galore, sending dirty looks at us carnivores (whether Indigenous or not). I think there must be a scientific lab somewhere spitting these people out.

Now I'm not a vindictive or petty person, but in my travels I have met many people who have pet peeves, or groups of people that annoy or irritate other assortments of people. I am no different. Over the years and after many a tasty veal sandwich, it has been my dubious pleasure to face many a renegade vegetarian who has strong, definite opinions about my diet and isn't afraid to express it to my face. For the record, I am a proud meat eater. I keep a pepperoni in my wallet for emergencies. When I die, I don't want to be cremated; instead I want to be marinated and barbequed. And unfortunately I have many an ex-girlfriend who would volunteer for the job. And some who wouldn't necessarily wait for me to die before starting.

In fact, an example of my devotion to DNA consumption can be observed in the oddest places, like during my occasional bouts of tequila festivities. Instead of doing the normal sequential routine of salt, tequila, and then a lemon to cleanse the palate, I instead opt for the more interesting salt, tequila, then a pork chop. Unconventional but definitely more tasty I think, not to mention the benefits of the additional protein.

Upon seeing this, one vegetarian woman I met told me that, on principle, she refuses to eat anything with a face. Poor woman, I couldn't help thinking, she must be terrible in bed! But then again, I guess nothing beats a good carrot.

Personally, I think this vegetarian/carnivore rivalry goes all the way back to Biblical times. It's all right there in the Bible, if you know how to read between the lines. Check out the first few books of Genesis. As you may remember, Adam and Eve are hanging around the Garden of Eden, looking for ways to screw up Paradise (you may know their great-great-great-great grandson, a gentleman named Columbus).

So there's our innocent Eve, with nothing much to do, hanging around this strange and unusual tree with a name plate nailed into the bark saying "Do Not Touch". She looks up and sees something in the tree, reminding her that she is hungry. So what does she pick from it that gets her, her hubby, and all their descendants tossed by God from the Garden of Eden and thrust forever into the Hell we now know as Urban Sprawl?

If my Bible studies are correct, I believe it was the proverbial "forbidden FRUIT." The operative word here is fruit! Not steak, not roast chicken, not even a lamb chop, but fruit! My question is, would all the troubles of the world have happened, would civilization be different if, say, instead she had picked some veal piccata? Or maybe we'd still be running around naked and happy if she'd had a craving for some chicken wings. Would we still be in Paradise if she had passed on the fruit for a beef and broccoli stir-fry? It does make a person wonder. Mental note: I must remember to send a copy of this column to the Pope. Could be some interesting theological discussions here.

So instead, all these thousands of years later, I get my jollies by telling vegetarians that we Native people consider pet stores on the same par with take out restaurants. The number of times I've told someone I was going by the Pets'R'Us to pick up some rabbits and then innocently asked, "Anybody want me to grab them some fish or maybe a kitten or two as an appetizer?" I mean, if you just hollow out the kitten from the top, they make dandy slippers, depending on your shoe size. For some reason, vegetarians don't appreciate my sense of humour.

Oh well, one thing I know for sure. When the end of the world finally does come, whether it's the next ice age or maybe global warming, I'm fairly certain it will be us big and fat meat eaters who'll end up eating the thinner, anemic vegetarians. Survival of the fattest. The good thing is, at least they'll be low fat!

Indian Humour—What a Joke!

I was recently in Winnipeg where I learned an important lesson dealing with the ticklish issue of humour, or what some people think is humour. I had arrived late for dinner with a group of journalists from the APTN network where I had just appeared on a talk show dealing with Aboriginal humour. I sat in the only available chair, beside a man I had been introduced to earlier in the day, and two young women I had not yet met. No sooner had I sat down when the guy beside me yelled to the two women in front of me "Hey, this is Drew Hayden Taylor and he's promised to give you each a screaming orgasm. And wait till you hear him scream!" That was my introduction to these women. For one of the few times in my life, I was speechless.

For the rest of the evening, he peppered the table with a non-stop barrage of jokes, most of which I'm fairly certain only he found funny. The evening ended with a series (I'm talking at least a good ten minutes worth) of constant Ojibway jokes aimed directly at me. Now I can take a joke as good as the next person, even more so since as a "professional" humourist (though some might argue), I have studied and experienced a lot of wit in the world. One would think I should have a higher tolerance for the more abstract forms of joking. I was wrong.

This man's constant attempts at being funny kept reminding me of boxing statistics, when the ringside announcers say that a particular boxer threw 112 punches in a round but only 13 were power shots. It was roughly the same ratio. And typically, the more he drank, the funnier he thought he was.... Sound vaguely familiar? At the end of the evening, the man's superior at work came up to me and apologized for the guy's behavior. I shrugged off the effect of the man's impact on me, thinking they had to deal with him more than I did. I was leaving the next day.

As everyone knows, comedy is subjective. Everybody has a different funny bone. Some laugh at the Three Stooges, others at *Married With Children*, and there's Shakespeare, and let's not forget the limited appeal of mimes. Truly, I have yet to meet anybody (who is not a mime) who will actually admit to enjoying and understanding the profession. Though the one universal element in the universe, after death and taxes (of which we as Native people have had more of one and less of the other) is everybody knows somebody who thinks they are funnier than they actually are. Someday they'll have a way of screening the DNA to prevent this.

In researching and editing a documentary I directed on Native humour for the National Film Board, I was privileged to explore and ascertain the wonderfully full and amazing forms of Aboriginal humour existing in this country, specifically the distinctive characteristics or aspects that seem to appear more in our humour than in other cultures (screaming orgasms not withstanding). And you don't have to be a "professional" humourist to figure this out.

For instance, teasing seems to be the predominate form of witty banter amongst our people. Everybody has been teased by a child, adult or peer. You ain't Indian if you can't tease or be teased—it's mentioned somewhere in the Royal Commission on Aboriginal People, Section 4.3.6: "The Federal Government will acknowledge the right of Aboriginal people in this country to tease, be teased, as well as hunt and fish and all the rest of it." In some Aboriginal cultures, it is a specific mechanism used in the society to keep people in line and maintain the status quo, the great social adjuster.

Also, our humour tends to be quite self-deprecating. That is to say, we tend to make jokes about ourselves, often at our own expense. How many people out there have told an "Indian" joke or made fun of themselves, family or friends? It seems quite natural. Again, it's also a way of maintaining social unity and keeping our feet on the ground.

Another unusual attribute deals with the ability to start a joke, and have it carry on, with various individuals building and adding on to it until a completely different joke finally emerges. Sitting around a table or fire, somebody tells a joke or teases somebody, and another person adds on to it until it lands in somebody else's lap. A soundly Indigenous practice I believe.

It's important to point out that these characteristics are not just limited to the Native community. There are exceptions to every rule. I for one, have seen many white people tease each other, and the mainstay of many Jewish comedians is the self-deprecating joke. However, I think over the thousands of years, we have created and mastered our own unique brand of it.

Some words of advice to wannabe funny-people out there. As somebody who's told a lot of jokes in his day and had a few of them fall flat, and also seen many people tells jokes that were funny and not funny, take notice of some experienced suggestions on tickling the funny bone, whether Indigenous or not.

Rule #1: The moment you try to be funny, is the moment you sound like you're trying to be funny. It's got to be natural and spontaneous (which defines the vast majority of Native people I know). You shouldn't have to push or force your jokes into people's faces.

Rule #2: Humour should amuse, not abuse. Most people tell jokes to entertain or obtain friends. Abusing them does not help you in your cause. I must remember to email that message to Winnipeg.

And I am tempted to urge people not to laugh at their own jokes, but there is another unique quality about some Native humour I forgot to mention. In some communities, particularly up north, you don't know you're being teased until they themselves start laughing. This is because the humour is so subtle and understated. I learned that the hard way.

And stay away from jokes about screaming orgasms unless you know the person.

And for the record, I don't scream.

GETTING THE N.A.C.*
(*NATIVE ARTISTIC COMMUNITY)

Where'd That Arrow in My Back Come From?

There are three things in this world I would urge people, if they have any sanity, never to be or do. The first two are unimportant but the third definitely would include the dubious endeavor of being a critic or reviewer in the Native artistic community. Because no matter what you may write, you can be sure somebody you know will not like it and make sure that you know they do not like it. Or they will never talk to you again.

It is undoubtedly one of the advantages of coming from a larger, dominant culture, when you can say or write what you want about other people's work, and conceivably never have to worry about running into these people and face the proverbial music (unless of course you're a proverbial music critic).

Not so in the Native community. In Canada, the Native population is fairly small. The Native artistic community is even smaller. And in a place like Toronto, most would fit in my mother's back yard for a barbeque. As a playwright, I know almost all the other Aboriginal playwrights in Canada, as well as the vast majority of the actors and directors. As a published author, I also know most of the other First Nations writers on a personal level. As a Native filmmaker … you get the picture.

And with the advent of political correctness, it's no surprise that many institutions that review books, plays, films etc. would prefer to avoid the hassle of seeming insensitive to the artistic aspirations of this country's Indigenous population, and at the same time, review their work without a potentially "racist" slant. So oftentimes, they call on a First Nations peer. That's where I often enter the picture, like a lamb to slaughter.

Everybody has an opinion. Some people have too many opinions. And in this insane world we live in, a very few people are paid for their opinion. These people are called critics and they make a few bucks sharing their opinion of other people's work. These are often, though not always, people who don't actually participate in the art they comment on.

So I think it's important to point out that, unlike many critics, I actually work in the fields I may review. Otherwise, what's the point of offering up an uneducated opinion? God knows there's enough of those in the world already. Critics can sometimes be like people who watch a lot of porn but never have sex. More akin to do as I say, not as I do.

In the past I have reviewed books by Tom King, Brian Maracle, Richard Wagamese etc., and movies ranging from *Dances with Wolves* to *Pocahontas*; and have written my opinion about various television shows, as well as many detailed articles on exploring and explaining the world of Aboriginal theatre. So needless to say, I've pissed off a lot of people. And as I have stated, eventually you will run into these same people at a Starbucks, a pow wow, or a book launching.

Some critics have the luxury of divorcing themselves completely from the people they write about. Because of the vastness of the non-Native art world, this is more than possible, even preferable. But as a participating member of both the artistic community and the Native community, that is not a conceivable option for me.

And the ironic thing is, I'm not an exceptionally brutal critic. I sometimes bend over backwards trying to find positive things to say about the material I am reviewing. And as a result, I have turned down more assignments than I have taken to avoid any unnecessary awkwardness or possible unpleasantness.

This is because, in the Native community, there is often perceived to be a fine line between those who support our artists, and those who feel the need to be critical and drag them down. It's often referred to in an over-used cliché known as "the crab story."

It goes something like this: A man was walking down the beach one day and saw this Native man approaching. In the Native man's hand was a pail. Inside the pail was a bunch of live crabs. The man commented to the Native man, "You better put a lid on your pail or all your crabs will get away." The Native man shook his head with a smile, saying "I don't need a lid. They're Indian crabs; the minute one of them makes it to the top, the others will pull him back down."

That is often the danger of writing from inside a marginalized group. I have been told numerous times: "After five hundred years of oppression and suppression, what our nations need is positive reinforcement and encouragement. Otherwise, you're playing into their hands, and dividing us in our time of cultural Renaissance. We must stand together and support our brothers and sisters in their endeavors" ... Or something like that.

As a result, the objectivity in reviews can be a little suspect. In many of the Native magazines I have read or seen in my professional life, the review section consisted of 99.9% glowing praise if the book/film/album was Native-originated. It got to the point where if I saw the word REVIEWS, I didn't bother reading the text because I knew instinctively it would be kind words and rabid support. Again, it's difficult to consider such support a fault after several hundred years of being told our stories and arts were worthless and meaningless. Thus the conflicted nature of being a Native critic.

I've been told this issue is not unique to specifically the Native community. Many have told me that such divided opinions on the merits of accurate and informed criticism have rallied opposing sides of many marginalized communities, e.g. the Gay and Lesbian community, the Asian, Jewish, Black, French-Canadian, left-handed walnut merchants etc. It is perceived that an objective opinion can quickly be misconstrued as a personal attack and the reviewer has been corrupted by mainstream sensibilities.

In my artistic community where the playwright population may consist of a dozen or two, every time you say/write something like "So'n'So's dialogue seemed a little clichéd and could have been a tad more original," it's not anonymous words from an anonymous patron. Especially when you've sat at the bar with this fellow writer, lent them money, called them a cab, or they've called you a cab; then it seems like a betrayal, regardless of the accuracy of your comments. I personally have received long letters deconstructing my reviews and pointing out, both rudely and politely, how invalid my opinion is. And that's what a review is, simply an opinion.

And as somebody who has received more than his share of criticism in the arts, some positive, some negative, I truly understand the value of accurate and insightful criticism. Many of my non-artistic friends have often said that they envied me and wished they could be a critic, be paid to read books or watch movies, or listen to music. Most don't understand that to be a movie critic, you need more than the ability to eat popcorn and say "I like it" or "I don't like it."

I've told them that if you like something, you have to be able to tell them why you liked it, concisely and intelligently. What stood out, what grabbed your nuts (or ovaries) and squeezed them until you felt something? Or on the other hand, "That movie sucked" doesn't exactly inspire confidence in the reviewer's capacity to eloquently present their case.

One of the reasons I don't review a lot of books or movies is I hate the detached feeling you must have in order to write about it—the ability to analyze while participating. Not something I find easy or enjoyable to do. And you'll find it's often easier to say why you disliked something rather than why you liked it, because the things that disturb or confuse you are more obvious and easier to put your thumb on.

So with all that being said, reviewing somebody's work is a huge responsibility. Reviewing somebody's work in the Native community is fraught with delicate considerations and potential social misunderstandings. However, growth comes from constructive criticism, be it Native or non- Native. Art, like reality and life, will have its detractors and benefactors. The real trick is to take what you can, and ignore the rest. Easier said than done, but it sure beats getting an ulcer, or an arrow in the back.

57 Channels and No Indians On

My suspicions as to the status of Canadian television, and to a lesser extent American television, were realized when I received a phone call while waiting in the Lethbridge airport to board a flight to Saskatoon. It was a call that couldn't have come at a better time.

To start off with, I was troubled and depressed. I'd spent almost the last two years trying to develop a Native sketch comedy show à la *In Living Colour* for the CBC, and like a poorly executed first date, the CBC said "not interested" and told me to take "Seeing Red" and go home.

The best metaphor (or simile) I can come up with for the process of series development is it's like white-water canoeing, except you're going against the current. Without a canoe.

Canadian television had once welcomed the Aboriginal perspective with open arms. For its nineteen year run, usually a third of the cast of *The Beachcombers* were Native, and then more recently there was *Spirit Bay*, *North of Sixty* and *The Rez*, all which broke new ground and let Canadians see how Native people function in this country. Today, as the summer sun of 2001 burns us all red, every one of these shows are buried in a collective grave, somewhere in the dark and dank cemetery known as the CBC archives or the Happy Haunting Grounds as we Natives call it.

Dead Dog Cafe, a brilliantly satirical radio show written by Cherokee/Greek novelist Tom King, kept CBC radio listeners amused for five years before voluntarily going off the air this year. "After writing eighty-five scripts, you sort of run out of gas after doing the same thing for so long. Luckily I hadn't run out yet but I didn't know how much more I had," explained Tom King. "At heart I am a novelist and [the show] prevented me from writing novels. Radio shows have deadlines, novels don't. It was time to kill the dead dog."

Though, according to CBC big wig George Anthony, reports of the show's death may be greatly exaggerated. Like a new Star Trek series, it may refuse to stay in the grave. "We're currently assessing at least three separate proposals to bring the CBC Radio hit *Dead Dog Cafe* to CBC

Television, including a fairly ambitious animated version." But like many a weary television writer has found, the road to series riches is often fraught with network executives.

But tonight, sitting on the couch, what Indigenous representations does that leave us with on Canadian television... supporting characters on *Blackfly* and the Evening News—the conclusion being the bloom is off the rose. Ojibway actor Herbie Barnes believes the fading interest was to be expected. "I think it's a natural progression. They found something new and it's not new anymore. That is the nature of television."

Movies too. It wasn't all that long ago when theatrical and television movies were being produced all over Canada that explored the Native reality: *Dance Me Outside, Where The Spirit Lives, Clearcut, Blackrobe, Spirit Rider,* and the most recent being *Big Bear,* to name just a few.

Carol Greyeyes, former Artistic Director of the Centre for Indigenous Theatre, blames our invisible status on television and film producers. "And when you think about it, it's not really their job [to portray Native people accurately]. Basically they're there to make money, and if Native people happen to be the flavour of the month, then they'll exploit that. And Native people are no longer lucrative, or Hollywood and the networks have gone "Oh, the trend is over. Let's move on to something else." Last year, if memory serves me correctly, necrophiliacs were the big ticket item in Canadian cinema.

When I traveled the globe, I was always proud to tell the world that Canada was at least a decade or two ahead of the Americans in the representation of Native people in the media.

Over the years, some American shows occasionally donated at least a token episode or two to Aboriginal causes—*Seinfeld, Barney Miller, X-Files, The Brady Bunch, The Partridge Family, The Beverly Hillbillies, Murder She Wrote* etc.—however accurate they may or may not have been. And let's not forget the TBS's laudable movie series about famous Native Americans or the ground breaking *Northern Exposure.* But to my knowledge, no particular show or series dealing specifically with Aboriginal life has ever been created south of the border.

In fact, proportionally speaking, I often felt the representation of First Nations people in Canada was almost directly proportional to the portrayal of African-Americans in the States. In America, since the 1960s, there were and are lots of television shows about the "Black" experience, again, however accurate. But no Native people. Now try and find an ongoing series about the Black community on Canadian television—*Air Farce, This Hour Has 22 Minutes, Black Harbour, Traders* etc., all exploring the mysterious and unknown world of Caucasian Canada. Do you realize there are more television shows on the air right now about aliens from outer space than about Native people? They must have a better agent than we do.

But attempting to be optimistic, perhaps this was just a dip in the cultural graph of television reality. George Anthony, one of the major shareholders in the CBC Brain trust, also informed me that CBC Children's is planning "two new series—*Inuk* and *Stories from the Seventh Fire. Inuk,* based on the work of acclaimed artist and illustrator Marc Tetro, is a show about an imaginative eight year old Inuit boy who is destined to be a Shaman. *Stories From The Seventh Fire* is a half hour animated (2D and 3D) and live action retelling of Native stories."

And rumours of a new *North of Sixty* movie and some new series called *"Harry's Case"* with Adam Beach as a sidekick may prove me wrong in the end. Perhaps there's hope after all. The spirit of *The Beachcomber's* Jesse Jim may ride again.

Keeping all this in mind, it's easy to understand how the introduction of the Aboriginal Peoples Television Network has changed the playing field substantially. Where else can you go to see re-runs of *Adventures in Rainbow Country* and that classic of Canadian identity, *The Forest Rangers*? As innovative and ground breaking as APTN's creation was, in its zeal to find suitable (i.e. Native tinted) and inexpensive programming, the fledgling network's options were a tad limited.

When it originally went on the air several years ago, most of the programming came from the voluminous archives of the North, where the Inuit Broadcasting Corporation and northern CBC affiliates in Iqaluit, Yellowknife and Whitehorse had been storing away programs about the changing face of the Aboriginal north for decades. My mother swore after watching the first few months of the network that she never wanted to see another Inuit/Dene hunting or seal/caribou gutting again.

Debra Piapot, APTN's Director of Communications, proudly hails the birth of the new network as being "an acknowledgement of the Grandmothers and Grandfathers of television broadcasting if you will, who brought forth and had this dream of including all of Canada's

Aboriginal people to start this network." Their dream for the future—"We want to be world-class and relevant. Ratings aside, if we're not relevant to each other, then we've already lost the battle, but if we do talk to each other and we are engaged in entertaining, and are relevant and authentic to each other, I think the ratings will go up. The rest of Canada will begin to watch."

To its credit, the network has become increasingly confident and experienced, and more interesting and broad-based shows have been making their appearance. Its two current affairs programs, *Invision* and *Contact*, carry all the news a First Nations person should know. The talk show *Buffalo Tracks* and the self-explanatory *Cooking with The Wolfman* both add variety to the programming. However, broadcasting *Shining Time Station* and *Dudley the Dragon*, only because they star Tom Jackson and Graham Greene, might need to be re-evaluated. And if I see either *Thunderheart* or *Billy Jack* aired one more time ...

James Compton, the Director of Programming for the APTN network, has had his own less-than-stellar experiences searching for corporate answers to why there are less tanned faces on a publicly funded network like the CBC, one that is supposed to represent the country's multi-faceted population. "I was at the Banff Television Executive Program; there you have representatives from Vision, History, CTV, CBC, BBC, the cream of the crop, all sharing ideas on how to run a Network.

"CBC came in with their fall launch, what they were planning to do in the upcoming year. When they showed us the promotional tape, I decided to count how many times they showed Native people. It was only a five minute video and I counted twenty-six shots of Aboriginal people. I said "Does this mean you're planning to do more Native programming?" Well, that went over like a fart in church. It was like I stabbed them in the heart. They didn't really answer the question, basically skirted the issue. Most of the shots were from the history series anyways."

But things are beginning to change, at least south of the border. And it all started with that call I received in the wilds of Lethbridge. American television may be waking up while Canadian television is going to sleep. That was the National Broadcasting Corporation, as in NBC—as in *the* NBC—that had called me.

It seems the network had recently polled its audiences and were shocked (their words—"shocked") to discover they had no programming for or about American Indians! And they wanted to do something about it. I was shocked that they were shocked. It seemed rather obvious to me—no more a revelation than "lard is fattening."

This American gentleman from New York who had found me in the Alberta prairies was on a quest to find Native people in the industry who might be interested in submitting material to the Network and work with them on dealing with this "shocking" imbalance. Thus the phone call.

We had a twenty minute conversation in the airport about the issue and all its potential ramifications until they started boarding my plane. And for a moment, I seriously debated missing my flight to continue this interesting conversation ... after all, it was NBC, and they had phoned me. Me! NBC or Saskatoon ... now there's a choice you don't make very often.

That was two months ago. Now NBC is taking a more broad-based approach to deal with this disproportional situation. The Network, along with the Oneida Indian Nation in Wisconsin, is launching a talent search for Native American actors, comedians and writers. Called *The Four Directions Talent Search,*" it aims to increase Native representation in television, and will take place across the United States and Canada, between August and November 2001.

The press release has been all over the internet in Indian country the last few days and the buzz has started. People on the Reserves can taste the Emmys. While the Prime Minister and Parliament has been worried about the brain drain of scientists and skilled technicians to the south, who would have thought there might be a similar exodus of Native artists and performers in the not-too-distant future.

Granted, right now it's a glorified talent search, an ethnic cattle call of humongous proportion. But it's something, a beginning. Just think, our own series snuggled between *Ally McBeal* and *Friends.* Between *Fraser* and *Law & Order.* I think the show should either be called *Touched By An Anglo* or *Cree's Company.*

Evidently I've Been a Bad, Bad Boy

It's beginning to look like the year 2000 is going to be a very interesting year for yours truly, the humble Ojibway scribe. As a writer in many disciplines, I primarily write for theatre, television and journalism. Now seemingly, I have been a very naughty boy in all three branches of literary expression; a few people finding fault with each genre of my examination of the Aboriginal world. And all I can do is sit there and just shake my head in disbelief. In my simple attempts to just make people laugh, I have inadvertently created some wrinkled brows and scowling faces.

It's only April, and in the last four months, I've received a bomb threat for a play of mine in Vancouver that an anonymous caller said was racist against White people, followed by a children's television show I have been writing for telling me quite explicitly that I am not to use the teachings of tobacco in any script I may write for them. And finally, an article I wrote for *The Messenger*, the AFN paper, has been banned and dropped for the spring issue. Evidently I am an irritant and didn't even know it. Could my ex-girlfriend be right?

The bomb threat, luckily a false one, said my play, *alterNATIVES*, made fun of White people. Odd, considering I am half White, half of the cast was White, and the Native characters in it had their own set of problems. All the characters were screwed up, in my opinion, much like real life. But the play was funny. But social criticism and humour evidently are not supposed to go together. I'm thirty-seven and still have so much to learn. And worst of all, my mother found out about the bomb threat and gave me a good scolding, telling me to "start writing good plays again!" Yes, Mother.

The children's show I was writing for (I cannot name them since I was told there were confidentiality issues at stake here and legal recourse was possible—people are so serious these days!) wouldn't allow me to mention, in one simple line that would involve no more than a second and a half of screen time, anything about tobacco. One of the characters wanted something (nothing greedy, more of a personal wish) and I wanted an Elder-type character to suggest the young character put down some tobacco as an offering, in keeping with the teachings.

Children's shown and tobacco. The two do not go well in the minds of the television networks. Even though I was talking about Indian tobacco, with no chemicals, not cigarette tobacco. Again we're talking one simple line of dialogue. Apparently it was an irrelevant issue. No different I guess than the wine you find in a bar and the wine you find at Communion. Again I have so much still to learn.

And finally, I wrote an article for *The Messenger* examining mixed marriages, primarily focusing on non-Native people who, because of their new current marital affiliation, now refer to themselves as being "Native." It was a situation I once heard referred to as "Indian by Ejaculation." Again, it was done with humour and what I hoped was keen social observation. But it was just more evidence that I was being a bad boy. Must have been all those George Carlin records I listened to as a kid.

I was asked to cut out several sections that they felt might offend some family members, particularly the "ejaculation" reference. That was a surprise to me because I was under the impression, however wrongly, that "ejaculation" was a real and legitimate word. I've even looked it up in the dictionary and everything. It's there, I assure you. I'm also quite sure I've actually read the word in a few academic articles and in some literary prose (not that I read a lot of writing that has the word "ejaculation" in it. Honest!).

Also a reference to a Jewish circumcision met with some unexpected resistance. Is it me or am I noticing a theme in that office's uncomfortability?

Be that as it may, I was willing to change the "ejaculation" to "intercourse" to be supportive, but I was told it wasn't enough. I was told the article was being dumped. I hope my mother doesn't find out about this one. She's been hinting about lawn furniture for Mother's Day and I may not be able to afford it if these unfortunate events keep up.

Taking all this into consideration, these incidents boggle my mind, and I assure you, it takes a lot to boggle my mind. As far as writers go, I've always considered myself a rather innocuous writer, as agitators go

I have not advocated the blowing up of one single bridge in my entire career, nor have I ever supported any Native terrorist organizations. Nor did I expect to ever consider myself becoming the Ojibway version of Salman Rushdie.

So being the bad, evil, naughty writer I am, have I learned anything from this experience? Are there any words of wisdom I can pass on to others should they find themselves in a similar situation? Yeah. Ask to be paid up front.

Mental Note—Start all future articles/plays/scripts with a warning: The following is meant to be funny. Do not take it seriously.

The Politics of Children

I'm a thirty-seven year old man, single child of a single parent, who at the time of this writing has no children (though the summer of '87 seems kind of foggy), and what's the one job that comes to mind that I would be completely unsuited for? Other than an aerobics instructor (though I do look good in spandex, if the lighting is low enough)?

I am talking about my recent splurge of writing specifically for children in television and on the stage. And let me tell you, Mr. Matthew Coon Come, running the Assembly of First Nations with over 600 squabbling and arguing Chiefs and Vice-Chiefs is nothing compared to the trials and tribulations of pleasing networks and producers in the fast paced and bizarre world of entertaining and educating the little ones.

In the past, I have had some experience. I've written at least four plays for young audiences (maybe more; as I said, the summer of '87 is still a little foggy). My first was a rather surprising hit called *Toronto at Dreamer's Rock*, which, ten years later, is still being produced and published. I affectionately refer to it as my retirement fund.

But more recently, I have been engaged in the lucrative, though frustrating world of children's television programming. Specifically, I have written three scripts for a Native-themed show involving animals, currently in production. I had a lot of fun and everybody was really nice to me ... until the rules came down from somewhere above about what you can and cannot do on children's television. Sort of the Television Ten Commandments. And some of them are bizarre. As a writer, I was only privileged to snippets of reasoning. Basically, anything beyond "don't do that" or "nice try but you can't do that with a turtle at 11:00 o'clock in the morning" was kept confidential. Evidently the television executive's mind works in mysterious ways.

Abbreviating the Commandments, I was frequently told that you can not have any violence, even a kick in the shin or a push. Now that kind of stuff you can almost understand. But did you know, you cannot have one character kiss another on the nose as I attempted to write in one script? It might corrupt the Aboriginal (and non-Aboriginal youth) of tomorrow. There might be rampant nose kissing across the nation. The courts would be clogged with nasal assault cases.

Other no-no's imparted to me included the fact that you cannot have one character call another character "weird" in an effort to explore self-image problems. Not even if you show the potential consequences of such an action. It seems it's better to avoid the whole situation completely. Yet, it's okay to have a male animal tug on the tail of a female animal. Am I the only one that sees some subversive subtext in a little "pulling tail?"

Luckily in theatre, it's a little easier. Actually a lot easier. I can safely say that, other than the normal dramaturgical process of developing the play, I never really received any flack or limiting directives from a higher up source. I even began my favourite play, *Girl Who Loved Her Horses*, with one of the main characters uttering a single word in astonishment: "Jesus!" Try that with the *Teletubbies* at 8:30 on Tuesday morning.

Granted, you still have to keep your audience in mind and what you are trying to say. Artistic freedom is artistic freedom, but spending fifty minutes of school time having characters swearing like a Chief who's been caught hiring relatives or wasting time exploring the wonders of bestiality would not be advisable. That's just common sense.

More recently, I have been working on a new young people's play titled *The Boy In The Treehouse*, which will be seen in Winnipeg, Toronto, Saskatoon and Regina. It deals with identity, parental longing, trying to honour ones relatives and vision quests. I was tempted to put in some tail pulling but somehow it did not seem appropriate.

I had not written a children's play in about five years and wasn't sure if I could capture that state of mind again. Writing for children is a unique and special talent. But as a former girlfriend once told me, I have nothing to worry about when it comes to thinking like a child. Oddly enough, I don't think she was the first girlfriend to tell me that.

In this play, a young boy must deal with the anniversary of the death of his Native mother by trying to embrace her culture. He does this by fasting in a treehouse. His non-Native father tries to be supportive but watching your kid starve himself up a tree tests the man's patience. In this piece, I got to explore concepts that many youth deal with. And as always, I was told the sky was the limit. Just the usual limitations when it comes to a touring show: not too many characters and try not to require a full scale castle or naval battle—they're kind of hard to tour. The only real concern I faced with this project was a kind and gentle word of advice from the Artistic Director informing me that people in certain parts of the Prairies are kind of serious about any mention of God or the Church.

But perhaps the most bizarre limitation that I was informed of did not come from any network executive or Artistic Director, but from the people who run kindergartens. My former girlfriend taught kindergarten for four months a few years back. It was a job she loved, almost as much as she loved the kids. But she was warned, and strongly urged, never to hug the kids. Even if they hugged her first, at no time was her arms or hands to touch the kids in an affectionate manner. She told me it was the hardest part of her job.

Then a few months later when I was in Labrador, I had the opportunity to tour the schools in a Native community, including a kindergarten. Over coffee, I chatted with the teachers about my girlfriend's dilemma. They informed me they had the same regulations. "But we ignore them," they happily told me. Unfortunately I was all too aware of the reasoning behind these restrictions, and sympathetic. But another part of me wished my girlfriend could hug all these kids as much as she wanted to.

So remember, anybody out there who is interested in writing or working with kids; under no circumstances should you hug a nose-kissing, weird, Church-going kid. No telling what trouble you'll get into.

Desperately Seeking Solutions

Over the past several years I have written many articles discussing the concept of the "blended blood" issue in the Native community. In fact, I have even been admonished by one Elder to, and I quote, "get over it." Evidently I am dangerously close to becoming the poster boy for People of Mixed Societies (otherwise known as PMS). If the truth be told, I have actually gotten over whatever "it" is, many years ago and revel in my unique perspective of the world. It's cheaper than therapy. However, every once in a while the whole damn issue raises its head yet again wanting another opportunity to be hotly debated.

No doubt we've all drunk far too much tea participating in these discussions about what makes an Indian an Indian. Is it nature or nurture? Is it time spent on a Reserve, or a simple matter of blood quantum as is popular in the States? Maybe it's the inherent ability to fascinate anthropologists. Or perhaps some indefinable combination of the three?

But this time I've decided to hang up my blanket on the issue and let other people answer this question for me. I've done enough talking (or in this case, writing) to last a life time. I've decided to look for answers out there in the grassroots communities.

The reason for this departure? A certain someone has approached me with difficult questions relating to this particular concern. And since my mother has frequently told me I am not all powerful or all knowing, I've decided to openly seek assistance.

Last year, Lee Maracle, Dawn T. Maracle (no relation) and I were having coffee one day when the topic of Native literature genres was brought up. We observed that Native writers seemed preoccupied with writing only about certain things, usually contemporary stories, on contemporary reserves leading contemporary lives. Occasionally there might be a legend, or a historical/period piece, or something tackling the mystical/mythological/philosophical side of Aboriginal life (e.g. If an Indian farts in the bush and a white person isn't there to hear him, has he actually farted?)

A vast part of our literature deals primarily with looking backward to our ancestors, at our culture, our language, our history, the colonization, the struggle to recover, etc. Usually, it explores or recounts the past and its relation to the present. Very little speculative work in the other direction has been created. We ended up discussing the topic of First Nations science fiction. There is precious little out there today. Gerry William's *The Black Ship* and the odd short story here and there are about all we came across in Canada.

Examples outside of Canada, even flying high above it where no Native has gone before, is Chakotay, the guy on Star Trek's Voyager. Basically I always thought of him as a Latino with a bad tattoo. They don't even mention what Nation he's from or how a self-respecting First Nations person could honour the Four Directions while deep in space. Which way is East? Towards the phaser banks I think.

Getting back to the point, Dawn T. Maracle decided to tackle this unusual literary possibility and is currently looking for Native authors interested in writing a Science Fiction short story for a planned anthology. It is hoped this book, for a change, will look forward to the future of the Aboriginal Nation. While searching for interested participants, she has landed smack dab in the middle of a dilemma—one dealing with that pesky identity issue.

A woman has offered to write a story for the anthology, but she has readily admitted that a distant ancestor (one of these all too familiar forebears whose first name often started with "Great-great-") was the proud owner of some Aboriginal blood, but she herself had never lived on a Reserve and hadn't delved that deeply into her "great-great" culture. So the question facing Dawn T. Maracle is—should she allow this woman to write a story for the anthology? And expanding on that particular issue, what are the guidelines for making a decision like this? God forbid, we do not want to go back to the ill-defined and nasty Department of Indian Affairs classifications; Status, non-Status or Métis. But at the same time, there must be some quality and accuracy control to make sure it is in fact the Native voice born of the Native experience writing these stories. It would be tacky to start out the new millennium with an updated W.P. Kinsella or Grey Owl.

Gerald Taiaiake Alfred, a Mohawk academic, uses the colourful metaphor of a Canadian flying to Germany, getting off the plane and self-identifying himself/herself as a German, thinking that's sufficient. Needless to say that wouldn't be nearly enough for the Germans. I've been to Germany. They require just a tiny bit more documentation. And it works in reverse. Some stranger showing up at an airport Customs office wanting to enter Canada simply by saying "I'm Canadian," just doesn't cut the mustard anymore. So why should that be good enough for the Native community, he asks. Simply saying "I am Native" isn't enough anymore.

On the other hand, the Aborigines of Australia have their own unique methods of determining who is what, and vice versa. Basically, as I have been told, you are considered Aborigine if 1) you have some Aborigine ancestry, 2) you self-identify yourself as being Aborigine, and 3) the Aborigine community acknowledges you as being Aborigine. It sounds logical but cynics have pointed out that anybody and their grandmother (or Great-Great-Grandmother) could consider themselves Aborigine. And Ted, the Aborigine down the street who runs the local gas station, could say that for $20, he (as a member of the community) will recognize you as being Aborigine.

Therefore, I ask the readers out there—what do you suggest we take into account? I dare you to pick up a pen/keyboard/telephone to provide us poor confused people some guidance and intelligent suggestions to help us define this thorny problem. Contact us and inform us of what you think the essentials of the Aboriginal voice are.

We humbly await your response.

Laughing Till Your Face is Red

"A smile is Sacred"

—Hopi Elder

It seems some people have no sense of humour. I am tempted to say some "White people" but that would be racist. Though I'm told that it is politically impossible for a member of an oppressed minority to be racist against a dominant culture because of some socio-political reason … but I digress.

A year or two ago, a play of mine titled *alterNATIVES* was produced in Vancouver. I don't know why I was so surprised by the non-Native reaction to Native humour, specifically that presented in theatre; it has always been something of a perception problem, as the art form continues to grow. With the ongoing debate over the suitability of political correctness, the dominant culture's willingness to enjoy, appreciate and accept the unique Native sense of humour quickly becomes a political mine field. Add to that the volatile atmosphere existing in British Columbia at that time by the fall out over the Nisga'a Treaty and the turmoil involving the Musqueam landowners, and it's no wonder a few people in Vancouver were less than enthused by a Native comedy/drama and began developing theatre appraisal via chemical interaction.

But looking at the larger picture, this particular reaction to Native humour goes beyond Vancouver and last December, at least in my experience. Several years ago I was fortunate enough to have an early play of mine produced at the Lighthouse Theatre in Port Dover, Ontario. It was a small, innocuous comedy called *The Bootlegger Blues* which detailed the adventures of a fifty-eight year old, good Christian Ojibway woman named Martha, who through a series of circumstances, finds herself bootlegging 143 cases of beer to raise money to buy an organ for the Church. Not exactly Sam Sheppard but it was based on an actual real incident that happened on a Reserve that for legal reasons I won't get into or my mother will kill me.

In this play there were no searing insights in the Aboriginal existence, or tragic portrayals of a culture done-wrong-by that we have grown to expect on the stage. In fact, it was the opposite of that. The director/dramaturge with whom I developed the project, my mentor Larry Lewis, came to me one day after having just directed the premiere of this little play you may have heard of, *Drylips Oughta Move to Kapuskasing*. He was somewhat burnt out by the process and said to me, "Drew, I want you to write something for me that has people leaving the theatre holding their sore stomachs from laughing so much, not drying their eyes from crying or scratching their heads from thinking too much." Thus was born *The Bootlegger Blues*.

This play, I was proud to say, had no socially redeeming qualities whatsoever. It was simply, a celebration of the Native sense of humour. Not my best work in retrospect but it was funny enough to beat the theatre's audience projections and subtly (don't tell anybody) raise some awareness.

But the thing I especially remember about that particular production was that it was my first introduction to the racially divisive line that sometimes exists when a non-Native audience is presented with Native humour, primarily on stage. Basically put, pigment-challenged audiences sometimes didn't quite know how to react to a Native comedy. And since Native theatre was still quite young, many of us Aboriginal theatre practitioners weren't too experienced in that field either. Prior to this production, *The Bootlegger Blues* had been produced on Manitoulin Island by a Native theatre company, so the audiences there were either primarily Native or sympathetic/interested people of pallor. After a two week run it then went on tour for a month.

In fact, it was on that tour where I received what I consider to be the best review of my life. Somewhere in Ottawa, this old man, an Elder I believe, shuffled out of seeing the play, walked up to me, and shook my hand, telling me my play had made him homesick. It was then it occurred to me that maybe this play was more than just a frothy comedy.

But in Port Dover, a small town located on the shores of Lake Erie, most of the pallid theatre patrons sported white or blue-rinsed hair, and were expecting normal summer theatre epitomized by frothy British comedies or usually mindless musicals. While my humble offering was a comedy (though I hesitate to say mindless), it wasn't the type they were expecting. I still remember the discussions with the Artistic Director who was concerned about some of the "strong" language in the show. Now those that know my work can attest that I am not one of the more profane playwrights. Hell no!

The strong language consisted of, I think, one "shit" and one "F.O.A.D. (fuck off and die)" in the two hour play. But that was enough to scandalize. A wall of beer, two Indians climbing into the same bed, and a veritable plethora of jokes about alcohol and drinking from a race of people most of the audience more than likely associated with drunkenness, didn't make the situation any more accessible. And a touch uncomfortable.

But what I remember most was the white audience's puzzled reaction to the show. It had a talented cast, and a fabulous director. Overall, it was a very good production. You would never know by the audience response. The first ten or fifteen minutes of the play was silence. All you could hear was the cast trying vainly to engage the audience, and the audience's breathing. For all the cast's enthusiasm, this could have been a murder mystery.

I puzzled over the audience's unexpected lack of involvement for some time. I knew it couldn't be the actors or the production. Heaven forbid, was it my writing? But the show had done well on Manitoulin Island. Then after one afternoon matinee, it occurred to me. It wasn't me. It was them, the audience. Proving my point, I overheard one pigment challenged lady coming downstairs from the balcony talking to her friend saying, "I guess it's funny, but I can't help get over the fact that if a white man had written that, he'd be in deep trouble."

That was it. Political correctness had invaded my career. Most of the audience were afraid to laugh, or were uncomfortable with the prospect of laughing at Native people, regardless of the context. After so many years of being told the miseries and tribulations we have gone through, the concept of funny or entertaining (outside the pow wow circuit) Aboriginal people was problematic. Other plays that had been produced, like Tomson Highway's, had some humour, but were darker, or more critical, and it seems that was what the audience was expecting, and I was failing to provide it.

Perhaps in some way they wanted to feel guilty by what they saw, to be kicked in the ribs by social tragedy their ancestors had caused rather than give in to the healing powers of humour. They did not expect Native people to be funny, let alone laugh at themselves. The audience had landed on Mars.

In this post-Oka society, people were still coming to grips with the concept that Native people were no longer victimized, they could be dangerous and volatile. These are notions of a definitely non-humourous nature. Maybe the wounds of Oka were still healing.

As an afterthought, I considered maybe doing a quick rewrite and throwing in a rape or murder somewhere in the text to shake the patrons up. Maybe blockading the bar or bathroom, something as a reference point for the overwhelmed audience. In fact, even though the play was about an aged female bootlegger, nowhere in the play does she or anybody actually drink a beer on stage. I didn't even give the audience that.

The other interesting fact of this production was that, as I've said, it beat the projection for audience attendance. By several important percents. So, obviously people must have liked it. I started to watch the audiences more closely in an attempt to answer this conundrum, and that's where I made my second observation. After about twenty minutes into the play, people began to laugh. Finally, the politically correct non-Natives were laughing at the Native actors doing the Native comedy. Laughing a lot, I might add. Above all else, true humour must be universal.

What the audience was waiting for, seeking in fact, was permission. They were looking for permission to laugh at this strange story about oppressed people that political correctness told them not to have their funny bone tickled by. As fate would have it, in practically every audience were several Native people enjoying the show. Luckily, Port Dover is half-an-hour from Six Nations, one of the largest Native communities in Canada, if not the largest population-wise. And with two members of the cast coming from that community, needless to say there were always a few trickling in to see their friends/relatives appear on stage. And they needed no permission to laugh. In fact, try and stop them.

In this audience of over two hundred people (on a good night), it was always the Indians who would start the chuckling and giggling.

It was laughter of recognition because seldom had this world been seen outside their own kitchen. Other than the rare movie like *Pow Wow Highway*, the humourous Indian was a rarely seen though thoroughly enjoyed animal. They were used to seeing the tragic, downtrodden and victimized Indian. According to the media, that was the only kind out there.

The laughter would start out scattered, sometimes embarrassed at being the only ones laughing, but eventually the rest of the audience got the hint that this was a comedy, and they were supposed to laugh. By the end of the performance, the whole audience was enjoying the play. A round of applause and an occasional standing ovation would follow. I think part of the catharsis was also a sense of relief from the Caucasian patrons that everything they had seen in the media wasn't always true, the fact that Native people weren't continually depressed, suppressed and oppressed. Yes, they found out, they have a sense of humour and a joy for life. That production was a learning experience for me, the cast and I hope, the audiences.

Several years later I wrote a sequel to *The Bootlegger Blues*, called *The Baby Blues*, part of a four part series I'm working on called *The Blues Quartet*. Its American premiere was at Pennsylvania Centre Stage, located at Penn State University deep in the heart of Amish country. And everybody knows what theatre animals the Amish are. Not exactly optimum territory for Native theatre, but I was getting paid in American dollars.

Again, this play was a celebration of Native humour in a country that knows practically nothing of its Aboriginal inhabitants post 1880 (except for Wayne Newton). Again I witnessed that awesome silence of an audience trying to connect, trying to find some neutral ground. It didn't help that there were numerous Canadianisms in the text— references to *The Beachcombers*, Canadian Tire money, and Graham Greene (for some reason, most American people thought I was referring to the English novelist, not the Iroquois actor) to name a few. But overall, I still felt it should have been an accessible play. It had been in Toronto.

I even ended up quickly putting together a glossary of Canadian and Native words with explanations i.e. sweetgrass, drumming, Oka, fancy dancing etc. to help the audience. But still, a Native comedy was difficult for them to grasp. Oddly enough, my production was sandwiched between *Man of La Mancha* and *Forever Plaid*. Maybe if my characters were insane and wore tartan, it would have been a different story.

In this case, there were precious few American Indians around to act as guides for the confused theatre customers.

One theory I came up with, then discarded, was that Native comedies being seen in a more metropolitan environment, might be a different story. Theatre patrons in urban climates tend to be more accepting and willing to embrace styles and forms of expression that perhaps are not as well known or familiar. I've seen plays with seventeenth century people trapped in a plastic room with no dialogue, just bouncing back and forth. A Native comedy then seems almost pedestrian. Yet witness the bomb threat in Vancouver and the success in Port Dover and Kincardine (maybe mad bombers don't have cottages).

Unfortunately, there's also a double-edged sword with comedies in the city. Though there are exceptions, urban companies prefer a more serious interpretation of life. As a result, most theatre companies tend not to programme comedies as they are often viewed as being too lightweight and frothy. The term I have heard is "It's more summer theatre." Thus I end up in Kincardine or Port Dover trying to explain what an intertribal dance is.

Native theatre as a whole has developed a fair amount of cachet in the last decade. With Ian Ross winning the Governor General's Award for his play *fareWel* (which admittedly had lots of humour), and the success of Tomson Highway and Daniel David Moses to name just a few, most major theatre companies (and many of the smaller ones) try to program a certain amount of Aboriginal theatre in their line-up. But again, their preferences lean more toward the angry, dark and often disheartening view of Native life. Thus I remember one Aboriginal woman telling me that she refused to see any more Native theatre because she found it "too depressing."

More recently, I wrote the play *alterNATIVES*, a comedy/drama this time, produced in that same Port Dover theatre in that same town. Except this time, it was more than a simple comedy. It was what I called an intellectual satire, meaning it dealt with serious and complex issues, but through humour. I've always thought the best way to reach somebody wasn't through preaching or instructing, but through humour. It seems to make the message more palatable—spoon full of sugar and all that.

This time the play premiered in two different small towns with primarily non-Native audiences. The result this time was markedly different. People, again mostly non-Native, laughed from the moment the lights came up. No waiting for permission or dealing with political guilt. In a scant six years since I had last visited Port Dover, colour-denied people had learned that it's okay to laugh at Native comedies. God (who, if my ex-girlfriend was correct, is a Mohawk woman) will not strike them down and send them to work at the Department of Indian Affairs if they laugh. It's amazing what can happen in a little over half-a-decade. The public looks at us now as being almost three-dimensional! It's astonishing what a good laugh will get you.

I think part of the reason, if not the whole reason, is the change in perceptions through the avenues of broadcasting. Analyzing the media, witness the number of television and radio programs that have embraced the Native appetite for humour. *Dance Me Outside, The Rez*—both of which were more-or-less successful—the delightful movie *Smoke Signals*, even the CBC Radio show *Dead Dog Cafe*, written and hosted by Mr. Amusing, Tom King. Substantially more programming than was seen in 1993.

Currently I am in the stages of early development for a television series of my own, a sketch comedy show titled *Seeing Red*. I see it as a combination of *Air Farce* and America's *In Living Colour,* Native oriented humour where we make fun of the perceptions and stereotypes surrounding the First Nations culture. It could be dangerous because myself and the other two writers plan to pull the leg of white people and Native people to the point of dislocation.

The CBC seems very interested and we are proceeding down the long-and-winding path of development and hopefully production. I think it shows a willingness of the public now not only to embrace the Aboriginal sense of humour, but also appreciate and revel in it. So much so in fact, that the powers that be at the CBC have specifically told me to concentrate on Native-based sketches only, and if possible to avoid writing any sketches not dealing specifically with Native issues. Perhaps we've gone a little too far in the other direction.

Add to that the documentary I recently directed for the National Film Board of Canada on Native humour, called *Redskins, Tricksters and Puppy Stew*, and by golly, it's almost enough to make you think

Canadian society has developed somewhat in the last decade. What was once the exception, has become a widely accepted rule. There is definite hope.

In my research, I have come across a term used by some Native academics to describe humour, specifically Native humour. They refer to it as "permitted disrespect." You have the other people's permission to tease or joke about them without getting into a fight. Maybe that's what some audiences need to understand. We Native writers are part of a specific community and have to answer to that community. We are allowed a certain amount of "permitted disrespect."

But it was Tom King who also told me in a recent interview that most of the negative letters the show received come from the non-Native population, most of which say something to the effect of, "If you guys (the producers/writers/actors) are white, you're not funny." Then Tom would tell them that, in fact, they are Native. These people would then respond grudgingly, "Oh, that's okay then."

If I'm to understand the meaning of that sentence, it's nice to know finally that you're only funny if you're Native.

Finally, people are catching on. Except in Vancouver I guess.

"It may be the one universal thing about Native Americans from tribe to tribe, is the survival humour."
—Louise Erdrich

The Voice of the People

One of the great adventures of being a columnist is that every once in a while, people out there who actually read the articles I write will find the time in their busy schedules to respond with a few written words of their own. This is usually delightful since it's often hard to tell if anybody has the slightest interest in what you have to say or write. Occasionally the remarks are positive, but more frequently, they are from people who have issues with my writing because, as the old newspaper axiom goes, "people only write letters to the editor about things that upset them."

Every columnist and professional writer is used to this, or should be. Every single person in this world has an opinion and very seldom do two match up identically. It certainly has made for some interesting correspondence over the ten years or so I have been doing this.

In that time, I have written almost a hundred and fifty articles about everything ranging from Native-oriented movies, to Buffy Sainte-Marie, to Matthew Coon Comb, to residential schools, to getting old, to ex-girlfriends, to being mixed-blood, to life on my reserve, to my cat, and trying to define the essence of Native humour, just to name a few topics.

But for me, the most remarkable and harshest responses to arise from the public have come from two noticeably vocal groups which have little to do with any of the more volatile subjects I have explored. Every year, for one reason or another, I write an article about the Native perception (and mine) of vegetarianism. Usually very tongue-in-cheek and based on experience. Why vegetarians? I don't know. Maybe because my mother forced me to eat too many vegetables as a child and I'm still dealing with the emotional scars.

But I would have to say that a good third of all the letters/emails I have received in my professional career came from irate vegetarians, of all people, who found displeasure in my humourist approach. Not from politicians I have skewered, or Nations I have teased or injustices I have examined. But vegetarians...! Perhaps all they are saying ... is give peas a chance.

The second most responsive readers of my work are people who are involved now, or in the past, with members of another race/culture. Being a half-breed myself who has dated women from several ethnic backgrounds, I often ruminate about the experience and the political implications of such a union, never saying whether it was good or bad, just exploring the adventure.

Well, simply put, a lot of people don't want it explored. They find the discussion uncomfortable. Or more accurately put, I am encouraged to give inter-racial marriages a complete thumbs up (love is colour-blind) or a total thumbs down (our society and blood must be protected). There seems to be very little middle ground. And God forbid, imagine the letters I receive when I write about someone that's involved with a vegetarian from another culture....

Other critical letters, though fewer and farther between, run the critical gambit that includes intelligent, well-thought out replies that have different opinions than mine and just want the opportunity to state them. I rather enjoy this type of correspondence and respect the time and effort the writer put into their notes. Other letters often have a different grasp of ... criticism.

One Native gentleman took the time to write a letter criticizing an article I wrote lamenting the poor nutritional value of all the white flour, sugar and salt that goes into bannock/fry bread. This fellow pointed out rather strenuously that I had not included the spiritual and cultural aspects that bannock/fry bread had in Aboriginal cultures. He finished off the letter by saying I had insulted the Elders and had no consideration for their teachings. All this over a piece of bread.

Did I mention he wrote this letter from prison? And he believed Elders were disappointed with me for writing about the high cholesterol in fry bread. Unlike whatever he did to be writing me from jail. It's a unique world out there. One, god willing, I am hoping to understand someday.

My favourite comes from a man who took the time out of his busy day to compose a letter to the editor complaining, right off the bat, that I used to write about my girlfriend far too frequently. How much longer was I "going to continue to shove my girlfriend down" the reader's throats, he inquired? I didn't realize that occasionally singing the praises of a girlfriend violated my journalistic integrity. My answer to his problem, don't read my articles then.

I now realize this may sound like that of a wounded writer whimpering in the dark ... I hope not because for most people, and especially writers, criticism should be a good thing. It should be constructive, not destructive. There must be logic and thought involved, not just emotion. The written word can be very powerful.

So with that written, all you vegetarians better quit pelting my house with rotten tomatoes or I'll get my ex-girlfriend to beat you up.

IDENTITY
(Stuff Psychiatrists Will Love)

Half Empty or Half Full

Not that long ago, a woman from my reserve told my ex-girlfriend, Dawn, quite casually in conversation, that Dawn and I have had it quite easy in this world because we don't look particularly Native. Somehow, having a fair complexion because of our mixed-blood made the world a far easier place to exist in and we should consider ourselves lucky to have been spared the tragedies reserved for really Native-looking Natives.

At the time, we thought it quite insightful and profoundly psychic of her to tell us how uncomplicated every single minute of our lives were up until that moment, and how horribly tragic the existence of all dark-skinned, brown eyed Aboriginal's lives were in comparison. Prior to then, I had somehow been unaware of my "advantaged" status in First Nations/Caucasian relations. It must have occurred that day I stayed home from school.

As the Galactic Birthing Gods would have it, I had grown up on the Curve Lake Reserve in Central Ontario, with just my mother. I lived the life of any Native person in the 1960s and 1970s, complete with wood stoves, water from a hand pump, all the usual accouterment that comes with that privileged reserve life. But at the time, nobody had ever commented on my bluish-green eyes making life less stressful. The outhouse in January was still the outhouse in January. The winter winds do not recognize blood quantum. Evidently I must have strong words with my mother's family about that negligent omission.

But in the years since I left the reserve, and oddly enough more recently in my urban environment, there seems to be a peculiar attitude out there aimed at people like me and our not-so-distinctive situation. For the last decade or so, I have written quite extensively about life on the reserve, the life of an urban Indian, and in some cases, my experiences as a person of mixed ancestry (though because of my childhood, my allegiance and consciousness is to my Ojibway heritage).

But like everyone, I had questions. I remember at one time, many years ago, running into Maria Campbell at a theatre opening party.

Ironically, I was halfway through reading the book she had written with Linda Griffiths, *The Book of Jessica*, about her own experiences writing a play about being Métis. I remember thinking it was providence that had guided her to this party, except in reality it was the director of the play. Often the two walk hand in hand.

After getting her to sign my copy of her book, I ended up telling her that occasionally, when I told people I was Native, they assumed I was Métis. So being still young and curious (I'm still curious but not so young), I naively asked her what was the difference between being a mixed-blood and Métis.

The lovely and patient Ms. Campbell told me the Métis are a culture unto themselves. They have their own brand of music, style of dress, even a language of their own. And since I was raised on the reserve by my mother and her family, also with a specific culture and language, and identified completely with that, to her I was essentially Ojibway, regardless of the melanin content of my skin. Needless to say, that cleared up a lot for me and answered a lot of questions. But unfortunately not everybody is as reasonable.

In more recent years, there seems to be a bizarre growing attitude of resentment towards that subject matter, and in some cases, my examination of the topic. One that reeks of potential internal racism within our community. And the irony is not lost on me. In the past, much like in the Black community, the lighter-skinned Native people were more acceptable in the mainstream society than darker-skinned people. And as a result, even within that marginalized culture, the lighter skins were favoured. Everybody wanted to look white, white was right.

"In the beginning, there was dark skin, and then God said let there be white … and it was good."

But today, with the advent of political correctness, the reverse is becoming the norm. The darker you are, the more acceptable you are. I knew a Native woman who refused to pursue a relationship with a half-breed friend of mine simply because she only wanted a full-blooded baby. Anything less was not acceptable. And I know other women who dated by the simple belief that the longer the braids and browner the eyes, the better.

Granted, there's a lot to be said for personal preference and having a cultural similarity to bond with. I personally prefer women with big screen televisions, but my point is that I have been lied to and misled. I am still waiting for that supposed easier existence in society that my friend in Curve Lake promised me, instead of what I have been experiencing up until now.

In reality, things have been getting harder the older I get. Not that long ago, I attended the launching of a documentary I directed on Native humour for the National Film Board. After the screening, there was a question and answer period where I revealed that two of the people featured in the documentary, Herbie Barnes and Don Kelly, were assisting me in writing a proposed television series I had pitched to the CBC.

Famed Aboriginal poet Michael Paul Martin raised his hand and commented that the three us were all half-breeds and he was curious if, because of that, we all shared some special connection and communication that allowed us to work so well together. For a moment I felt that our secret was out and our alien telepathy had been revealed, necessitating the postponement of our invasion. Instead I replied that if we get the series, we were going to give our production company a name based on the fact that the three of us were half-breeds. The company would be called … A Buck And a Half Productions.

The battle continues. Things have gotten to the point where, I'm told, my name is now officially a swear word or insult. Several months ago I received an email from the West Bay Reserve located on Manitoulin Island, from a gentleman whom this insult had been directed at. It seems he and a visual artist in that community have had difficulty in getting along, and for some reason, this visual artist had referred to this person in anger as that "Drew Hayden Taylor, half-breed, Métis wannabee."

Now somewhere along the journey of my life, my named joined the vernacular of reserve cussing. If only I could get royalties. 1 guess I am now immortal. And I have no idea why or how this has happened. And specifically in this implication, I think there is a number of technical errors in reference to the term "Drew Hayden Taylor, half-breed, Métis wannabee." It's repetitious, inaccurate and a legitimate case of overkill. Oh well, I guess I should just be happy that I'm mentioned in conversation.

And perhaps one of the most outrageous examples I am personally familiar with came in the form of a letter to the editor. A gentleman named Paul Sayers had, rightly or wrongly, issues with an article I wrote for the Toronto magazine called *It*. But more importantly, he had issues with me and he wasn't shy about demonstrating it.

Not only did he misspell my name in his letter, but in reference to a book I wrote titled *Funny, You Don't Look Like One: Observations of a Blue-Eyed Ojibway*, he concluded his critical letter by writing "PS. Funny, I do look like one, tales from a proud BROWN-eyed Ojibway Man." The strenuous capitalization was his. In the end, *Now Magazine* decided not to print the post-script because they felt it was uncomfortably close to being racist.

Now I can take criticism as much as the next person. I have a spot underneath the dresser where I frequently curl up into a fetal position, because I know no writer is perfect and not everybody agrees with the writer's opinion. But I'm not sure what my having blue eyes has to with an article I wrote that had nothing to do with looking Native. The article was about a lack of professionalism exhibited by some Native organizations and people. Again, the irony was not lost on me.

In Bonita Lawrence's essay, titled "Mixed-Race Urban Native People: Surviving a Legacy of Policies of Genocide," she is quoted as saying "Most of the people I interviewed, however, did not have much sense of the extent of the daily privilege they enjoyed from having white skin ... Their concerns about not fitting in within the Native community at times appeared to overshadow their awareness of the fact that their lives were made much easier by the virtue of not looking Native." Again, I find it admirable that so many people know every single moment of my life as well as all my darker brothers and sisters. I must put a better lock on my diary.

Is the White looking drunk I see on the street any more fortunate than the Native looking one? And I realize the examples I have discussed here are small potatoes compared to the tragedies of residential schools and other atrocities visited upon our Nations. But like most of my Native-looking family, I too am living in fear of diabetes. I am worried about and touched by the same issues any dark-haired First Nations person, any place in Canada, might be.

And while I may not face those prejudices forced upon my darker skinned cousins, they do not have to face the reverse preconceptions people like I must deal with. It all evens out in the end.

It's a strange and weird world out there, even in this new millennium. And as I'm told, I should be just breezing through life easier than my darker-skinned brethren. I'll believe it when I no longer have to write articles like this.

Living the Indigenous Myth

Several years ago, my then Mohawk girlfriend and I, a fellow of proud Ojibway heritage, found ourselves in the history-rich halls of Europe, lecturing at a university deep in the heart of northeastern Germany. Our talk dealt with issues about being Native (or Red Indian as we were often referred to), the propaganda vs. the reality, how our two different nations viewed life, just to mention just a few of the thousands of Aboriginal topics discussed that day by an interested crowd.

Then this one young lady, a student at this former communist university, put up her hand and asked a puzzling, though oddly naive question. It went something like, "Do Indian women shave their legs and armpits like other North American women?" It was not the most anthropologically inquisitive question I have been asked, but unbeknownst to me, the shaving of lower extremities and armpits in Europe is a largely unexplored area of female hygiene and evidently this topic warranted some investigation as to its Aboriginal application.

Other than the obvious follicly oriented aspects of the question, it presented a rather obvious example of the same issue that also troubles our fair country known as Canada, thousands of miles away from that far-off country in distance, language, culture but not that far in perception. I am referring to the myth, the number one myth in my perception, that permeates the collective North American unconscious (and conscious). The Myth of Pan-Indianism. As stated, this young German lady began her question with "Do Indian women … ?" A common beginning for many Canadians, though First Nations, Native, Aboriginal, or Indigenous may be substituted for Indian. There is a persistent belief that we are all one people. These are obviously people who have never compared a Blood with a Naskapi.

Somebody with a lot of time on their hands once estimated that within the borders of what is now referred to as Canada, there were over fifty distinct and separate languages, and each distinct and separate language and dialect emerged from a distinct and separate culture.

So, I began telling this woman, there is no answer to her question because technically, there is no "Indian/First Nations/Aboriginal … " nor could we speak for them all. To us there was only the Cree, the Ojibway, the Salish, the Innu, the Shuswap, etc.

I find myself explaining this concept annoyingly frequently, not just in Europe, but here in Canada—at The Second Cup, Chapters, the bus station. The power of that single myth is incredible. When people ask me or the government or God, "What do First Nations people want?" that's a tough question to answer (but then I can't speak for God). Some of the Mi'kmaq want to catch lobster, some of the Cree want to stop flooding and logging of their territory, the Mohawk want the right to promote their own language, and I know bingo is in there somewhere. That is why every time I see a newspaper article or news report talking about the plight of the Aboriginal people, I find myself screaming at the offending method of communication. "Which People! Be specific!"

That is why I never watch television in public.

That is the power of myths. By the very definition of that word, they are wrong and incorrect. That is why we as Native people (see, I do it myself) prefer not to use the term myth when referring to the stories of our ancestors, as in "The Myths and Legends of our People." There is just something inherently wrong about starting a traditional story with "This is one of the myths that was passed down from our Grandfathers …" Literally translated, it means "This is a lie that was handed down by our Grandfathers …"

The correct term preferred these days is teachings—as in "Our teachings say …" It's certainly more pleasant and accurate because it recognizes the fact that most myths exist for a purpose. Once you put aside the "lie" aspect, there is usually some nugget of metaphor or message within the subtext. And in the Native (there I go again!) way, we like to accentuate the positive and reject the negative.

However, the word legend can also be used instead of myth or teachings, provided you have oral permission from a recognized Elder, or written permission from an Aboriginal academic (any Nation will do), or the thumbs up from any Dene named Ted.

Culture by Association

Not long ago, I read in a Native newspaper a brief biography of someone I have known for going on two decades now. For most of those two decades, this Torontonian had identified herself as being white, with a mild interest in Native issues. More recently, I was surprised to learn that since she married a Native gentleman, and had a child by him, she was now referring to herself specifically as an Anishnawbe-qua, an Ojibway woman. Suddenly out of nowhere, she had a completely different ancestry.

You know, you hear in the news all the time about scientists experimenting with gene and DNA swapping, but you never think it will come into your own neck of the woods. Or maybe I just shouldn't have taken her to that Billy Jack Film Festival in the 80s. Or that damned *Dances With Wolves* film again!

Seriously, this is a delicate topic to explore, one that could get me in a lot of trouble, depending on who reads this and where they stand in the minefield I call "spousal cultural appropriation," otherwise known as SCA. I refer, of course, to individuals who have married people of the Aboriginal persuasion, and now repeatedly identify themselves as having the same status (no pun intended) in that same community.

In many cases, this practice is referred to rather vividly as being "Indian by ejaculation." God knows I've done my share of passing out citizenship, but it sure beats the hell out of all the Bill C-31 paperwork and that pesky lineage requirement.

And to be fair to the other sex, I know of a similar case in Six Nations involving an Iroquois woman who took her non-Native husband to several clan mothers in a desperate attempt to get him adopted into one of the Nations. Eventually she was successful and he now successfully identifies with one of those Nations.

Technically this is not all that new an idea. Marrying somebody for their nationality has been an age-old immigration scam for years. I was once asked, by a friend, to marry a woman from Czechoslovakia so she could become Canadian. Needless to say, I didn't jump at the chance or I'd be writing this from jail.

But of the women I have been lucky enough to date over the years, and those exceptional ones I ended up having special relationships with, I can't help wondering if my "familiarity" with them makes me a member of the Filipino, Irish, Delaware, Cree, Puerto Rican, Mi'kmaq … (and this was just my Vegas vacation last year) nation and a proud representative of their culture?

More recently, I had an excellent relationship with a marvelous Mohawk woman, and though I have great respect and honour for her people and culture, I never felt the urge to "become" Mohawk. My lacrosse skills are just not up to it yet. So that's what puzzles me about the SCA issue. At no time during my current or past relationships, did the thought of ever wanting to call myself a Mohawk man, Filipino man, or the host of other cultures I was privileged to briefly be exposed to, occur. Granted I have a Métis belt, a Mi'kmaq sweater and a Salish painting, but I drew the line there.

I don't believe it's like becoming Jewish where you can take certain classes, get something snipped off, and then convert, and finally be legitimately called a Jew. I am curious at what it currently takes for a non-Native to call themselves a Native person. Must you take Ojibway 101? Show a marked preference for French braiding your hair? Learn how to kill a deer with a corkscrew? Make bannock with your elbows? Maybe we've allowed it to be too easy to join the Aboriginal bandwagon. Perhaps if we snipped something off, the interest might wane.

In the end, I am somewhat mystified by this constant fascination and obsession many non-Natives feel towards our culture. I just find it a little odd and slightly annoying that thousands of years of culture and tradition can be appropriated for the cost of a marriage license (if that). Perhaps it's the fact we have one of the highest suicide rates in the civilized world (and I do use that term loosely). Maybe it's the fact our life expectancy rate is substantially lower than the national average. Could it be the constant turmoil with the various levels of government over land claims, hunting/fishing rights, reparations, etc.? Possibly it's that the standards of living on most reserves are a national disgrace. Conceivably, it's the fact that in the next thirty years, of the over fifty

Aboriginal languages once spoken in this country, it's estimated only three will be left—for possibly another thirty or forty years. But hey, we've got cool hair and funky pow wows.

THE PLACES I'VE BEEN, THE THINGS I'VE SEEN

(An Aboriginal Travel Guide)

Columbus Merely Had a Better Publicist

It's generally accepted that the Vikings and Columbus were the first to visit the shores of our beloved Turtle Island, "discovering" all of us savages in the process of building monumental cities, developing complex social and political structures, creating amazing works of art, and suffering from the delusion that anybody who had a God that had written "thou shall not kill" or "thou shall not steal", might actually be worth inviting to stay for dinner. Unfortunately, the vast majority of the European population at that time couldn't read. And it showed. It's amazing how much trouble a simple boat can get you into.

Modern scholars, however, now concede that perhaps the Vikings and Columbus were not the first to darken our eastern (or western) shores. Evidence exists supporting the claim that, in fact, there were a multitude of non-Turtle Island residents sharing tea and bannock with our grandfathers and grandmothers in the last five thousand years.

The following is a list of eight possible explorations of our noble land by non-Italian or Nordic heritage.

Hsi and Ho (c.2640 BC)

It is argued that these two Imperial Chinese astronomers were ordered by their Emperor to make studies of lands to the east of China. The two men sailed north to the Bering Strait, then south along the North American coastline, spending time with the Pueblo in the Grand Canyon, and eventually journeying to Mexico and Guatemala.

Votan and Wixepecocha (c.800-400 BC)

According to Hindu legends, Hindu missionaries sailed from India, and island hopping, made their way to Central and South America. Votan, a trader, lived amongst the Mayans as a historian, and his contemporary, Wixepecocha, was a Hindu priest who settled with the Zapotecs of Mexico.

Hui Shun (c.458 AD)

Official Chinese documents propose a Buddhist monk named Hui Shun, accompanied by four Afghan disciples, sailed from China to

Alaska, then continued his journey down the coast by foot. Reaching Mexico, he preached Buddhism to Central Americans, supposedly naming Guatemala in honour of Gautama Buddha. He returned to China after forty years.

St. Brendan (c.550 AD)

Two medieval manuscripts tell of the journey of an Irish priest, who with seventeen other monks, sailed west from Ireland in a leather hulled boat. They supposedly traveled as far as Newfoundland and the Caribbean.

The Albans (8th Century)

According to Farley Mowat's book, *The Farfarers*, these Scottish sea people not only settled Iceland and Greenland centuries before the Vikings, they also had thriving and extensive trade and business arrangements with the Indigenous people of Baffin Island, Labrador and Newfoundland.

Prince Madog Ab Owain Gwynedd (c.1170 & 1190 AD)

Due to political conflicts with his brothers, this Welsh prince sailed west from Wales and landed somewhere in the Americas where he built and fortified a settlement. After several years he returned to Wales, leaving behind 120 men. He crossed the Atlantic again in 1190 to discover the settlement was destroyed and all his men had been annihilated.

King Abubakari II (c.1311 AD)

After learning from Arab scholars that there was land to the West of the Atlantic, King Abubakari, a Muslim from Mali, became obsessed with extending his kingdom across the ocean and ordered the creating of a fleet to sail to this unclaimed land. It is believed they landed in Panama, traveled south, and settled in the Incan Kingdom.

Johannes Scolp and Joao Vaz Corte Real (c.1476 AD)

Portugal and Denmark arranged a mutual expedition to find the fabled sea route to China. The combined fleet sailed across the Atlantic, exploring Labrador, Hudson's Bay, St. Lawrence River and the Gulf of St. Lawrence. Failing to find a route to China, they quickly returned to Europe where their discoveries were ignored.

It seems everybody was trying to get here. A word of advice, next time you're at the beach, keep watching that horizon. No telling who's next.

Deep in the Heart of Winnipeg

Just last month I had the privilege of spending several fabulous days in the heart of wonderful downtown Winnipeg. I had been to Winnipeg many times in the past, and have many wonderful and close friends living somewhere in its depths, but I had never visited under these auspicious circumstances. I was an invited guest at the Winnipeg International Author's Festival! I felt like an adult—one with a free plane ticket.

At this literary festival, authors from all over the world were there to read from their latest brilliant works, generate some publicity, hob nob with other fellow writers (whatever a hob nob is—I think it's a small furry animal that lives somewhere up in the Arctic), and sample the hospitality of this prairie city. During the festival, I met some great people, ate some wonderful food, and generally left the province with many more magnificent memories to tell the kids (should I ever have any—mental note: casually bring up this issue with girlfriend, she may have input).

But as with everything in life, you must take the bad with the good. And much like the newspapers, we often tend to remember and report the not-so-great occurrences. For instance, I learned an important lesson about Winnipeg and its festivals: they really put you to work in this town. In the incredibly short time of a scant forty-eight hours, I did nine, maybe ten readings—it got fuzzy after a while. After about the fifth or sixth reading, I even found myself boring.

On top of that, I was there to promote my new book, a collection of humorous essays and articles titled *Further Adventures of a Blue-Eyed Ojibway: Funny You Don't Look Like One—Too—Two*. In fact, a book launch was planned for my final night in Winnipeg. One minor problem. No book. It seems the company that printed the books had problems somewhere in the process which resulted in no book for the launch. Now, I cannot speak for most people, but when I go to a book launch, generally I'm expecting to see a book. Call me a radical but that is what I have been conditioned to expect. The result—one cancelled book launch and one depressed writer. Not Hemingway depressed, more Lord Byron depressed.

But that still left me with the nine readings I already mentioned. Nine readings that none of my dozen or so friends in Winnipeg bothered to attend. But I'm not bitter. Really. I'm sure they had nine other separate things to do.

Then things took a different tack. At two of these readings I had the pleasure of working with Greg Scofield, the noted Métis poet. We were both at an inner-city high school, reading and answering questions from the student body. First Greg got asked this question by a young man hidden somewhere in the audience, then it was my turn to answer the question while on the stage. "Have you ever tried to kill yourself?"

Both of us hemmed and hawed, awed I think by the blasé nature in the delivery of the question. Its not every day you get asked a question like that by a teenage audience at a reading. I remember blurting out an answer, my mind reeling with what would motivate a sixteen-year- old to ask such a question, twice in the same day, the same hour.

I remember responding to the suicide question with some half-hearted joke about, "Only when I open my American Express bill," but even then I knew I wasn't doing the inquiry justice. I was probably just deflecting the uncomfortableness of it. In my travels I've been to Davis Inlet and a host of other communities where suicide is a real and ever present issue. My second answer of simply "No," seemed to pale beside the ramifications of the question.

I spent the rest of that day, in between other readings, thinking about that teenager's question. Perhaps Greg had a better perspective for answering. In his recently published autobiography, Thunder Through My Veins, he talks quite freely about some of the harrowing times he's gone through and how he has managed to survive the darker times. I have such great respect for people who have gone through that and come out the other end. That which does not destroy us, makes us stronger. The German philosopher Neitzche had it right I guess.

I hope that Neitzche is on the course list at that school.

How to Plant a Legend

I've been a bad boy. A very bad boy. And if I'm lucky, it won't come back to haunt me. And to all the Native people out there who travel the world, it was just meant as a joke. Really.

The name of the country is Belgium. Brussels to be exact. I was there at a theatre conference lecturing about the wonders of Aboriginal theatre in Canada. One of the organizers, a lovely older Jewish lady, offered to take my girlfriend at the time and myself out sightseeing. So sitting at a picturesque cafe, drinking really strong European coffee, she asked us if Native people celebrated any traditional holidays or seasonal ceremonies. My ex instantly began to regale her with a proud litany of Iroquoian rites. Then this curious lady asked me about Ojibway examples.

I don't know why, but for some reason, perhaps the innate trickster in me, I answered "Well, it's a little known fact that the most respected and revered holiday in the Ojibway year marks the death of Elvis Presley." She looked confused for a second before nodding in sympathy and respect. Sitting next to her, my ex-girlfriend rolled her eyes (did you know you can actually hear eyes rolling in their sockets if they're done with enough annoyance?)

And for some reason I don't remember, the conversation continued quickly in another direction and Elvis' elevated position in the Ojibway pantheon of ceremonies gave way to other fascinating conversation. I never did get the opportunity to correct my failed attempt at humour. Now I am back in Canada with a guilty conscience and possibly responsible for a growing, if inaccurate legend. So now this woman, who is a respected member of the University of Brussels, attached to a department that teaches/studies Canadian theatre, now thinks Ojibways have an unnatural attachment to Elvis Presley. And the scary thing is, she might not be that far off.

In this new millennium, I still occasionally see older Native men walking down rez roads, sporting what looks like vintage ducktail hairstyles—heavily slicked back, listening to classic rock n' roll music, and wearing clothes that would have seemed outdated the day the music died. In many Native communities it's called "The Time Warp" effect, ancient cars, outhouses right next to the satellite dish, copies of People magazine read by women who still cover their hair with colourful handkerchiefs.

And, I'm ashamed to say, this isn't the first time I have been known to bend the cultural truth a little when pressed. A long time ago, a fellow Ojibway friend and I decided one summer that we had time to kill and money to spend. With that extremely rare revelation, we found ourselves several months later in New Zealand, hanging out with the Maori, the indigenous people of that far off South Pacific island.

After several weeks with one particular family, that of the noted Maori author Patricia Grace, we were faced with an unusual dilemma. A challenge was thrown to us. This cultural exchange was a little one-sided. Since we had lived with them, shared in the Maori lifestyle, ate Maori foods, this family was curious to sample North American, specifically Ojibway cuisine. So here we were, two Ojibways with our culinary backs against a wall, in a land where lamb and red pickled beets rule. How does one prepare a traditional Ojibway meal under such conditions? Head to the zoo and see if there are any deer or moose handy? Not to mention my corn soup talents are a little rusty.

Our solution!? The tasty and nutritional food that has raised many a generation of Ojibway and still continues to grace our indigenous kitchen tables. These humble Maori were treated to the unique delicacy known as Macaroni and Tomatoes or also known as, depending where you come from, hangover soup. Two huge pots full. One robust Maori had three bowls full. That is one of the proud Ojibway legacies we left behind.

I try and reason to myself that I'm not all that inaccurate or evil. Elvis did actually have some Native blood, I'm told. Cherokee I think. But in America that's like saying politicians occasionally lie. And tomatoes are actually Native (no pun intended) to the Americas. But maybe that's stretching it a bit.

So to all those who may visit other places on this fabulous planet, don't be surprised at what you may hear about the Ojibway wherever you may go. It's a colourful world out there and evidently I'm doing my bit to make it a little bit more colourful. It comes from having a creative spirit. I guess I won't even begin to tell you what I told the Cubans and the Fijians. I think it may have dealt with us being the best lovers or something like that. And that every Thursday was "Take An Ojibway To Lunch Day." I wish!

I just wish I could remember when Elvis' birthday really was. Should this woman ever come to Canada, I may have to arrange something pretty quick.

FUNNY, YOU DON'T LOOK LIKE ~~ONE,~~ ~~TWO,~~ THREE:
Furious Observations of a Blue-Eyed Ojibway

ADVENTURES IN INDIAN COUNTRY
(Stories From the Edge of Turtle Island)

First We Take Turtle Island,
Then We Take Berlin

I waved good-bye to Turtle Island as my girlfriend and I left its familiar shores and flew out over the Atlantic. We were on our way to a country that is widely known to Aboriginal people across North America as a land curious, intrigued, and downright infatuated with us Injuns—a place known as Germany. It was Dawn's first trip and my third to that fabled land where beads, fluff, feather, and leather are always in fashion—even for those who look more German than Native. Nobody really knows why.

Some theorize it's because of a turn-of-the-century writer named Karl May who wrote several books romanticizing the North American Indian. Others believe it's because Germans were once tribal themselves, never fully conquered by even the mighty Roman Empire. Or perhaps it's our connection to a wilderness that is practically non-existent in Europe. I promised one Teutonic woman I would kiss a squirrel for her.

We were attending a Canadian Literary Festival in Berlin, with a lecture/reading tour to follow, to support the recent publication of my seventh book, a collection of short stories called *Fearless Warriors*. The tour consisted of stops at six universities, spread across much of the northern part of the country, all with significant Canadian/Native Studies programs.

During much of the trip, we had the opportunity to play tourist. One of the things we noticed was how much people over there smoked. In Canada, we've all gotten used to (except for the smokers of course) not being able to smoke in any government building, restaurant, university, airport, train station, elevator, bathroom, closet, refrigerator, etc. (bingo halls notwithstanding). In Germany, smoking is still socially acceptable. Boy, is it acceptable!

Let's see... as tourists we had a hamburger in Hamburg, but, unfortunately, didn't have the time for a frankfurter in Frankfurt or a berliner in Berlin (which is actually a type of glazed donut, minus the hole—I stored these in my wallet).

More interestingly, since the reunification of the country in 1989, massive building construction and renovations have taken over the skyline of the country. In Berlin alone, I counted at least twenty-three huge construction cranes hovering over an eight-block radius. The running joke in the country is that the crane is now the national bird of Germany. And if I'm not mistaken, isn't the crane or heron one of the clans of the Iroquois Confederacy—famous for its Mohawk ironworkers? A conspiracy … I wonder?

In Rostock, located along the Baltic Sea in the north part of what was once East Berlin, we were taken out by a teacher and her boyfriend to sample some of the local establishments the town had to offer. It was a cute little town, with an adorable traditional (by European standards) town square decorated for its yearly Christmas market. Everything with a yuletide nature could be found and bought. It was very Heidi-esque. Except when we found ourselves in an ancient basement dancing club, crawling with students from the nearby university, all smoking heavily. Evidently this was a student hang-out/pub, and we had to pretend to be part of their ensemble as they (and we) danced to 80s music, like I remember dancing to 50s music. I felt old.

And crouching in that low basement, I couldn't help thinking how strange life is. Here I was, in the labyrinth-like basement of some building older than most of Canada (politically and architecturally), on a book tour of Germany (East Germany, to make it weirder), surrounded by students who were studying Canadian Studies.… And to think I always thought I'd end up working at the Band Office embezzling money from the Department of Indian Affairs. Who'd a thunk it?

In many of the stores lining the sidewalks of Berlin, Osnabruck, Kiel, Dusseldorf, etc., it wasn't hard to find such things as the omnipresent dreamcatchers (I guess it doesn't matter if you dream in German) and day-timers with pictures of some Native guy with "Indianer 1999" written under his chin. Maybe that was his status card number?

In Greifswald, Dawn was presented with a beautiful, beaded deerskin purse by a German teacher. The professor had beaded it herself and it looked as authentic as any I had seen in my more domestic travels. I just hope the Germans don't end up doing with beading what the Japanese did with cars and cameras.

In our travels we also discovered several plaster busts of Indians, never donning less than three large feathers. I knew we forgot to pack something. Practically everywhere we went there were posters saying "Kanada" in large letters, showing a picturesque shot of the Rockies with a Native Elder in full regalia, standing in the foreground and looking off into the distance. We saw these posters on posts, walls, and fences, but we never did figure out what they were advertising. That you can get a Native Elder cheap in "Kanada?"

In one restaurant, we saw a tall blonde man sporting a "Mohawk haircut," wearing a grey-and-white camouflage bomber jacket. Then I remembered hearing something about an autobahn (a German highway) being blockaded or something.

Another fascinating aspect of Germany was the amount of good quality beer and wine. After all, this is a country famous for both.

Hey … wait a minute … beer and wine, vast amounts of smoking, dreamcatchers, Mohawk haircuts and camouflage outfits, beaded pouches, pictures of Indians everywhere … maybe we didn't go to Germany. Maybe we just went home for the weekend instead.

Nah, I don't think so. At home we don't talk about Native literature nearly as much as they do in Germany. Actually, upon reflection, I think that says something quite sad.

Brother, It's Cold Outside

In case you haven't noticed, it's cold outside. And on these cold and chilly days, I find myself contemplating a cultural and historical curiosity, one that leaves me with a burning desire to ask my often equally frigid non-Native friends a question. The query goes something like, "Tell me again why your ancestors picked this country to move to?" A simple question. One I ask because *it's so cold outside*. I mean, being of Native descent myself, I *have* to live here. Several dozen millennia of freezing your buns off sort of make you attached to the place. But I will admit, being half-White makes staying warm in this environment a little more difficult.

So to all the non-Native people shivering around their televisions at this very moment, I ask you once more: Why did your people come here voluntarily? *It's cold here.* Or didn't your ancestors read that in the pamphlets? And this is only Toronto. I won't even bother discussing the distinctive winter weather of Regina or Winnipeg.

Now being somewhat of a history buff, I understand the whole "seeking to escape oppression" concept. We Native people have faced a little oppression ourselves in our history but you don't see us running to one of the coldest countries in the world to try and improve our lives. Of all the countries in this big old world, why pick The Great White North (no ethnic pun intended)? I know Tourism Canada is gonna kill me, but need I remind you, *it's cold here!* Couldn't the white folk have planted potatoes in Florida? There were a lot of wide, open spaces in the Bahamas. There were railways being built in Venezuela and lots of places in St. Lucia in which to hide from despots and dictators. *It's not cold there!*

Now trust me, this isn't some anti-immigration rant, it's an anti-frostbite one. I mean, I practically live in Thai restaurants, have a fondness for Italian leather, and have several Mexican quilts on my bed to keep me warm on these cold, cold nights. Now think about it. What's the common denominator of all these countries? They're warm. *And it's cold here.*

To me, it's just a question of sheer logic, like, "Tell me again? Why did you vote for the Tories?"

Two Sides of the Coin

Davis Inlet. Mention that name and dark, depressing images immediately come to mind. At least they did to me when I learned I'd be making a day trip to this infamous community. I envisioned scenes of poverty, anarchy, and substance abuse, just to name a few. You remember Davis Inlet. That's the community of people that was forcibly relocated thirty years ago. These people ended up on some small island in the middle of nowhere, put there by the government for some obscure bureaucratic reason. And didn't they do that same thing to an Inuit community back in the 1950s; bundle them all up and ship them from northern Quebec to an island in the far, far north, to an area they were not familiar with? All in the name of furthering Canada's claim to the Arctic Archipelago by populating it with people. Much like Davis Inlet, these people are saying "enough is enough." They want to go back home and are petitioning the government for compensation.

Putting it in a different context, it's like saying, let's put everybody in Sudbury on some island in the middle of James Bay and see how they survive. But it seems to me that the government doesn't do things like that to non-Native communities. Why am I not surprised?

So I came to this community on the stunningly beautiful shores of Labrador and saw some of the things I expected to see. Many of the walls in Davis Inlet are covered in graffiti, including some disgusting suggestions on the door of a Nun's home in the community. I noticed most of the public buildings no longer have glass windows. Instead, it's more logical to use a form of unbreakable plastic. The entrance to the school I visited looked like a bunker under siege: dark, decorated with heavy mesh screening, ominous looking, and heavily fortified. I admit it, I felt sorry for this community.

But there were other things I saw in this windswept, frozen village, things that I had not been expecting that made me realize this community had been getting a bum rap. For instance, I have never been to a place where the children are so quick to smile. Walking down the hallways of the school these kids would come up to me with a big smile and boldly ask, "Hi, what's your name?"

At the airport—a postage-stamp-sized, flat piece of snow-covered land—I watched four young kids, all younger than seven, running around the building and through the office in glorious celebration of anarchy. They climbed on everything, played everywhere, and they were having fun. Not just average fun, but the kind of fun that comes with complete freedom. The parents were busy working, processing the half-dozen or so passengers in a cold aluminum room, completely oblivious to the chaos their kids were creating and enjoying. These were happy kids.

And in the same school that I described as a bunker, the students were rehearsing a play they had written and were performing for the community. It was a play about solvent abuse, specifically gas sniffing, and how it's often cyclical; the parents drink, so the kids think it's okay to do similar stuff. And the play was completely in Innu, the students' Native language. Even though I had only been in Davis Inlet for a few hours, I felt proud of these students.

During the Skidoo trip back to the airport, I looked over at the setting sun, and back at my very brief encounter with this community. Thoughts were running through my head. We passed a tame wolf that lived in the town, a beautiful animal with a glorious winter coat that a family had adopted. I saw the new houses being put in. And then the Skidoo blew up. Or more correctly, the voltage regulator shorted out and smoke started pouring from the engine. On the walk up to the airport, in the increasingly frigid twilight, I had more time to reflect.

It will be at least another five or six years before the new village the government is building for this community is ready for occupancy. And these kids will be young adults by then. There is hope for Davis Inlet.

You Know You're Old When …

As winter slowly turns into spring, and the continuous cycle of the seasons completes another full year, it occurs to you that yet another birthday is soon approaching. And you have mixed feelings about it. In your early years, you measured birthdays by different milestones.

For instance, you turn thirteen, and you are officially a teenager (parents be afraid, be very afraid). You turn sixteen, and you can get a driver's license (other drivers be afraid, very afraid). You turn nineteen, and you are legal for just about everything. And conversely, you are also responsible for everything you do. You turn twenty-five, and you are no longer eligible for youth-oriented job-employment programs—the first kink in your imaginary armour of agelessness. You crest the hill known as thirty, and well … this is a particularly difficult birthday because you now begin to realize that you're getting ever so slightly older. At age thirty-three Christ and Crazy Horse died. You wonder: what have you done with your life?

And from here, the years and pounds begin to add up a little too quickly and comfortably. And it's your turn to be afraid, very afraid.

Our culture and teachings have taught us to revere and respect our Elders. Growing old is part of the cycle of life, like the seasons. I have trouble benignly remembering that fact when it takes at least two days to recover from pushing a car out of a snowdrift. And it was a small car. And it wasn't a particularly deep snowdrift.

Recently I have begun to notice various uncomfortable signs that "the times they are a changin'" (for those old enough to remember that song), and they're a changin' none too easily. In my own life, I've observed numerous signs from the Creator gently reminding me that I am not a young man anymore. At the age of thirty-six, soon to be thirty-seven, I am a little over halfway past the life expectancy of a Canadian Aboriginal male. Evidently, physically speaking, it's downhill from here. The Elder years are fast approaching. Well, maybe someone will carry my luggage from now on and people will actually listen to what I have to say.

I have taken the liberty of recording some of those "gentle reminders" for your interest. Feel free to add your own reminders, or just cry along with me. The choice is yours.

You know you're old when:

You realize the Zorro t-shirt you put on might not be appropriate for somebody your age. You begin looking for beer and sport t-shirts favoured by your uncles. If you're lucky, you might be able to find that prized golf or fishing shirt. Welcome to the club. You now dress like your uncles.

You are at the dentist, and as the dental hygienist is cleaning your teeth, she comments casually that she saw one of your plays when she was in high school. "But I don't remember which one it was. That was so long ago." You refrain from responding as your heart cries out because, at that moment, she has several sharp implements deep inside your mouth. You decide to overlook it this time.

Every time you put on a sweater, your girlfriend can automatically tell which decade you bought it in. Nobody told me velour was out!

Your girlfriend steals all your batteries for her own personal reasons and refuses to tell you why. And you don't care.

You find out fifty percent of the Native population is under twenty-five. You do the math and realize you have underwear that is older than half the Aboriginal community.

And scariest of all, your mother makes sense.

And this was just today!

The Seven "C's" of Canadian Colonization

On June 24, 1997, all of Newfoundland celebrated the five hundredth anniversary of the landing of John Cabot's ship, the Matthew, on the island. Back in 1597, Cabot's was the first European ship to visit Canada (not including the Viking's short stay in Canada's tenth province, back around 1000 A.D.). A fabulous party was held, including a cameo appearance from her Majesty, the Queen herself.

But not all were happy with the planned festivities. The Assembly of First Nations, as well as many other Native organizations and individuals, didn't really see this as something to celebrate. Some consider Cabot's arrival as the beginning of a campaign of genocide and cultural destruction that has lasted five hundred years. As an example, less than three centuries after Cabot's landfall, the Beothuks, Newfoundland's Indigenous people, were extinct. And while that blame can't be laid directly on Cabot's shoulders, most Natives believe it started with him. At least in Canada.

But Cabot had a lot of company. History has shown that many European explorers laid the foundation for the colonization of our little country. Other explorers of the unknown have had effects on Canada and its Native people. And a surprising and interesting fact is that the names of many of these explorers start with the letter "C." Perhaps this is the prerequisite for conquering Canada. For instance:

Columbus: The man who made getting lost an art form. He is the prototype of men refusing to believe they are lost and ask for directions. While not specifically or directly connected to Canada, his arrival in the Bahamas can be viewed as one earthquake starting several tidal waves. It is ironic that many White people every year still like to "discover" the Bahamas, and other spots in the Caribbean and Mexico that he came upon. Perhaps White people are migratory.

Cortez: Again, while not directly related to Canada, his actions have had wide-reaching effects. He conquered an empire (the Aztecs) and was actually one of the few conquistadors to die a rich man. At one point, he took a Native woman as a mistress and Christianized her to make her more acceptable. Known for his ambition, womanizing, and twice being arrested for breach of trust, it's no wonder that he was a politician—a mayor in a town in Cuba.

Cabot: Cabot's real name was Giovanni Caboto. Probably the first of many men to change his name to get into Canada. He was amazed by the number of fish available offshore. It is rumoured the crew attached ropes to baskets to lower them into the water, and pulled them up overflowing with fish. Ahh, the memories. The first case of foreigners plundering the Grand Banks.

Cartier: Founder of Quebec City in 1534. Misunderstood what the local Natives were saying when he asked them, "What do you call this land?" as he indicated the countryside with his hand. Unfortunately the Native people looked where he was actually pointing, at their village, and replied, "Kanata" (a group of huts or a village). Kanata is now Canada. The first misunderstanding between the French and Native population. Not the last.

Champlain: The explorer of much of Central Canada. Though he spent decades in the New World, Champlain never, oddly enough, bothered to learn any of the aboriginal languages of the people he worked with and exploited. Even then, Quebec's Language Bill 101 was in effect.

Cook: Explored much of the coast of British Columbia after discovering Tahiti and the Hawaiian islands while looking for the Northwest Passage. His first claim to fame was his meticulous charting of the St. Lawrence River—in preparation for the British assault on the French at Quebec. He is also known for his precise charting of the whole length of the rugged coast of Newfoundland. One of the first cases of Easterners moving to the West Coast.

Christ: Subject of the world's first and bestselling biography."

Christ did more to change the lives of Canada's Indigenous people than all the explorers put together. Unfortunately, this change was usually for the worst: think of the Jesuits and, more recently, the residential schools. But many have embraced the teachings of this man and found happiness. The church brought more than just Christ's messages to the Native people, it also brought bingo.

Other honourable mentions of people "discovering and conquering" this continent whose names begin with the letter "C": Clark (of Lewis and Clark fame), who went to the Pacific Northwest looking for dinosaurs, and Custer, every Aboriginal's favourite example of "do onto others as you would have them do unto you." But they lack that specific Canadian connection.

Most of these men were crawling through Canada's coast and interior looking for gold, jewels, and spices, or, more specifically, a new trade route to India or China. On June 24th, 1997, I thought it would be ironic and fitting for there to be a whole line of Native protesters waiting on shore for the landing of the *Matthew*, all holding signs saying "India and China: That Way," pointing north to the Northwest Passage. It would have done more to honour the spirit of these explorers than what the people in Newfoundland had planned.

Or, better yet, they should have had some Chinese or South Asians waiting on shore. That would have thrown them for a loop.

A Lexicon of Aboriginal Trivia,
From A to Z

With the growing interest in all things Native, a few small but interesting details of everyday (or not so everyday) Aboriginal life sometime fall through the cracks. The following are tidbits of trivia for the reader to do with what he or she pleases.

Apache: In the movie *Rambo II,* Sylvester Stallone's killing-machine character is reported as being half-German and half-Apache. One government agent in the film sums it up by saying "God, what a mix!"

Break a leg: In reference to the two famous confrontations that happened in Wounded Knee, South Dakota, Native actors, hoping for a good show, use the term "Wounded Knee" instead of "break a leg."

Crum: George Crum, a Native cook working at the Saratoga Springs Resort in New York, accidentally invented the potato chip in 1853. When a customer complained that the fried potato wedges he was served were too big and not salty enough, Crum retaliated by serving the gentleman wafer-thin potato slices covered in salt—as a joke. Evidently the joke took off.

Dartmouth: This top-notch American ivy league university located in New Hampshire originally started out as a seminary for educating American Indians. An institute for redskins instead of bluebloods.

Education: Having an MBA now stands for having Mixed Blood Ancestry. Or Me Big Aboriginal.

F.B.I.: Amongst Native Nations in America, F.B.I. stands for Full Blooded Indian, while in Canada, DIA (Department of Indian Affairs) now stands for those "Damn Indian Agents."

Grey Owl: While known as a famous Aboriginal imposter, this Englishman claimed to actually be half-Jacarilla Apache, not Ojibway or Cree as Canadian mythology would suggest. He may even be related to Rambo.

Hui Shun: A Chinese Buddhist priest and explorer who also supposedly "discovered" America in 458 A.D. and tried to convert local Indians to Buddhism. Allegedly he named Guatemala in honour of Gautama Buddha.

Indian Summer: The politically correct now refer to this time of fall as "First Nations Summer." I kid you not.

Jobs: Though Native people in the United States make up less than one percent of the overall population, they are estimated to make up over ten percent (a lot of them Iroquois) of the high iron workforce, building skyscrapers, bridges, and the like.

Kemosaabe: Kemosaabe is an actual word in the Ojibway language. It means "to peek or look through," i.e., a mask. A liberal translation might also include a "peeping Tom."

Little Bighorn: The only non-Native survivor of Custer's Seventh Cavalry was a horse ironically named Commanche, ridden by a Captain Keogh. The horse suffered seven wounds, three of them serious. Treated as a war hero, the horse lived till 1893 when it died at the age of thirty.

May, Karl: One of Hitler's favourite authors was Karl May, who wrote a series of books at the turn of the century romanticizing the American Indian in the Old West. May's books are still in print and popular in Germany. Many people believe them to be the root of the German preoccupation with Native people.

Names: Pocahontas was not her real name. It was actually a nickname given to her by her father meaning "playful one." Her real name was actually Matoaka.

Ouch: The translation of this word varies from community to community. In Curve Lake you would say "owe-ee," where as on Manitoulin Island the pronunciation would be "eye-yow," and in at least one Reserve in Southwestern Ontario it would be "eee-yow." The Tyendinaga use the term "agee" and claim that the term hockey is derived from it; when White people saw Mohawks being slammed against the boards, they would cry out "agee" in pain. Agee/hockey... think about it.

Pool: These days, in playing the game of pool, after sinking the first ball, instead of calling stripes/highball, or colours/lowball, trendy Natives call "half-breeds or full-bloods."

Quipu: Elaborately knotted strings with which the Incas recorded virtually every important aspect of their civilization. The position and number of knots on each individual string had a precise meaning. It was their form of writing and accounting.

Recreational Vehicles: The Winnebago Nation, located along the shores of Lake Superior, has officially changed its name to Hocak Wyijaci. Put that on a RV.

Saugeen: A Native Reserve in Ontario that is investigating the possibility of unionizing the Band Office, a first in First Nations. Saugeen Local 001. Only problem: who would care if the Band Office went on strike?

Tonto: The actor who played Tonto was actually from the Six Nations Reserve near Brantford, Ontario. Jay Silverheels was his professional name; his real name was actually Harry Smith. Perhaps a distant relation to Pocahontas' John Smith?

Ukrainians: There seems to be a bizarre artistic connection between Ukrainians and Native people. Note author W.P. Kinsella, playwright George Ryga, and actor Michael Zenon. Zenon is, no doubt, familiar to millions of older Canadians as Joe Two Rivers from the ancient television series, *The Forest Rangers.*

Vegetables: Native contributions to international cuisine include the potato and the tomato. So the Irish and the Italians owe us an amazing debt of gratitude.

Wannabes: People who "wannabe" Indian. Not to be confused with "should-a-beens," people who are not Native but for one reason or another, should have been.

Xinxa: A fictional tribe of Indians from Guatemala that gave Lamont Cranston, otherwise know as the pulp and movie hero "The Shadow," a fire opal ring to assist him in fighting crime. "Who knows what tribes lurk in the heart of Guatemala? The Shadow knows!"

Yuchi: An Aboriginal nation that was moved from Georgia to Oklahoma in 1836, and is believed to be, by some authorities, one of the "Lost Tribes of Israel." As recently as 1975, *Newsweek* said that "some specialists in American folklore think the customs, language and appearance of the Yuchi … imply an old Jewish heritage." Oy!

Zero: The Mayan base twenty number system, which included zero, had been developed a thousand years in advance of its use elsewhere, and Mayan astronomers were capable of astonishing precision in charting the heavens.

Reasons Why You Should Be Nice
to Native People

In this era of unsettled land claims, government cutbacks, and the continuing unacceptable levels of unemployment and mortality, it's no wonder Native people across Canada are sometimes viewed as, shall we say, pissed off at the world. And those are just a few of the many larger issues that happen to make the evening papers. On a smaller level, a more personal and everyday kind of existence, the complaints and irritants continue.

I refer to the minor annoyances that make living as an Aboriginal person in Canada less than enjoyable. So, since the education of those who just don't know what life is like as an Aboriginal person in Canada is always half the battle, I humbly present six minor irritations in the everyday life of a Canadian Native person for your consideration.

1. Non-Native people who try to "out-Indian" Native people. Ever sit in a sweat lodge of an approximate temperature of sixty to eighty degrees Celsius with a non-Native person that is reciting an incredibly long prayer thanking the Grandmothers, the Grandfathers, and everybody else who could possibly be listening up there, as various parts of that non-Native's anatomy shrivel up and fall off from the heat?

2. The fact that it is rapidly becoming unsafe to wear traditional clothing made of buckskin or fur because of spray paint-wielding lunatics on a mission to destroy thousands of years of heritage. Why can't they destroy something really horrible, like polyester?

3. People called New Agers who chase Native people around because they think there's a spiritual connection there somewhere. If I see one more New Ager approach me at a pow wow or a conference, shoving those damn crystals at me, I hereby refuse to be responsible for my actions or where those crystals may end up anatomically.

4. The fact that it's customary for Native people to expect everything they do or every decision they make to have repercussions seven

generations down the road. And how amazingly true that's become concerning the settling of land claims in this country. We'll be lucky if they get settled by our tenth generation. Looking on the bright side, at least it's job security for treaty researchers, lawyers and politicians.

5. The fact that the Native people of this country are constantly being referred to as "Canada's Tragedy," "The Dispossessed," or "The Sad and Unfortunate Story of Canada's Native People." It's always something depressing like that. And if you're always called names like this, pretty soon you'll start to believe it. I refuse to be tragic, or sad, or depressed; there's too much to be delighted with in our cultures. Someday I want to see headlines like "Those Happy People of Manitoulin Island" or "Those Laugh-a-Minute Crees in Northern Alberta."

6. The millions upon millions of people you meet in bars, airplanes, classrooms, libraries, etc., who say "I've got some Indian blood in me too." If every Native person I know gave the government a nickel for every non-Native person who has claimed this, the national debt would vanish with money left over to reinstate all the funding cut to Native programs. I once knew a girl in high school who told me that she had a drop of Native blood in her. "A long time ago, my Great Grandmother was raped by a Mohawk." Now there's a proud lineage.

All the stupid questions we get asked. Like, "Can you ride a horse?" Or, "What's it like living on a reserve?" "Do you know Graham Greene?" "What did you think of *Dances With Wolves*?" "Last week I had a dream about a plaid horse and a talking feather. What does it mean?" Perhaps that you should get help.

A HORSE OF A DIFFERENT COLOUR
(Pros and Cons of Being Who You Are)

Checking Under the Bed

For the past six-and-a-half years, it seems I have shared an apartment with some unexpected guests. As luck would have it, the rental gods had seen fit to bless me with a rather large two story, two bedroom apartment, located on a lovely street in Toronto. What I don't remember seeing in the lease involved some unforeseen boarders living in the second floor room that doubles for the guest bedroom and office. I am a writer and it's been in that second floor room where I have created some of my (hopefully) great works of art. Alone, I originally thought. But unbeknownst to me, somebody or something else had a prior claim to that patch of space—which as a Native person, the irony was not lost upon me. It all started a year or two after I had moved in. A fellow playwright, also Native, was staying in that spare room while in town working on a production. I was away but she later told me about the night she was sitting on the steps, directly underneath the window of the mystery room, having a cigarette. Out of the comer of her eye, she thought she saw a shadow cross the house directly in front of her— meaning the "thing" that cast the shadow came from the room in which she planned to sleep. Puzzled, she watched the house where the shadow had been moments before, only to see it pass by again. Unnerved, she investigated but found nothing. An uncomfortable night of sleep followed.

Several years later, another friend, this time a Native filmmaker, told me she thought she saw a person in that room once when she too was staying under my roof. It was only a fleeting glance, out of the comer of her eye, but it was enough to make her comment on it to me. She, like the other woman, shrugged it off and nothing else happened. Now this was where I began to puzzle. While having nothing more than a passing interest in the supernatural, I began wondering if maybe, we had a … dare I say it … ghost in the house. I had never seen whatever this thing was, but then again, when I'm in that room it's usually to write, and I become pretty focused at that time. A walking corpse would have to tap on my shoulder pretty hard to get my attention.

The final, and perhaps most perceptive experience came when my girlfriend's best friend came for a visit. The morning after she spent the night in that room, she calmly asked if we had any "Little People" living in our house. Evidently she had felt "somebody" tugging on her hair as she lay in her bed and assumed that's what they were.

I was not unfamiliar with "Little People." The concept and reputations of "Little People" extends well beyond the famous Irish Leprechaun version. In fact, most cultures around the world have numerous legends detailing the adventures of these diminutive creatures that can live anywhere and everywhere. In this case we are talking of a more Indigenous clan. The multitudes of Native societies existing in Canada and the States are no different in these beliefs. My people, the Ojibway, have many stories about them; so do the Iroquois, my girlfriend and her friend with the tuggable hair.

They are indeed a select bunch. One odd aspect of these miniature inhabitants is that, to my knowledge, they have only revealed themselves to Native women, at least in my house. All three of my guests were Native women. Maybe they have a predilection for the double X chromosomes. Or perhaps the men who have stayed in that room don't have hair long enough to tug. Two of the three were artists of one sort or another, the other a student. Maybe they were more open to the possibility. Accountants or stockbrokers might not be so receptive. But regardless, as a sign of respect, I have been very careful with mousetraps. But this issue is fast becoming an irrelevant point. For in the next few weeks, we will be moving. A new house beckons, on a new street, with new adventures. But I must not be too confident. Little People can move too. Maybe they will decide to join us in our new house. Or maybe they will stay behind and play games on the next tenants. The will of these tiny dwellers are unfathomable to us people of a more blessed vertical stature.

As is the custom of my people, we will put down a little tobacco when we leave, as a parting gift to them. We hope they will accept it and remember us fondly. Or they might consider it a bribe to travel with us. Whatever their decision is, we will accept it.

But one thing does bother me, Little People or ghosts ... they were there in the room with me as I wrote and struggled with many different writing projects. Often I would reach a dead end, or face writer's block as I stared at a blank computer screen. Then suddenly, out of nowhere, I would receive a flash of inspiration. It wouldn't be long before I found myself typing "The End." So if my unforeseen houseguests were responsible for such stimuli, does that make them my ghost writers?

The Bomb Waiting

Tick, tick, tick. The older I get, the louder that relentless reminder becomes. Each year, each day: tick, tick. Evidence of this internal biological bomb is everywhere around me: my family, the news, government statistics. Inside of me, a Native man in his mid-thirties, lies a ticking bomb. Dormant for the moment, thank God, I know it lies there waiting for the biochemical fuse to be lit.

What was once unknown to most Native people, has almost become inevitable. Diabetes is a full-blown epidemic in most Native families and communities. A recent study taken in the small northern Ontario Aboriginal community of Sandy Lake showed that almost twenty-nine percent of the population was diabetic, with another fourteen percent showing the early symptoms. That's forty-three percent. And that's just one village. Tick, tick.

While working on a project in Pennsylvania last summer, I saw a documentary on the Pima people located somewhere down in the American Southwest. For uncountable centuries these people eked a living in the desert, drawing water from a small river nearby. As with many of their neighbours, their diet was high in grain and vegetables, with a little meat thrown in. Refined or store-bought food was a rarity.

Then sometime during the 1930s, the American government felt the need to divert the river, the lifeblood of the community, in another direction. Robbed of their water, the Pima were also robbed of their ability to provide their own food. Feeling responsible, the government stepped in and began providing the community with relief supplies and provisions. Needless to say, much of it consisted of canned meat, processed food, and sugar.

Sixty years later, the diabetes rate is almost fifty percent, with one quarter suffering from some physical ailment brought on by the disease, and one in ten having had some form of amputation due to the condition. Obesity is the norm.

These are just statistics, and statistics are meaningless. Faceless numbers that are delightfully removed from most people's everyday existence. I know. I've ignored a lot of statistics. Then I began to hear that sound coming from my body.

Tick, tick, tick.

Last Christmas I was at my Aunt's house on my reserve. I was there with several members of my family enjoying dessert after a hearty Christmas meal. Various pies and cakes were being passed around when one of my uncles mentioned how this was going to affect his blood-sugar level. As I sat there, with a huge slab of apple pie on my lap, I saw the conversation take a decidedly different turn. This was a room full of my aunts and uncles, all of whom were casually comparing and discussing the various levels of insulin they all take. I felt the pie on my lap getting heavier.

Of the thirteen surviving children my grandparents had, six, including my mother, are diabetic. That's a little over forty-six percent. Higher than in Sandy Lake. Tick, tick.

I didn't even know my mother suffered from the disease until I visited her in the hospital for a minor operation several years ago. As she lay there in her bed, I noticed the identification tag on her wrist. It indicated the patient was a diabetic. Concerned for my mother's welfare, I was going to report the potentially dangerous mislabeling to a nurse, but my mother assured me it was no mistake. She was a diabetic. So was my grandmother. The affliction had found them both late in their lives and these things were always viewed as a private matter.

That's why the Christmas incident caught me by surprise. It was the first such conversation of that sort I can remember hearing. People are talking and acting—facing it. There are now full-time Aboriginal diabetes health workers and workshops. Before, in my youth, I'd never heard of such things, let alone a need for them.

I still hear the ticking, and it does worry me, but I manage to hold that omnipresent sound at a distance. There's a good chance, somewhere over fifty percent, that it will pass me by.

Those are dangerous odds.

Luckily I don't have much of a sweet tooth, unlike one relative I grew up watching put four tablespoons of sugar into her coffee. My only weakness consists largely of soft drinks and the occasional bowl of ice cream. Still…

There's an old saying about death and taxes being the only things you can really count on in this world. Well, most Native people who live on reserves don't pay a lot of taxes. Maybe for them, and for me, it's death and diabetes that are the reality these days.

Tick, tick, tick.

No Time for Indian Time

If there's one thing I (and I'm sure a g'jillion others) hate in this world, it's stereotypes. No surprise there. In fact, much of the work I do as a playwright and journalist deals with addressing those inaccurate and often damaging images, particularly the Native ones. But if there's even one thing in this world I hate more than aforementioned stereotypes, it's people who use those stereotypes, quite often of themselves, as an excuse for their poor behaviour.

I was recently in Vancouver where a play of mine, with several Native actors in the cast, was in production. During the rehearsal, one of the actors was proving annoyingly difficult for not having the ability to show up on time for rehearsals and run-throughs. A decidedly naughty no-no in the world of theatre, not to mention any other respectable business. Needless to say several stern lectures were administered to the actor. Several days later, his best friend, oddly enough a non-Native person, phoned the theatre office to complain. He accused the company of being racist and not understanding that Native people are "culturally unable to be on time." Evidently he informed the office staff that the Aboriginal people of this country are ethnically and racially late for everything, and the company was being unsympathetic in its inability to recognize and respect that cultural quirk. Basically, forcing Native people to watch the clock was a form of colonial oppression.

One of the people who took the call was a Native woman. One, whom I believe, was never late for work. This simple fact, strongly delivered by this stranger on the phone, seemed to surprise her, as it did me. I was not aware that being tardy was one of those Aboriginal rights constantly being argued about in treaties.

This concept, commonly known as "Indian time," is quite popular and well exercised in the Native community. And on most occasions, it serves a logical purpose. The concept behind "Indian Time" is that things start or happen when they need to, not by some artificial beginning. There is no need to rush something that does not have to be rushed. A pow wow Grand Entry is supposed to start at 12:00, if it starts at 1:00, it is not worth having a heart attack. If people are an hour or two late for a party or some other gathering, nobody panics. Time is not rigid. That is true "Indian Time" and I practice that myself.

But often, some people use this ancient concept to escape or shift blame for the carelessness of their actions. If there is a meeting or some important event that has repercussions beyond this individual, and they are late, I've heard them shrug it off blaming it on "Indian Time" and not taking responsibility for it themselves. I wonder if any of these people have ever tried to catch a train or plane. I also wonder if they would be as nonchalant if their pay cheque was a little late due to "head office time."

What makes this so annoying is that traditionally Native people did respect time. If a trip was planned for dawn, it was guaranteed people would be ready to depart in the canoes when the sun first peeked over the horizon. Those that practiced "Indian Time" had better have an extra pair of moccasins for the long walk ahead of them.

Same with the first sighting of a buffalo herd or the arrival of migratory ducks and geese. It's not in the nature of these animals to hang around waiting for people to find the time to kill them. The Native people had to be able to move and react instantly. Nature waits for no people.

That's why I've always had a problem with those who abuse the concept of "Indian Time." My mother, who has spent most of her life on the reserve, whose first language is Ojibway, and who can be classified as being as "Indian" as anybody, prides herself on never being late for an appointment. Most of the time she's early. There's nothing more annoying for a young Native boy than your mother making sure you're early for a dentist appointment. But since this West Coast gentleman and his friend seem to believe that being late is "culturally correct," my mother must not be that Native. That will be a surprise to her.

Lillian McGregor, a well-respected Elder currently living in Toronto, perhaps put it best when she talked about a watch she bought with her first pay cheque. "This watch is very meaningful for me as it taught me to value time, both mine and that of others. I learned that promptness was a form of respect. I grasped how quickly time passed, and that each hour, minute and second was a gift from the Creator."

Maybe somebody should buy this young actor from the West a watch.

White May Not Be Right

You mention that somebody is in a black mood, or perhaps a friend of yours has a red hot temper, and you can immediately get a grasp of the temperament of the individual you are talking about. Colour, for the longest time, has often been used as a descriptive element in describing the emotional and moral fibre of people, places and things. But, oddly enough, it seems the darker the colour mentioned, the more dangerous or ominous those people, places and things become.

For instance, if you notice bad, stormy weather by remarking how dark the skies look, or if you've heard the Devil referred to as the "Lord of Darkness," you'll get my point. I looked up the word "black" in a dictionary that partially defined the word as gloomy or dismal, sullen or hostile, evil or wicked, and indicative of disgrace.

Yet, you mention the word "white," and a completely different concept emerges: images of purity, virginity, cleanliness, immediately pop to mind. In fact, just recently in a newspaper I came across the phrase "linen-white landscape," used to describe an earlier, more innocent era of time. Let us not forget the famous "little white lie" which means doing something wrong for the right (or white) reasons. Ancient racial intolerance and biases are more than likely at work here. But what I find so ironic is that when you actually look at the pigment of the many things available to modern Canadians today, the opposite is true. Especially when it comes to the tasty world of food. Many of the most dangerous, most unhealthy, and most evil edibles we consume are in fact white in colour. Your cupboards are potential death traps. There may be a need for rigorous readjustment of colour perceptions in the near future.

The colour white may do its most widespread damage in the world of edibles and nourishment. Practically everything white used in the culinary arts has been confirmed as being dangerous to one's health. Sugar has long been viewed as a menace. Salt is like playing with a loaded gun. White rice, while not particularly dangerous, is basically viewed as a pot of unhelpful starch. Each dab of cream or whole milk can be viewed as a potential nail in your coffin.

Need I mention the reputation white flour has in the health community? Add to that its many by-products—white bread and the like—and we're talking empty calories with little nutritional benefits. Might as well inject the glucose directly into your thighs and waist. Why waste (no pun intended) time on the stomach?

And finally, at the top of the pallid pyramid lie fat and the infamous brick of lard (basically rendered fat). Both are white, and both are notoriously bad for your health. Unless heart disease and strokes appeal to you. Death does indeed ride a pale horse.

What I find equally scary is the realization that one of the most common and trusted forms of sustenance known to Native people— the proud, mighty, and eternal bannock/frybread/scone—is, in fact, made of white flour, white sugar, white salt, and white baking powder, and is usually fried in white lard. I am a great believer in tradition, but I do not think it would be disrespectful to consider, perhaps, throwing a vitamin or two into the mix.

And taking a slight detour, but still on the subject of "not really good for you." I do believe heroin is white in colour, although I am no expert on the subject, I assure you. Cocaine and crack are also that familiar milky hue, if I'm not mistaken. And let us not forget the ever-popular white rum. If the more innocent past can be "linen-white," I assume the more jaded present may be alluded to as having a "heroin-white landscape."

And yet, on the other hand, the darker the shade of these same foodstuffs, the more beneficial they are perceived to be for your body. Brown sugar, or even honey, is observed to be better than its white counterpart. The same goes with brown rice, and whole wheat flour and bread. I'm not sure where the jury stands on dark rum though.

Casting our net a little wider, there are numerous other ivory- toned purveyors of pain and death out there in the world. It would take far too long to mention all of them ... but how about the Great White shark and the polar bear, both having a reputation for the most attacks on humans? Then there's Melville's *Moby Dick*, the great white whale, the KKK ... the list goes on and on.

At the risk of sounding racist (which I'm not—I'm more of a foodist), it looks pretty much like everything white is bad for you. It makes you wonder what all those white supremacists are so damn proud of.

Who's to Blame and Who
Has the Right to Blame?

I have a great respect for those who have educated themselves and have taken the time to think about the world and their place in it as both individuals and as Native people in general. But every once in a while you bump into people who have taken that education, and those wonderfully complex thoughts, and have done strange and questionable things with them.

Case in point: While attending an Aboriginal academic conference, I happened to be part of an informal gathering where a friend of mine, in conversation with several other scholarly Aboriginals, expressed her confusion over white people's—or those we call the Colour Challenged—die-hard refusal to accept guilt or culpability for what has happened in the five hundred and six years of colonialism. Basically, but severely paraphrased, she said, "When are White people going to accept their guilt for what their ancestors have done? I don't think they seriously understand their responsibility." Somewhere deep inside me, I could feel DNA picking sides.

These words, and the meanings behind them, reverberated within my head. I don't know if it was simply my white-half that rebelled against such a broad statement (when asked, I tell people every other cell in my body is Caucasian), or if my own inherent Aboriginal sensibility questioned the accuracy of that belief. While I was raised Native, in a Native community, with no connection to my non-Native half, I am still conscious of it. My friend is a very smart person, with clear-cut beliefs, but also a gentle and well-liked individual. I respect her greatly. But that understood, I wondered where I stood in the wide spectrum of accusations inherent in her statements.

My problem, I think, is that I have trouble assigning complete blame to an entire race. To me, it harks back to the Germans and the Jews. It's a brutal comparison, I grant you, but fifty years ago the Nazi party attributed blame for the ills of the Depression and a multitude of other social problems in Germany specifically to the Jews. Today, equally unfairly, many have painted Germans rather broadly for the actions of some of their ancestors.

So, to say all White people are to blame makes me incredibly uncomfortable. Where would my friend and her associates begin to lay blame? With all Asian complexioned people in general? What about White people who themselves were discriminated against? Like, for instance, the Irish and Scottish, who have a long history of repression, or again, the Jews (though I've heard some argue about whether Jews can be classified as Caucasian). What about immigrants in general? I recently met a Bosnian woman who had just moved to Canada. I do believe I noticed her skin being of the milky shade. Is she to be included in the blame?

Or is there a residency requirement before blame is extended, much like health benefits? Ten years maybe? Twenty? How about thirty? Or perhaps we should be counting generations instead. Must the pallid-enhanced person be first generation Canadian? Second? Definitely third or fourth I'm sure. I'm a little fuzzy as to where the line of guilt begins. I won't even go into all the White people I've met who claim they were Native in another life. Actually, if pressed, I would say, "Well, you're not one now."

On a realistic level, when I go to my local Second Cup for my daily latte and am served by a gangly, pimple-faced teenager, I just can't seem to look at him and think, "You, as a member of the pigment-challenged majority, are personally responsible for my reserve having only a few thousand square acres to call home, when once we roamed freely across the land." The fact that he probably works for minimum wage makes it even more difficult.

Another provocative statement to be issued by my friend is even more politically volatile in nature: "It's impossible for Native people, or people of any other minority, to be racist. Only white people can be racist. You can only be racist looking down, not up." Again, I'm sure there's some legitimate pseudo-political understanding behind that declaration. I'm just not sure I want to know what it is.

Because of the academic psychobabble that interspersed the conversation, it seemed to me that a fancy, academic coating was covering old-fashioned intolerance. Paraphrasing a fable, the Emperor may have new clothes. But he's still naked. Disliking someone because of the colour of their skin or their cultural background works both ways. At least that's what I've always been taught by my Elders. I realize I might be incredibly naive about all of this, but I just don't see how it's okay, even acceptable, to discriminate one way, but not another. Maybe you learn these things in university.

I am aware that I am probably boiling these complicated and intricate sociopolitical arguments down to overly simplistic terms. Tough. I like simple terms. How many of us operate our lives in strictly sociopolitical environments? How many of us would want to? I certainly don't. I like to think I live in the real world with real people. I learned long ago that the more blame you assign to other people, the more blame you accumulate yourself. It's an Aboriginal karma thing.

However, I don't want people to think I am letting the dominant culture off the hook for past injustices. Not by a long shot. The status card I carry with me all the time is a constant reminder that there are still a multitude of concerns to be dealt with by the government and society at large. All I'm saying is beware of the shoe that fits on the other foot. And maybe the moccasin too.

I heard it best put at a discussion I attended in Montreal several years ago. One person-of-pallor stood defiantly and asked a row of Native people seated at the front table how long they expected him to feel guilty for what his ancestors had done.

The table spokesman said quietly, "No, I don't expect you to feel guilty for what your ancestors have done. However, if things haven't changed in twenty years, then I expect you to feel guilty."

I hope they teach that in university.

STRANGE BEDFELLOWS
(Politics, Scmolitics [an Ancient Ojibway Word])

Half Empty or Half Full

Not long ago I received a letter from a woman whom I shall call Lynda. Unfortunately the envelope with her return address has been lost in transit. In this letter she struggled to share some of the anger and confusion she felt at being a person trapped between two cultures. She was a product of an Irish mother and a Mohawk father; they had evidently separated when she was young and, as a result, she had practically no contact with her Aboriginal roots during her adolescence. She writes: "I still feel I have to somehow prove a connectedness with full-Natives in order for me to be accepted … I feel like I'm in a nowhere zone of cultural identity … I've had some very ignorant remarks made towards me by non-Natives, but what really hurts is being shunned by full-Natives and Native organizations." One Elder even questioned the existence of her reserve, the Mohawk community of Tyendinaga in southern Ontario. "Never heard of it," she said to Lynda and turned away.

Anybody who is familiar with my work knows that I pride myself on being an "Occasian," somebody of Ojibway and Caucasian ancestry. I have written quite extensively on that particular subject, both examining the issue from a personal point of view and sometimes joking about the concept. As an Elder once told me, "You either are something or you aren't. You can't be half. But it is possible to be two things, not just one." Lynda, wherever you may be, I went through the same thing you did.

I have bluish eyes and a fair complexion, but one of the few characteristics I do seem to share with my Native family is my troublesome belly that keeps showing that Native fondness for high-calorie food.

Most of my life I grew up with, "You're not Native, are you?" and "You don't look it," and a dozen other variations. Recently I was walking down the street and a Native panhandler accosted me for money. Being in a hurry for a meeting, I waved him off. As I hustled away, he saw the First Nations jacket I was wearing and screamed after me, "First Nations!

I don't think so!" Another time I was entering a money machine alcove in a bank. There was a young Native woman standing there warming herself. She took one look at my jacket, sneered and said, "What tribe, Wannabe?"

My advice to Lynda? Get used to it. I don't mean that to sound harsh but for every one of those types of people out there, I have met a thousand who will welcome you. It just seems that sometimes in the great balance of life, the ratio of good to bad will get a little erratic and bunch up on the bad side. Sometimes it will seem like the "unbelievers" are the only kind of people you'll meet.

One final note of confidence. What these people are failing to acknowledge is that it's pretty well accepted that after five hundred and five years of occupation and intermarriage, there are precious few individuals out there who can claim complete full-blooded Native ancestry. They're just seeing in you what they refuse to see in themselves.

Lynda, I know of Tyendinaga. I hear all the best people come from there.

The Dating Game—Who Should Date Whom in the Native Community

The last time I was in Edmonton I got asked the question again. It's a question I find myself getting asked quite frequently, as if I am the spokesperson for all Native men in Canada (if I am, I want a better salary). And to tell you the truth, it's getting annoying. This time it happened on a radio talk show hosted by a Native woman. Logically, it is always a Native woman who asks this question.

"Why is it that Native men, when they reach a certain level of success and power, end up dating and marrying only White women, and not Native women?"

Often they point to Ovide Mercredi, Graham Greene, Tom Jackson, etc., as examples. All well known, prosperous men whose partners are of the Caucasian persuasion. This is a question and issue that is of specific interest to many Native women, who regard this practice as a rejection of both them and the preservation of Native society.

Many Aboriginal nations are either entirely matriarchal or have elements of strong female interaction embedded in the culture. There is a belief that women are the protectors and teachers of the culture, especially when it comes to raising children. So when a non-Native woman enters the scene, it can disrupt what some see as the continuing cycle of cultural preservation.

But understanding that, is the talk show host's question still a valid one? True, you go to many functions and social gatherings where the successful Aboriginal intelligentsia gather, and it does seem like the majority of the Native men do sport non-Native spouses. Jordan Wheeler, Native writer for *Sixty Below* and *The Rez* (whose wife, by the way, is a lovely Native woman) blames it on the circles in which "prosperous" Native people are forced to circulate.

Since there are more "successful" white people than Native people and more "prominent" Native males than females—this is relatively speaking, and I use the terms "successful" and "prominent" loosely— the women a Native male is likely to meet, interact, and develop relationships with will have a mathematical probability of being non-Native. Unfortunate but true.

However, I do seriously doubt this is the only reason. Life is not that simple. Some who like to dabble in amateur (or not so amateur) sociological examination believe there is a deeply subconscious (or maybe not so deep) belief that a non-Native girlfriend is a symbol of success and achievement in both White and Native societies. Or then there's the theory that White women are just easier to find in the dark. I don't know which is the correct answer, or even if there is an answer. One could say that maybe two people just fell in love, but for reasons that I've quoted above, their love has taken on a political taint.

If snuggling with people of no definable Native heritage is a crime, then it is one I am guilty of. Rightly or wrongly, I am a graduate of the "colour-blind school of love." But taking into account the last four girlfriends I have had, I've noticed a disturbing trend developing in my personal life. One that on the surface, may lend credence to the argument.

One of the first serious relationships I ever had was with a Native woman. Sometime afterward I fell in love with a woman who was a half-breed like myself. Then I found myself with a Filipino woman (still technically a visible minority but not Native and not Caucasian). Finally, I spent several years with a White woman. If this trend keeps up, my next girlfriend will either be an albino or an alien.

To the best of my knowledge, none of these relationships were politically or socially motivated. I'm not that bright or ambitious. They just developed as most relationships do. You see each other in a room, make eye contact, you mumble to yourself, "Oh please God, please," and the rest I'll leave to your imagination.

One older Native woman, a strong proponent of Native men marrying Native women, even verbally chastised me for dating a White girl, urging me to break up with her and start seeing a Native woman she had just recently met. Even though her three daughters had married, had children by, or were simply dating White men, I was the one at fault here. The irony of the situation was not lost on me.

This begs a different angle to the original dating question. Why is it never questioned why successful Native women marry White men (i.e. Buffy Sainte-Marie or Tantoo Cardinal)? Granted the ratio is substantially different, but still I think it is a valid issue. I even posed that question to the hostess on the radio show. She looked at me blankly for a moment before answering, "I don't know. I don't have an answer for that."

And is it only the White culture that's at question here? The issue of the dominant culture absorbing and sublimating the much smaller Aboriginal culture? What about, for sake of argument, a Native and Black combination? There was no noticeable reaction to my relationship with my Filipino girlfriend—in fact, many people jokingly commented that she looked more Native than I did. What about the Asians, both South (the real "Indians") and East? And if you really want to throw a wrench into the works, what about the Sami, the Aboriginal people of Scandinavia, otherwise known as the Laplanders? They all have blonde hair and blue eyes but are recognized as an Indigenous people. I've been claiming to be half-Sami, half-Ojibway for years.

And does this question only relate to heterosexual couples? What about gay and lesbian relationships? I've never heard of any grief being given or received over an inter-racial relationship in either community. It all gets so confusing.

So I sit here, a single man, afraid to pick up the telephone and call somebody. For, depending on whom I phone, I will no doubt be making a very important and major political statement. And I just want somebody to go to the movies with.

How Native is Native if You're Native?

Within the growing and diverse Native community, an ongoing ideological battle seems to be raging. One that seems to have become reversed from what it was decades ago. I remember that when I was growing up, the more "Native" you looked—i.e. dark-skinned with prominent Aboriginal features, the lower you were on the social totem pole (no cultural appropriation of West Coast symbolism intended).

White was "in" and Native people (and, no doubt, many other ethnic cultures) tried to look it, dress it, or act it. Those that didn't were often made fun of. Being dark was no lark. In the Caucasian world, people whose family history included a drop or two of Native blood bent over backwards to keep the scandal a secret. The skeletons in those closets would thrill anthropologists and museums the world over.

These days, it's a completely different ball game. Native is "in." The darker you are, the more you are embraced, the more "Indian" you are thought to be. The lighter your skin, the more difficult it sometimes is to be accepted by your Aboriginal peers (and the non-Native world). White is no longer right. And heaven forbid that those in the dominant culture with some barely remembered ancestor that happened to tickle toes and trade more than some furs and beads with a Native person, should let a conversation slip by without mentioning that at least four of the twenty-four chromosomes in their body don't burn in the summer sun.

But it's often more than simply how you look. It's how you think, act, where you live, and point with your lower lip. Consequently, something more representational of the existing philosophical schism is the difficult question of determining "What makes a Native a Native?" What set of qualifications or characteristics will allow an individual to speak as a Native person, or have an opinion representative of the larger Indigenous population? Sure as hell beats me. But, as sure as there are a hundred websites devoted to "Xena the Warrior Princess," there are a vast number of "experts" in this world eager to tell you what defines a Native and will more than happily tell you whether you fit into that category.

Personally I think it must be great to have all the answers. My ambition in life is to be such an expert. I have done the necessary amount of research. God (or the Creator) knows my bluish-green eyes have allowed me a unique entry into such discussions. Drew Hayden Taylor: Aboriginal Attitude and Attributes Assessor (DHT: AAAA).

One example in the broad spectrum of modern Aboriginal acceptance relates to the world of education. Many reserves and Native educational organizations are constantly encouraging and extolling the virtues of education to the youth. Yet, there are many individuals in these communities who believe that the more educated you become, the less "Native" you become. They scorn and disdain those who want to or have gone through the conventional educational process. Evidently, scholastic knowledge and learning deprives an individual of their cultural heritage. I must have missed that in the sweat lodge.

Conversations with Elders and traditional teachers have convinced me that this is not a traditional belief or teaching. Many Elders urge and encourage the pursuit of education. In fact, the two worlds of traditional and scholastic education can, and often do, travel the same roads, albeit one on horseback and the other on a vintage 1953 Indian Scout motorcycle. In fact, those that are often wary of formal education are usually locked somewhere between both worlds; they're neither traditional nor particularly well educated. Unfortunately, it is their own insecurity that is being revealed, proving the need for educated Native psychologists.

Another example on the flip-side involves the disquieting story of a reserve education counselor in a southern Ontario community. Practically every year this person would ask at least one, and who-knows-how-many, off-reserve students, "Why should you continue going to university?" She would then strongly hint that this student almost owes it to the community to quit school, saving the reserve money.

So, if some students on the reserve are being urged not to go to university, where is all the university-fund money going? This is what's called the I-don't-know-if-I-should-go-to-school-or-stay-home-and-collect-welfare-or-possibly-scratch-out-a-living-telling-students-what-to-do paradox.

I have a column in a Regina newspaper/magazine jokingly called "The Urbane Indian." I was telling this to a Native woman at a meeting and she asked me what urbane meant. I told her it was similar to sophisticated, refined, or knowledgeable. She thought for a moment before responding, "I hope I never get like that." Evidently being suave and debonair (or as we say on the reserve, swave and debone-her) is not a Native characteristic worth having.

There are also those who believe that the more successful you are, the less Native you are. If you have money, toys, a nice house, two accountants, and a vague idea of where the Caribbean is, then you are obviously not one of the Indigenous people. I remember reading an interview with a successful Native prairie businessman who was looked down upon by his brethren because he had made a financial success of his life. And he rationalized it as, "If being Indian means being poor, then I don't necessarily want to be Indian." A harsh statement indicating that he did not think there was any middle ground. I know many successful Aboriginals who are every bit as "Native" as those who still subsist on Kraft dinner and drive 1974 Dodge pickups with multi-coloured doors.

A friend of mine severely criticized another friend because she had made the decision to live in the city while he had moved back to the reserve. He felt that you could only be Native, or really call yourself an Aboriginal person, within the confines of those artificial borders. Yet he had moved back home in his mid-thirties, having never lived on a reserve and having grown up in urban environments. I guess he finally and officially considered himself an "Indian."

Taking all of this into consideration, I guess this means the only true "Native" people are uneducated poor people with limited vocabularies who live on the reserve. Yikes!

As cliché as it may sound, I think everybody has their own unique definition of what being Native means. Very few of us exist in the world our grandparents lived in, where their definition was, no doubt, far from ours. And this definition will no doubt further evolve in the coming millennium. My career as "DHT: AAAA" will have to wait because I don't have all the answers. I don't know the boundaries and the necessary factors for making these decisions. To tell you the truth, I don't even care anymore.

I do know one thing though. Passing judgment on other people isn't a particularly Aboriginal thing to do. I know this because an eagle came to me in my dreams, along with a coyote and a raven; they landed on the tree of peace, smoked a peace pipe, ate a baloney sandwich, played some bingo, and then told me so.

That should shut them up.

STRAIGHT FROM THE ART
(Movies, Plays, and Books, Oh My!)

My Name Soars Like an Eagle

In a magazine (that shall remain nameless) specializing in new ways of looking at life, there's an ad for a "spiritual development" workshop called "Cry for A Vision." "Join us for four-and-a-half days on the land as we traverse the shadow and retrieve the light. Ceremonies and teachings are based on ancient shamanic wheels and keys. Set your intent for the coming year and dance it awake." The last names of the two dancing workshop leaders are Crystal Light Warrior and Butterfly Dreamer.

I must say that, as a First Nations person, reading stuff like this makes me wish we had colourful names like that on our reserve. I'm almost ashamed to say they sound a hell of a lot more interesting than Taylor, Jacobs or Knott.

With the growing popularity of the New Age and other movements sympathetic to the Native cause, taking on Aboriginal names and personae seems to be an ongoing and ever-popular hobby among people searching for a new way of looking at life. Pseudo-Indian names currently abound and prosper on the shelves of most bookstores with sizable sections for books of a more metaphysical nature. It seems odd but fitting that after five hundred years of taking our land, language, culture and ways of life, these people are now reduced to taking our names. Or what they think are our names. A casual perusal of titles in a bookstore specializing in New Age literature provides a cornucopia of pseudo-traditional Native author names. Ones that make you wonder, "Who the hell are these people and why do they feel the need to mix and match various animal and nature words randomly?"

Personally, I know very few people of Native ancestry who feel the need to write self-help books promising universal peace and a cosmic path to follow. It isn't exactly kosher. Even if they did, they probably wouldn't do it under pseudonyms that sound like Nintendo games— Crystal Light Warrior?

I think you definitely have to be White with far too much time on your hands to come up with colourful names like that today. And a closer examination of these New Age-coloured Native names reveals some interesting characteristics. First of all, most of them usually have one of four specific references in them: wind, fire, feather, and wolf (a bear or deer can be substituted with proper authorization). Secondly, they're all in English. And thirdly, they're all beautiful examples of nature/animals-turning-into-human metaphors.

Even in this age of political correctness, these perpetrators of cultural appropriation still seem to be getting all the breaks. And if you actually read the author biographies in some of these books, you'll notice how vague and non-exact the descriptions of the people behind these expressive names are, probably on purpose. They include lines like this: "Hairy Turtle Sneezing lives in the deepest, darkest part of the woods where he communes regularly with nature when not astral projecting."

One cannot help but get the impression that the only Native people most of these writers know are in the *Dances With Wolves* video tape they keep perpetually cued in the VCR. Names such as Blackwolf, Gary Buffalo Horn Man, Sherry Fire Dancer, White Deer of Autumn, and, my personal favourite, Summer Rain with her faithful Indian companion, No-Eyes, described as "her beloved Indian Shaman Teacher" (I kid you not!), are just a cross section.

Mysticism and the belief in a world outside the physical one we inhabit is a strong and honoured belief among most Aboriginals, but I must have been astral projecting the day they gave out beloved Indian Shaman teachers. But, fortunately, my birthday's coming up. Besides, I'm starting to see how this works. My girlfriend is studying for her Master in Education; that makes her a teacher, not to mention my beloved teacher. She's also Mohawk. So she's a beloved Indian teacher. Luckily she has some Irish blood—so in total, I guess she's my beloved Indian Shamus Teacher. It seems to lose something in the translation.

And the authors you read about on the backs of these New Age book jackets are just the lucky ones with decent publicists. Out there, on the pow wow grounds, in the craft shops, and hanging out at the Friendship Centres, are masses of uniquely named individuals, keeping low profiles, and generally hanging out looking for spiritual guidance and, if possible, an even better-sounding Indigenous name.

Of course, the Aboriginal world isn't the only one that induces cultural envy. I've seen people of many different cultures explore and dabble in the exotic elements of a variety of cultures other than their own. I, for one, have been known to wear Italian leather, eat a lot of Thai food, and dare I say, wear cowboy boots. But, to the best of my knowledge, my name has always been Drew Hayden Taylor.

Traditionally, those who were given a special "Indian" name were usually required to use it on special occasions only; it was a personal, private name. Putting it on business cards seems to defeat that purpose. I know many Native people who have a traditional name. Sharing it with somebody is a sign of great respect. Putting it on a book cover to make money is not.

Again, different culture, different priorities. Let us not forget that in some Native communities "colourful" family names are frequently used. I've known some Whiteducks, Many Grey Horses, New Breasts, Tailfeathers, and the odd Goodstriker, to name just a few. But somehow, their attitude toward their last names is a little less esoteric and a little more natural. There isn't any "traversing shadow and retrieving the light" involved. Maybe after the occasional beer, but not much.

Another point, traditionally, is that glancing through books dealing with Aboriginal history provides an interesting, if not downright ironic, twist. A simple assessment of authentic Aboriginal names of the past includes such mystical and beautiful titles as Sitting Bull, Crazy Horse, Dull Knife, Bloody Knife, Roman Nose, Old Man Afraid Of His Horses, Big Foot, Black Kettle, Crow Dog, Gall, Rough Feather, Wild Hog, Hairy Bear, Lame Deer, Leg-In-The-Water, Low Dog, and Stumbling Bear, to name just a few. But would you buy a self-help book from Bloody Knife?

In all fairness, I believe people should be allowed to do whatever they want. So, maybe, as a point, I should write my own book. L. Ron Hubbard was once quoted as saying something like: if you want to be rich someday, start your own religion. I can do that. But Drew Hayden Taylor does not exactly exude Aboriginal confidence and ancient Shamanic wisdom. I must concoct one of these awe-inspiring names.

My book will be called *Spiritual Enlightenment in the New Millennium—How To Receive Completion of your Spirit's Journey Through The Adoption of Caucasian/Christian Names*. It will be written by me,

Spread Eagle, and my girlfriend, Eager Beaver. I'm ready for Oprah (which spelled backwards is Harpo).

How to Make Love to an Aboriginal Without Sexually Appropriating Him or Her

It wasn't too long ago when Lee Maracle, the well-known Native-writer-turned-actress, and I were having a lively conversation at a downtown watering hole. The subject at hand: the exciting growth and expansion of Native literature, something we both have a familiarity with. In recent years, there have been many inroads made and directions explored by Native writers hitherto unseen; we have produced biographies, comic adventures, dramatic novels, searing political attacks, and a plethora of theatrical plays.

But we also noted that there were still a few avenues of expression that had not been, as yet, tested. Erotica, for some unknown reason, sprang to our minds.

Pooling our experiences, we both had come across a few poems and some theatre that bordered on the erotic, but other than those few samples, the pickings were pretty lean in that department. And knowing that Nature hates a vacuum (not to mention two writers in search of a good idea), we toyed with the idea of co-editing a book of native erotica (not to be confused with Native "neurotica" of course). Between the two of us we knew we could put together the finest samples of literary love Native writers had to offer; page upon page of pounding pulses, sweaty skin, heaving bosoms … why should white people have all the fun?

The closest I had ever come to the concept of Native erotica was a book of so-called erotic legends I had read as a teenager. Called *Tales from the Smokehouse*, it featured a series of amorous adventures with such characters as Big Arrow, and was narrated by men in a sweat lodge. Compiled and written by a white writer, some of the tales had a decidedly contemporary setting and feel. The fact that one of the stories takes place in Montreal during Expo '67 leaves me to doubt the collection's authenticity.

The more we talked about our little project, the more excited we became. First we had to discuss what the parameters of the collection would be. Specifically, how would we define Native erotica? What separates our erotica from other types of erotica? My argument was the real difference between the two was that in Native erotica there are no tan lines.

However, the former journalist in me saw the need to research this properly before the writing could take place. Some have argued that one type of Native erotica (stories about Natives, not by Natives) is already alive and well, and available at your local bookstore. Much like *Tales from the Smokehouse,* non-Native writers have tapped into the lust-filled Aboriginal angle long before Lee and I came up with our hot-and-heavy little idea.

Visit the historical romance department of any substantial bookstore, and you'll see an amazing selection of literature that features a magnificent Native man (well-muscled, dressed in a taut, laced-buckskin breech cloth, and always leaning at a forty-five-degree angle) with a mane-and-breast-blessed woman (almost always fiery, independent, and White) that is willing to loosen the ties that bind, if you know what I mean.

Here is a random sampling of what's available:

Wild Thunder by Cassie Edwards

"You have come to see the horses," Strong Wolf said. Suddenly, alone with him, his night-black eyes stirring her insides so pleasurably, Hannah went to him, framing his face between her trembling hands, hardly able to believe that she could be so bold, so reckless. She brought his lips to hers.

When his arms pulled her against his iron-hard body, his head swam with the ecstasy of the moment. Strong Wolf whispered against her lips, "You want to see the horses now?" His fingers stroked her back. The heat of his touch reached through the thin fabric of her cotton blouse. "Later," Hannah whispered back, her voice unfamiliar to her in its huskiness. Strong Wolf whisked her up into his arms and held her close as their eyes met in unspoken passion. He kicked the door shut, then kissed her feverishly as he carried her towards his bed....

An awful lot of whispering going on. I must learn to whisper more. And why do they always have names like Strong Wolf, never anything like John or Ted or Herbie or ... Drew.

Comanche by Fabio

She was tired of fighting him. She curled her arms around his neck and let herself succumb, only a little, to the potent feeling White Wolf's nearness aroused. He trailed warm kisses down her face, the curve of her neck. Then she felt his hot breath and wet lips tickling her. Maggie moaned softly. She had never known such rapture could exist. The intensity of the pleasure racked her with chills. With a devastating urgency, her resistance faded.

Maggie felt free of her shadow of control. Her heart hammering, her flesh crying out for her husband's heed, she mused that she might be out of her mind, and she was in the arms of a wild, totally aroused savage, determined to have her....

Strong Wolf, White Wolf. They must be brothers. The Wolf brothers. They live just down the block. Sounds like Hannah and Maggie could be related too. It seems they both have a fondness for "totally aroused savages," but then, who doesn't?

Song of a Warrior by Georgina Gentry

Passions flamed! "Green eyes, you are too innocent to know what might happen if I stay." Her heart skipped a beat. She was playing with fire, like a small child, suspecting the danger but too fascinated by the flame to back away while there was still time. Her whole being seemed controlled by heat and she couldn't control her words. "Don't go," she said again. With a muttered curse, Bear turned and swept her into his embrace, holding her close against his powerful body. Willow knew she couldn't stop him now even if she wanted to.

She was horrified when she realized she didn't want him to....

Just another typical day on the reserve. Bear and Willow at it again, sweeping and embracing everywhere. I tried sweeping and embracing once. The woman thought I was going for her purse. I couldn't walk properly for a week.

Shawnee Moon by Judith E. French

When his Shawnee mother died, handsome half-breed Sterling Gray left the noble tribe that raised him and crossed an ocean to become a British soldier and gentleman. Now he's returning to his homeland with a breathtaking new bride.

A Scottish hellion, wearing an ancient Celtic necklace, whom he rescued from a hangman's noose. Though his very presence inflames Caitlin's heart with a vengeful fire, Sterling knows the dangerous beauty is his destiny. A love foretold in mystic visions, a love for which he must risk his passions, his pride, and his future to win…

I'm a half-breed. I've been to England—well actually, it was three hours in the Heathrow airport, but it was still England. Yet, for the life of me, I don't remember running across any Scottish hellions during my breakfast. Must have been an off-day for them.

All things said and done, someday Lee and I will get this book off the ground. Is the world ready for it? Who knows? The world's just getting used to us not being stoical and silent; I don't know if it's ready for a little First Nations' slap and tickle.

And what should we call the book of Aboriginal ardour? Again Lee and I argued. My suggestion? I want to call it *The Night was Dark and so was He/She*.

FUNNY, YOU DON'T LOOK LIKE ~~ONE,~~ ~~TWO, THREE,~~ FOUR:
Futile Observations of a Blue-Eyed Ojibway

AN INDIAN BY ANY OTHER NAME, WOULD STILL SMELL AS SWEET

Where Do I Sign Up?

It has been said (and proven) that revolutionary principles and great ideas often come from places of higher education, like universities or colleges. Well, according to a very good friend of mine located in wonderful downtown Edmonton, the University of Alberta has done such a thing. Students there noticed that Native society, ever in a state of ebb and flow, was in need of a new social organization on campus; one that administers to the needs and wants of its wounded student body. Specifically, Native men in pain. The name of this new self-help group is called S.A.W., which stands for Survivors of Aboriginal Women. Definitely a long needed support group with thousands of potential members.

According to my friend (who's capable of breaking quite a few hearts in her own right), this organization is set up to help men deal with the repercussions and recovery that resulted from dating Aboriginal women. The pain, the agony, the scolding, the tears—sort of a combination therapy group/frat house thing, I assume. Evidently, as a result of prior painful relationships, these men don't have hearts anymore, just scar tissue. My first reaction upon hearing of this organization was, "Where do I sign up?" I want to start a Toronto chapter. I feel their pain. If you can believe it, my ex-girlfriend once chewed me (the bastard) out for almost fifteen minutes because I returned a hamburger to the counter at Wendy's incorrectly.

Before you immediately dismiss the idea of such an organization as silly as a home for unwed Native fathers, try to picture these delicate, wounded men sitting in a circle, hands on each other's shoulders, eyes gazing at each other sympathetically.

"Hi. My name is Ted, and I've dated a Cree.

"Hi Ted."

The next logical step would be to develop some sort of a twelve step program to be drafted into the charter. Indians like twelve step programs.

It should probably go something like this:

Step #1:

Admit to yourself that Native women are beautiful and you are not at fault for falling in love with them.

Step #2:

Admit that for every door that is slammed in your face, another one will open ... usually a divorce lawyer's.

Step #3:

Love hurts. Some love more than others.

Step #4:

It is not her fault that she broke your heart or your fishing rod, or your pool cue. You will live.

Step #5:

Always remember ... your mother is an Aboriginal woman too.

Step #6:

Without women in your life, the world would be a very boring and gay place ... and so on, seven through twelve, various other assorted pearls of wisdom to ease the pain.

I applaud the University of Alberta for their fortitude in founding such a gathering of kindred spirits. It probably won't get them many dates, but that's not the point. We're talking about larger issues to be wrestled with. There may be a little more "self-snagging" on the pow wow trail this summer but it's all for a good cause.

Wanting to know what women thought of S.A.W.; I mentioned the organization to a female acquaintance of mine. A glazed look fell over her as she went through a quick assessment of past partners. Her comment: "Geez, I bet I got a couple of ex's in there. Come to think of it, they all drink Molsons Ex too." Another friend had a slightly worried look. "They don't actually name names ... do they? I gotta make some phone calls." She then disappeared with her hand full of quarters.

An organization such as this poses some interesting questions. Is it strictly a men's organization with males bonding over female troubles? Is the organization about dealing with female fraternization recovery? This asks an even more interesting question ... can lesbians join? I'm sure they have their share of women problems. How about people who have issues with their mothers? Transsexuals? The 21st Century can be so complicated.

Now I know what you're thinking. This came up frequently in my research. If there's a S.A.W., there has got to be a S.A.M., Survivors of Aboriginal Men. In fact, many would argue there's a more pressing need for a S.A.M. But it has also been argued that there is already a place where women congregate to discuss and complain about the current and past men in their lives. It's called Bingo.

Recreational Cultural Appropriation

F. Scott Fitzgerald once wrote "The rich are different from you and me," to which everybody usually responds, "Yeah, they got more money." On a similar theme, it's been my Ojibway-tainted observation over the years that "Middle class White people are different from you and I."… Yeah, they're insane.

Much has been written over the years about the differences between Native people and non-Native people, and how differently they view life. I think there's no better example of this admittedly broad opinion than in the peculiar world of outdoor recreational water sports and the death wish that surrounds it. As a member of Canada's Indigenous population, I've always cast a suspicious glance at all these water-logged enthusiasts for several reasons. The principal one being the now familiar concept of cultural appropriation—this time of our methods of water transportation. On any given weekend, the Canadian rivers are jam packed with plastic/fibreglass kayaks and canoes, practically none of them filled with authentic Inuit or Native people, all looking to taunt death using an Aboriginal calling card.

Historically, kayaks and canoes were the lifeblood of most Native and Inuit communities. They were vital means of transportation and survival, not toys to amuse bored weekend beige warriors. To add insult to injury and further illustrate my point, there's a brand of gloves used by kayakers to protect their hands from developing callouses. They are called Nootkas. To the best of my knowledge, the real Nootka, a west coast First Nation, neither kayaked nor wore gloves. Perhaps my argument can best be articulated with an example of the different ways these two cultural groups react to a single visual stimulus. First, in a river, you put some Native people in a canoe, right beside some White people in a canoe. Directly in front of them should be a long stretch of roaring rapids. With large pointy rocks and lots and lots of turbulent white water. Now watch the different reactions.

Granted, I'm being a bit general but I think I can safely say the vast majority of Native people, based on thousands of years of travelling the rivers of this great country of ours, would probably go home and order a pizza. Or possibly put the canoe in their Ford pickup and drive down stream to a more suitable and safe location. And pick up pizza on the way. Usually, the only white water Native people prefer is in their showers. Hurtling towards potential death and certain injury tends to go against many traditional Native beliefs. Contrary to popular belief, the word portage is not a French word, it's Native for "Are you crazy? I'm not going through that! Do you know how much I paid for this canoe?"

Now you put some sunburned Caucasian canoeists in the same position, their natural inclination is to aim directly for the rapids paddling as *fast* as they can *towards* the white water. I heard a rumour once that Columbus was aiming his three ships directly at a raging hurricane when he discovered the Bahamas. I believe I have made my point. Yet even with this bizarre lemming-like behavior, there are still more White people out there than Native people.

I make these observations based on personal experience. Recently, for purely anthropological reasons, I have risked my life to explore this unique sub-culture known as white water canoeing and sea kayaking. There is also a sport known as white water kayaking but I have yet to put that particular bullet in my gun. So for three days I found myself in the middle of Georgian Bay during a storm testing my abilities at sea kayaking. I, along with a former Olympic rower, a Québécois lawyer who consulted on the Russian Constitution, one of Canada's leading diabetes specialists, and a 6 foot 7 inch tall ex-Mormon who could perform exorcisms, bonded over four foot swells and lightning. All in all, I think a pretty normal crosscut of average Canadians. The higher the waves, the more exciting they found it.

Still, I often find these outings to be oddly very patriotic in their own unique way. I cannot tell you the number of times I've seen many of these people wringing out their drenched shirts, showing an unusual array of tan lines, usually a combination of sunburnt red skin, and fish-belly white stomachs. For some reason, it always reminds me of the red and white motif on the Canadian flag. Maybe, back in the 1960s, that's where the Federal government got their original inspiration for our national emblem.

But this is only one of several sports originated by various Indigenous populations that have been corrupted and marketed as something fun to do when not sitting at a desk in some high rise office building. The Scandinavian Sami, otherwise known as Laplanders, were very instrumental in the development of skiing, though I doubt climbing to the top of a mountain and hurling themselves off it to make it to the bottom as fast as gravity and snow would allow, was not a culturally ingrained activity. The same could be said for Bungee jumping. Originally a coming-of-age ritual in the South Pacific, young boys would build platforms, tie a vine to their leg and leap off to show their bravery and passage into adulthood. I doubt the same motivation still pervades in the sport, if it can be called a sport.

I have brought this issue of recreational cultural appropriation up many times with my friend who usually organizes these outdoor adventures. The irony is, she works at a hospital. And she chews me out for not wearing a helmet while biking. She says there is no appropriation. If anything, her enthusiasm for these sports is a sign of respect and gratefulness.

That is why I think these people should pay a royalty of sorts every time they try to kill themselves using one of our cultural legacies. I'm not sure if a patent or copyright was ever issued on kayaks or canoes; it was probably conveniently left out of some treaty somewhere, but somebody should definitely investigate that possibility. Or better yet, I think that every time some non-Native person white water canoes down the Madawaska River, or goes kayaking off Tobermory, they should first take an Aboriginal person to lunch. That is a better way of showing respect and gratefulness. And it's less paperwork.

Indians in Space!

It wasn't that long ago when the Aboriginal media was raving about the launch of the first person of Native ancestry to be launched into space aboard the Space Shuttle Endeavour. His name is Commander John Herrington, a member of Oklahoma's Chickasaw tribe. I believe he took an eagle feather with him on his historic flight. He boldly went where no Aboriginal had gone before. He took one small step for man, one giant step for First Nations. He must have thought, "Today is a good day to fly." His heart (and the rest of him) really did soar like an eagle. Aye Captain, the Injins canna take it! ... and so on and so on. This event caused me to ponder the concept of Native people and outer space. Now there's two things you rarely see in the same sentence. First Nation people are seldom thought of when it comes to space technology or science fiction. Come to think of it, neither are country music and bannock. Hmmm ... I wonder if there's a connection.

There is Chakotay from the *Star Trek Voyager* series; but, most would agree he's more of a Latino with a bad tattoo. They've never really defined what nation he comes from, although there are tantalizing hints that he's Central American with possible Aztec or Mayan roots. I love the palm pilot thingee he has that speeds up vision quests. It's quite a remarkable device. Place it in your hand, turn it on, and in a few minutes you're communing with your spirit guide or ancestors. In terms of vision/dream quests, it's quite the little time saver. I want one. Fasting for days can really eat away at your space exploration time. It's a pity there's no such gadget for land claim settlements.

Other than Commander Herrington, the skies and stars are a little lean on Native influences. Perhaps it's because Native people are often thought of as being more historical in reference. When the public thinks of us, it's often in terms of the vanishing Indian. Even today they imagine images of yesteryear: living in teepees, riding horses, chasing buffalo—all that nostalgic stuff. When we think of ourselves, it is also often in terms of the past and of all the things we've lost in the last five hundred years: land, language, customs, resources. In terms of our future, we always seem to be looking back to the past to recover what we lost.

What does the future hold for the Aboriginal population of North America? Who can say? On a philosophical level, the possibilities of space travel do present some interesting questions for those traditional Indians who might want to consider a life above and beyond Turtle Island. For instance, one of the things that have made us strong and allowed us to survive all those years of oppression is our connection to the land. It's one of our strongest beliefs. Now, the question of the moment is, is it just this land or will any land do? Does Mars count as Mother Earth? Mother Mars perhaps. Will we take that connection to Turtle Island with us to other parts of this universe? How will that change our beliefs?

What about this whole concept of colonization? Imagine our Native astronauts landing on some far-off land, and saying, "We claim this land in the name of... Turtle Island... ?!?" Will our ancestors be spinning in their graves if we end up suckling on the colonial teat too? Heaven forbid if there's an indigenous species living on that planet. That would scald the bottom of the corn soup pot for sure. Is there a traditional teaching or an Assembly of First Nations policy to address this potential situation?

For instance, what would happen if we managed to design, construct and launch our own space ship or space station? Like the Space Shuttle Buffy St. Marie or Space Station Kahliga. The problems would begin almost immediately. First of all, tradition dictates we would have a sweetgrass ceremony (or sage or tobacco) to bless the place in the closed environment of space with all sorts of fire suppression gadgetry about. Smoke is a definite no-no in the closed quarters of interstellar existence. Plus, the concentrated levels of oxygen might make things a little more dangerous.

More puzzling, how can you honour the Four Directions when there are no directions? Do you choose four directions arbitrarily? Perhaps a larger constant, like using the plane of the solar system, or even the galaxy itself? Or maybe we could use some complicated computerized method of relating Earth-based directions to your current position on board whatever it is you're on board. I don't remember Chakotay having these problems.

It's all so complicated. Maybe that's why we never bothered to think about it. Horses and buffalo are easier to deal with.

HOLIDAZE AND BIRTHDAZE
(The Operative Word Being Daze)

An Aboriginal Christmas Perspective

Ask any Native person what they want for Christmas and they might tell you their land back, an end to economic and social racism, or possibly better cable selection. And what do I want this holiday season? I want this festive season to bring me a better understanding of the love/hate relationship Native people have with Christianity and its celebratory offshoots. Oh, and a new computer.

This seasonal quest for knowledge came to me just last week when I made a pilgrimage to the General Synod Archives for the Anglican Church of Canada located on Jarvis Street in Toronto. Ironically, I was scheduled to pick up photographs of Aboriginal residential schools and their students/conscripts for a documentary for the National Film Board. Oddly enough, the documentary is on Native erotica. Immediately upon entering into the lobby, I felt uncomfortable and ill at ease; a feeling I've encountered before while touring other religious edifices. It is a feeling that someone is watching you, knows what you've been up to and knows that Native people believe in living in harmony with Nature, not having dominion over it as indicated in the Bible. The sensation stayed with me until I left the building and had made my way down the street. Makes one wonder if Christian churches and organizations can carry bad Karma.

Consciously, part of me began wondering if this was a uniquely Native thing—to be aware of the ghosts of generations of Aboriginal people who had the word of God beaten into them, were kidnapped from their families and abused, in order to be shown the way to Heaven. The missionary zeal of "Worship our God (or we'll beat you until you do)" tends to leave a bad aftertaste. The Golden Rule, "Do unto others as you would have them do unto you," must have been edited out of the North American edition of the Operator's Guide to Civilizing Heathens.

However, after some serious pondering (in a coffee shop, of course), I came to realize that my questionable appreciation of such theological organizations is not unique to just the Aboriginal people of this continent.

Many different cultures over the world had religious orthodoxy forced upon them by conquering nations. That was part of the inspiration for Columbus' voyages and the Islamic expansion during the 7th Century. Remember, history and hymns are written by the winners.

After Cortez's destruction of the Aztec Empire, the Spanish government, along with the Pope's blessing, decided to instigate what was called the *Requiermento.* Feeling a little guilty over the rampant destruction of Central American civilizations, Church and State decided to give the people a chance, a voice, in their own destruction. As conquering Conquistadores marched into the Aboriginal villages, there was someone at the head of the column who read aloud from the *Requiermento,* a proclamation telling all citizens of the village they had a choice of voluntarily becoming vassals of the Pope and Spanish King or to be utterly destroyed. A minor point is that the document was read in Spanish. Needless to say, the ability to choose did little to stop their destruction. *Feliz Navidad.*

Soon, the introduction of Christmas to the Americas, with its message of peace and love, came between waves of epidemics and forcible relocations. This unique co-existence has remained until today, resulting in groups of Native people both suspicious and loyal to the Church. A confusing, though understandably, schizophrenic existence. I've been lucky enough to travel to over 120 Native communities across Canada and the U.S. The most unusual thing I have seen in many poor and economically disadvantaged communities, are two financially disproportionate displays of wealth: satellite dishes and massive Christmas lights and holiday adornment on houses that appear barely strong enough to hold them up.

Christmas, commonly viewed by most historians as a pagan rite dressed up in a priest's collar, is a hard tradition to turn down regardless of the sexual abuse its progenitors condoned in the aforementioned schools. Native people have a soft spot for stories about babies being born, and it really wasn't *HIS* fault what happened two thousand years later.

Most of my family loves Christmas, as does practically every Native community in Canada. Even the ones hurt and damaged by the effects of residential schools. Christmas carols really are that addictive. Even the more traditional communities that embrace First Nations beliefs still get a week off from work during the Yuletide season. Eggnog knows no spiritual boundaries. Personally, I still like Christmas although I hold no particular allegiance to Jesus Christ or Santa Claus, two popular White men with far too much say in the Native community. I hum the carols when I hear them on the radio. I spend way too much money on gifts. My blood sugar level drifts dangerously close to the endemic diabetes that is constantly knocking on the Aboriginal door. The bottom line is that Christmas is fun. Any man who's willing to die for your sins (and there are plenty of them on both sides of the ecclesiastical line) is worth roasting a turkey for.

Just think; if Jesus were around today and was Native, he'd probably be in therapy from residential school trauma. Happy Birthday, Buddy.

It's Not Just an Age, It's a State of Mind

What does one normally do on their 41st birthday? Blow out candles, read birthday cards too, I suppose. Put up with half-hearted birthday greetings from various friends and acquaintances. And, let's not forget pondering one's own mortality. Turning forty was traumatic enough, but it was more akin to going for a swim in a chilly lake, cold and shocking but manageable. Add one extra year and there are no more excuses. You just jump completely into the bone chilling river of your fifth decade of existence. You. Are. Completely. In. Your. Forties. Abandon all hope. This year seems unusually aggressive in its attempt to welcome me into that decade. The gods are letting me know I am entering a new phase of my life. Recently, I went to a play with a friend and her eight-year-old daughter. On the way home, this little girl looked at me and innocently asked how old I was. I told her. She paused for a moment, then responded, "Wow, my grandmother is only eight years older than you." That hurt. It still hurts.

Shortly after, a lovely woman asked me out on a date. She was twenty-four-years-old. (For a moment I was flattered. "I still have it," I thought). Then a startling revelation occurred to me. I was in high school when she was born. I was chasing girls when she was chasing rubber balls. Not wanting to be rude, I accepted her invitation. I have many faults in life, but being an "ageist" is not one of them. So, we started seeing each other, and on one of our dates, we went to work out at the YMCA. You really don't know a person until you've seen them sweat. We got on adjoining treadmills and inputted our information into the gizmo (speed, weight, incline). I jokingly commented that running on the treadmill reminded me of the opening credits of *The Six Million Dollar Man,* where the treadmill he's running on shows sixty miles an hour. Not hearing a response, I looked over and saw complete confusion on her face. She had never seen *The Six Million Dollar Man* television show, had never heard of Steve Austin, Lee Majors or bionics. That also hurt. It still hurts. I hurt a lot.

Perhaps the most searing pain to hit me this year came from an academic source. I was at a Native literature conference at the University of Windsor, when a gentleman walked up to Daniel David Moses and I at a wine and cheese party. He introduced himself as a professor from the university. He said he was delighted to meet us as he had taught both of our dramatic works in his theatre history class. It was official— it was not a regular history class but a theatre history class course! That really hurt. It still does. Thank god there was wine.

But what can you do? Aging is a part of life. You cannot fear the inevitable, death, taxes and all that. Getting older becomes increasingly more inconvenient as evidence of the past follows you around. For instance, I've dated ladies from Wikwemikong, Tyendinaga, Moraviantown, Nova Scotia, B.C, and various other communities. There are 633 reserves in Canada but the list is beginning to get a little thin. I'm running out of reserves I can visit.

One thing that does allow me to get up in the mornings and face the day are the little victories I can claim against the inevitable march of time and age. Last month when I was home on the reserve, a friend asked me at the last moment to attend a wedding. It was summer and I had only brought a t-shirt and shorts with me. Not discouraged, my friend, who is a little older than me, took it upon herself to find me suitable clothing for the wedding dance. When she asked what size pants I wore, I told her I had a thirty-two-inch waist. She burst out laughing. Evidently I was the only forty-one-year-old man on the reserve who could claim such an accomplishment. Even one of my cousins, who is about thirteen years younger than me, and my height, could only muster a thirty-six inch waist ... and on the eighth day, God created the Stairmaster.

A few days later, after visiting the gym, I rushed home and threw on an old t-shirt I had hanging around the house, and went to visit this same friend. Bad idea. The t-shirt I put on was from a television show I had worked on when I was starting out sixteen years ago, called Spirit Bay. She recognized the t-shirt and growled at me, "How dare you wear a sixteen-year-old t-shirt into this house, one that you can still fit!!" Since then, she has not returned any of my calls.

There's no point in whining. Instead, I shall lie back and try to find that inner glow, which the Elders we all know and love have. I am not an Elder, and I still haven't found that inner glow yet, but I refuse to play shuffleboard or comment on how they just don't write music like they used to. And, there are still plenty of reservations to visit in the States.

ON THE ROAD AGAIN
(Things I've Seen and a Few I Shouldn't Have)

My European Pow Wow

When Europeans first landed on these shores so many years ago, it was estimated there were approximately 100 million Native people waiting here to welcome them with local delicacies like tomatoes, potatoes, tobacco and corn. In the intervening five hundred plus years, our effects on the land across the big pond known as the Atlantic is often thought of being limited to produce, canoes and kayaks. Imagine my surprise when I found myself in Italy, at the Turin International Book Fair, on what turned out to be a positively Indigenous travel experience. Since Canada was a featured exhibit at the Fair, I was one of twenty-one Canadian authors (with a heavy focus of Italian-Canadian writers) invited to introduce Italians to the wonders of Canadian literature. Nino Ricci bought me a cappuccino. Steven Heighton, Jeffrey Moore and I gossiped about our lovely writer wrangler. John Ralston Saul asked what one of my books was about. I asked Canada's resident philosopher, "John, what's it ALL about?"

As usual, I was the only First Nations author at the Fair and the only writer not translated into Italian. Evidently Native theatre and humour are not of particular interest in the land of Columbus and Cabot (born Coboto in Venice). I was there for colour. Or so I thought. During the seven days I spent in Italy, I was absolutely overwhelmed by the amount of intentional and surprisingly random amounts of Aboriginal influence and representation in Turin. At the Book Fair itself, home to three huge venues of publishers exhibits amounting to thousands of different Italian books for every taste, I found one book titled *Guida alle Riserve Indinae di Stati Uniti E Canada,* It was a guide to every Native community in North America. While I doubt it was a best seller, it was still a shock. I'd expect this from the Germans, not the Italians.

One night I was asked to attend a book launching, of an Italian translation of a Canadian book. I was shocked to discover it was *Racconti Eroti Ci Degli Indiam Canadesi,* better known to thousands of Native readers across Canada as *Tales From The Smokehouse.* This book is a collection of supposedly Native erotic tales compiled by a not so Indigenous sounding gentleman named Herbert T. Schwarz and published way back in 1974. Its pedigree as a respectable source of authentic legends is suspect though, since one of the "tales" takes place during the 1967 Montreal Expo. During the launch, an Italian anthropologist delivered a quick lecture on the nature of First Nations erotic storytelling. I sure wish I could have understood the man. It sounded interesting. Then, a professional storyteller proceeded to read one of the tales. Again, it sounded interesting. I had read the book many years ago, but it sure looked and sounded different in Italian.

The book was translated and published by an organization called Soconal Incomindios, a non-profit organization whose goal is "to unite all those who are interested in the Aboriginal Peoples of the Americas—in their cultures, as well as in their various political, social and cultural conditions." Located in downtown Turin, they even have their own magazine called *TEPEE: Comitato Di Solidarieta Con Popoli Nativi Americani,* which has been around since 1984. In the current issue, No. 28, topics explored include *"Culture Native Ed Ecosistemd"* and *"Philippe Jacquin, L 'Indiano Bianco Dell 'Universita' Francese."*

A few nights later, Soconal Incomindios presented a reading by Lakota poet Gilbert Douville, originally from Rosebud, South Dakota, and now living in Turin via an Italian wife he met while on tour with an American Native dance troupe. When not writing poems, Douville makes jewelry, and ironically, teaches English as a second language.

More surprising, a week prior to the Book Fair the Universita' Degli Studi Di Torino invited me to a conference titled *Indian Stories Indian Histories: Storia e Stone degli Indiani d'America*; but due to other reasons I was unable to attend. It looked like a fascinating conference with topics such as "Framing the Text: Bill Miller, Buffy Ste. Marie and Modern Native Visualization Imagery," "Trickster Shift: Art and Literature (from the University of Helsinki!), "Contemporary Tales among Cree and Blackfeet" and "The Early Collecting Practice of the Museum of Anthropology at the University of British Columbia." I'm glad I missed that last one.

My European journey got stranger and stranger. After the book launch of the Italian/Aboriginal erotic tales, a young Turin lady drove me back to my hotel. Along the way we chatted. I asked if she was a student. With her makeshift English and a thick accent, she managed to convey that she got her degree in Native Studies last year. I wanted to make sure I understood her correctly, but indeed, she got her degree in Native Studies. In Italy. I guess that proves the saying that anything is truly possible.

On a walking tour of Turin, I was further inclined to wonder if these awesome adventures were some sort of practical joke. Too many things were proving to be a tad too coincidental for your average Native tourist to believe. Our tour guide told us that before Italy had consolidated into the present country we all know and love, it was a collection of city states. Turin was a particularly important one. It was run by the House of Savoy, which has a close connection to the French Crown. As a sign of solidarity and support, the city of Turin sent 1200 of their best soldiers in 1666 to Quebec to help the French fight the Iroquois. Eight hundred returned home as several hundred elected to stay behind in this new country, which explains why there are so many French Canadians with Italian last names. Also, local fable has it the soldiers brought back an unknown number of people of an Aboriginal nature who were curious to see the strange new world where all these strange folks had come from. They ended up settling down and being absorbed into the population. They soon disappeared into legend. I suppose that's why so many Italians have dark complexions and even darker hair. You think? These first Italian/Indian Métis today are affectionately known, (politically incorrectly), as Awopahos.

Several years later, when the new palace for the House of Savoy was being built, the architect wanted to honour those soldiers who went off to battle the savages. Above all the first floor windows in the new palace are large brick images of Native people designed by an architect who had never been out of Europe. There are eight of them in a row; all with four brick feathers standing straight up. They sadly smile down at the Turins as if to say, "I only came for the Gelato."

The best and most indicative observation to top off this surreal trip happened on the way to the airport. When the taxi stopped at a red light, I gazed out the window, pondering transcontinental Native thoughts. In the car right next to us was a small Fiat with a dream catcher hanging on the rearview mirror.

Why did I bother leaving Canada?

REZ POLITICS
(Who's Doing What to Who, How Often, and for How Much)

Art and the Regular Indian

I have a very good friend who has gone to great pains to inform me of two startling facts about the average Native community that I was unaware of. First of all, the university degree she earned many winters back has allowed her the educated insight to break the Aboriginal population of Canada down into two categories: *with-its* and *regular* Anishnawbe (Ojibway). Secondly, *regular* Anishnawbe have the only true understanding and appreciation that can be considered legitimate forms of Aboriginal artistic expression. *With-its* are Aboriginal artists doing what they do because they have been corrupted by the dominant society. This concept made me re-evaluate my career.

Perhaps an explanation is in order. We were having a discussion about a project I'm working on (a documentary on Native erotica) and how I'd spent the last eighteen months researching the reclaiming of Aboriginal sexuality. The discussion derived from her belief that there is no such thing as Native erotica (which may or may not be true). I told her that celebrated poet Kateri Akiwenzie-Damm was in the final throes of putting together a book on First Nations literary erotica, so evidently some people in the community were talking about it.

My friend completely dismissed both projects, saying they were of complete non-interest to *regular* Indians on the reserve because erotica wasn't part of our everyday life. She argued that *regular* Indians on the reserve didn't care about things like that; it's something they wouldn't discuss; it was an influence introduced by the European culture; and those who participated in avenues of exploration *like that* had capitulated to the dominant culture. *With-its* were just playing into their game. Regular Indians wouldn't buy Kateri's erotica book or see my documentary but white people would … maybe *with-it* Indians too. She wanted to know who had asked me to do this film.

"The National Film Board of Canada. I worked with one of the executive producers at the Toronto office."

She asked me if it was a White woman.

"Yes, a White woman," I responded.

She said something like, "Well, there you go," as if she'd won some big victory, Then proclaimed, "A *White* woman wants you to do a documentary on Native erotica."

I pointed out that I had suggested the topic, researched it, and if the funding came through, I would direct it too. I told her I got the idea after seeing an art show called *Exposed*, a collection of erotic Native visual and installation art, curated by Native people, which toured the country. That's about the time the term *with-its* was introduced.

"These are not things *regular* Indians would be interested in," she said. "Only, I guess those you'd call *with-its*. I don't think you should do the documentary. You're only contributing to the artistic desires of White people."

As she talked, I looked around the room admiring at least a dozen stunningly beautiful quilts, which she had created, scattered throughout her home. I wanted to comment that I hadn't seen any quilts or quilt-like images on any of the pictographs or petroglyphs seen on my travels; but I thought the better of it.

The people who had put together the erotic art show had had similar concerns about their project. Not wanting to be disrespectful, they consulted an Elder in southern Saskatchewan who congratulated them on the project and said that it was about time someone reclaimed our sexuality. To which my friend commented, "How do you know she was a real Elder? Could she have been an Elder of convenience?" Now it was my turn to enter the discussion with more than a "but…," "I…," "You don't… "

"As a playwright, film maker, and television writer, no one is more aware than me of the changing face of Aboriginal society. I've had eighteen years on the reserve and twenty-two in the urban environment. I've visited at least 120 Native communities across Canada and the United States. Suffice it to say, I have some experience with nearly all aspects of the Native community. It has often been said that we have gone from telling stories around the campfire to telling stories on the stage or television. People change. The Ojibway spoken by my mother is no doubt different than that spoken by her grandparents and their grandparents. Cultures are evolving. Constantly."

"Exactly," my friend said. "But what is making it happen?"

"The environment."

She nodded, "And what's evolving our culture today?"

Taking a wild guess, I answered, "The 21st Century."

"Exactly. White influences."

I couldn't help but think how this implied that Native people have no noticeable influence in the 21st Century (which I found kind of depressing, if not defeatist).

Then she added, "Not our ways."

"So you aren't really comfortable living in this split level house with heating and plumbing?" I said.

It was here she got really upset.

"I resent you for asking me a question like that. That's the kind of question a White person would ask."

I was tempted to point out I am half-White but, she knew that already. Come to think of it, she is half-White too. "It's a stupid question. Where else do you expect me to live? Would you expect me to go back and live in a shack?"

I was puzzled. "Traditionally, I never heard of Native people living in shacks."

"Now you're just arguing." With a wave of her hand she dismissed me, abruptly ending our conversation.

Granted, my seventy-one-year-old mother whose first language is Ojibway and who is as Native as they come probably wouldn't be interested in a book or documentary on Native erotica. But, I can guarantee a few uncles might hazard a peek. This kind of generalization does a great disservice to the *regular* Anishnawbe. In my travels I have met many reserve Indians who have a legitimate interest in non-reserve issues and the arts. I should also mention that conversation with my friend happened over a glass of traditional California chardonnay, which not long after she had finished while watching regular soap operas on regular television.

But I will admit I am in true awe of my friend. It is seldom that you meet somebody who has the authority to speak for an entire population of people and can categorically maintain what they will or won't be interested in and, ironically, with utter confidence. Perhaps she should get a job in marketing.

Oh well, what do I know? I'm just a *with-it*, not a *regular* Anishnawbe. Evidently, somewhere along the pow wow trail I went from being a Reserve Indian to an Urban Indian to an Urbane Indian.

Who's Stealing What From Who and is it Stealing?

Cultural appropriation in the arts has been a bugaboo in many a bonnet for the last fifteen years or so. The concept of somebody from one culture telling another culture's story has been discussed, argued, fought, and frequently dug up again to be rehashed in a dozen different ways. Often the major sticking point deals with when is enough, enough. When does respect and political correction begin to infringe on the creative process so much in fact that it hampers, even compromises, the art? The argument often drifts to: should non-Native people write Native stories, should men write female characters, should heterosexuals write about the Gay experience, should dog people write about cat people? The lines of demarcation become blurrier than promises at closing time.

More recently, there's been a new development in the cultural appropriation issue; specifically, deep in the Native community. Renowned Cree playwright Tomson Highway is no stranger to the argument. He is a proponent of colour-blind casting and has often said art is colourless. This whole discussion annoys him to no end. In fact, several weeks ago at the Native Playwrights Summit in Toronto, he confessed that someday he plans to write a play in French with three White girls as the central characters.

This January, his first main stage play in fourteen years, titled *Ernestine Shuswap Gets Her Trout*, opens at the Western Theatre Company in Kamloops, British Columbia. The play takes place in Kamloops and all the major First Nations characters are Shuswap, Okanagan or Thompson. The playwright is Cree. Is this an issue? Somebody familiar with the area asked that question. Tomson said no. He had direct consultation with the local Aboriginal cultural centre to keep him honest.

Several months back, I was approached by the Toronto organization, Red Sky Performance (a sister organization to Native Women in the Arts), which is run by the amazing Sandra Laronde. She asked if I would be interested in adapting the Tlingit creation story, *How The Raven Stole The Sun,* into a dance theatre piece for her company. I am Ojibway from the wilds of central Ontario and truth be told, I know very little about the Tlingit culture other than they are located along the northern B.C coast, as well as in Yukon and Alaska. I know there's probably salmon involved in the story.

Raven legends are ancient oral stories. The version I was to use was put down on paper by Alaskan Tlingit Maria Williams, who was flown into Toronto as a consultant for the original discussions. I asked Sandra if my being Ojibway (and herself, being from Temegami) would be an issue. Would we have hordes of politically correct Tlingit storming the Red Sky Performance offices? Sandra didn't think so. We were both Native, we were sensitive to the mistakes that could be made, and we had the blessing of Maria herself. But one Tlingit writer/actress/storyteller that was at the Native Playwright's Summit said, "Why not get a Tlingit writer to do it? Hire me. What's their number?"

In my own and Tomson's defense, there is a sense of collective understanding that seems to exist between the First Nations of Canada regardless of what part of the country or nation you are from. It's something akin to a sense of shared experiences, born of oppression, of survival, of disenfranchisement, of too much baloney. I believe this allows us to relate to each other's existence regardless of individual tribalism. We revel in our connection to this land.

My very first writing assignment, a thousand years ago, was for an episode of *The Beachcombers*. There I was, writing a story about Jesse Jim and his wife Laurel, two of the Native characters in the show. They were Salish if I remember correctly, I was not. I had never even been to British Columbia at that point. In the end, the episode turned out pretty good and I managed not to culturally embarrass myself.

I was also a writer on *North of 60*, a show about the Dene of North West Territories. Again, I was not Dene, (unless there is something my Ojibway mother has not been telling me). A Dene critic of the show was once quoted as saying "It's a show about my people written by Jews and Crees." And, I guess, unbeknownst to him, one lone Ojibway.

It seems that when you're writing a script for television, or some form of the dominant cultural media, the specifics of your Nation becomes irrelevant. Non-Native producers seem only to care that you can wave around a status card and can tell the difference between a bagel and bannock.

Ojibways can write about the Dene or whoever. The Haida can write about the Innu. I can even write about white people if I've got the inclination. Hey, I've been known to throw a few Caucasians into my scripts, just for lack of colour, and to find out if anybody would accuse me of culturally appropriating Burlington culture. Hasn't happened yet. The ears prick up in our own community when we Native writers start looking over the fence at other First Nations stories. One woman on my reserve was a little uncomfortable with the idea when I raised it, but then shook it off saying, "Well, at least you, being the writer, will be Native. That's something." Maybe it is something. Maybe it's nothing. It is a question for those far more intelligent than I am. In the meantime, I've got an idea for a story about a handicapped Black albino lesbian from South Africa … but it's okay, her car has a dream catcher hanging from the rearview mirror.

The Things You Learn
When Not in School

"Education is an admirable thing, but it is well to remember from time to time that nothing worth knowing can be taught."
—Oscar Wilde

One day while I was having lunch at the Governor General's Rideau Hall residence (it's not often I get to start a story like this), I bumped into Matthew Coon Come, Grand Chief of the Assembly of First Nations at the time. While we chatted, he mentioned hearing my name and asked what I did for a living. I summed up a fifteen year writing career into a few sentences about being a playwright with a dozen books and over fifty productions of plays to my credit. He seemed mildly impressed and then asked where I'd gone to University. That's when the bubble burst. I told him I never went to university, that I was a member of the great uneducated masses. Everything I learned, I had learned by being a student of life. The tuition was cheaper. He laughed and said something like: Well, there goes that idea. I asked, "What idea?" He said that for a moment he thought I might be a great role model for Aboriginal youth. Evidently the idea quickly evaporated due to a noticeable lack of degrees.

This reminded me of a similar incident several years earlier, which occurred at a birthday party for a professor at York University. The slightly tipsy birthday boy, an expert on Native literature, asked how I could validate myself as a contemporary playwright whose work was being studied in many different universities without having any academic credentials behind my name. It seemed he thought the situation was an ironic oxymoron. I didn't take his comments personally, since the alcohol and potato chips were free.

It is a touchy subject for many people. The definition of what proper education consists of. There is a universally accepted belief that education is important in many cultures in societies. Especially in today's society when technology, politics, economics and practically everything changes on a yearly basis. Education is good. The more the merrier. Especially in the Native community which suffers an appalling school drop-out rate. What often puzzles me is the narrow definition of what is considered acceptable education.

At one time amongst Aboriginal people, education often came from the Elders. Everything we were taught came directly from those who had experienced it. Many still follow that tradition and understand the importance of using diverse sources of knowledge. For example, Matthew Coon Come's homecoming to his people, the James Bay Cree, is now part of Aboriginal folklore. Returning home from McGill and Trent University where he studied Law, Political Science, Economics and Native Studies, Matthew's father promptly took him out onto the land to complete an equally important part of his education. Unfortunately, not everyone understands the variety of educational opportunities out there, and potential venues of education are ignored in favour of popular European models.

In the Ontario Aboriginal community of Curve Lake, a prime example of this contradiction is running its course. A young woman named Pattie Shaughnessy applied to the Band's Education Committee for funding to attend the Centre for Indigenous Theatre's (CIT) Native Theatre School, an organization devoted to teaching young Native people the art of theatre from both contemporary and Native perspectives. To be fair, I must admit a conflict of issues here. I am a member of the Curve Lake First Nations with several relatives on the Education committee; I am also on the Board of Directors for the CIT. I should also point out that I know Ms. Shaughnessy casually.

Ms. Shaughnessy, an aspiring actress with solid ambitions, was turned down by the committee. She has also recently auditioned for the prestigious National Theatre School in Montreal, and I thought supporting such a lady in her artistic endeavors would be a real feather in the community's cap. Evidently I was wrong. As a board member, who had written Ms. Shaugnessy a letter of support, I pursued the issue in an informal manner and was told the Education Committee prefers to financially support applications only to accredited institutions. This committee policy was told it was a way to make sure students and the Band didn't throw their money away on "fly-by-night organizations." I informed the woman I was talking to that the Native Theatre School had been around since 1974 and practically every Aboriginal actor in

Canada had once been a student there. "Then get the place accredited," was the response. When Ms. Shaughnessy informed them that a good chunk of CIT's funding came from federal rather than provincial sources, which limited eligibility for accreditation, "Then tell them to get provincial funding." Ahh. If only the world were so cut and dried.

During a discussion later with a senior committee member, I asked how many of the Education Committee members had any post-secondary school education, to which I received what seemed to be an oddly indignant but firm, "That's completely irrelevant." "Irrelevant." As an artist, I liken it to someone with reasonable arts experience or background, sitting on an arts adjudication panel. You would think it would just make sense to know of which you judge.

Luckily this is not a policy held by too many Native communities. In the past, Rama First Nation in Ontario has funded students to the CIT. For the last two years, Wahpeton Dakota Nation in Central Saskatchewan has not only funded at least five students a year, but has also hosted CIT's summer theatre school. They understand not all forms of education have lecture halls and tests or involve tossing a graduation cap into the air.

In the end, it's not a matter of which form of education is better or worse. I'm sure Grand Chief Coon Come appreciates that both forms of learning are equally valuable. It's a pity more people don't.

"Training is everything. The peach was once a bitter almond; cauliflower is nothing but cabbage with a college education."
—Mark Twain

My Elder is Better than Your Elder

It seems that in the simple world of Eldership (i.e. the fine art of being an Aboriginal Elder), there is a hierarchy that I was not aware of. This hierarchy recently became apparent when I was involved in a conversation about a certain Elder who shall remain nameless for obvious reasons. This one individual openly scoffed at the idea of this person being considered a wise and respected Elder, citing the fact that he was a raging alcoholic once. "He was the worst drunk in the village!"

Now it's no surprise to anyone how one's past experiences and mistakes can follow you for the rest of your life. Elders are no different. Mistakes are buoys on the river of life that can help you either navigate the river or send you up shit creek without a paddle.

I didn't realize how those mistakes can also negate the positive achievements a person might accomplish during the remaining days of their existence. I was truly surprised to find that only those who never drank, never lied, never abused tobacco, never swore, never walked counter-clockwise at a clockwise ceremony or were ever human could be considered the only real Elders. I learn something new every day.

I suppose priests and nuns who hear their calling late in life can't really become true priests and nuns since, more than likely, at some time in their past they've either taken the Lord's name in vain, had sex with a Protestant or sampled some Devil's Food cake ... maybe all three at once.

It is no secret the best drug and alcohol counsellors are people who have lived the darker side of life and know of what they speak. Otherwise, counselling sessions would be like learning to water-ski from someone afraid of the water. You can read all you want and take as many workshops as you like but unless you've wrestled with those demons yourself, there's only so much hands-on experience you can bring to the job. Which is why I'm puzzled by this reaction to an Elder who had a life before they became an Elder.

Handsome Lake, a Seneca Chief in the late 1700s considered by many Iroquois to be the second great messenger after the Peacemaker himself, was sent to his people by the Creator to teach the wisdom of the Great Peace, part of the Iroquois philosophy/beliefs. Yet, his vision came to him during a four-day coma induced by a rather severe bout of drinking. The point being, Handsome Lake cleaned up his act to become a well-respected orator and teacher. Gandhi, a different type of Indian I'm fairly certain can be included in the classification of wise Elder, was a lawyer before he became the man of peace we are all familiar with. Now that's a hell of a bigger obstacle to overcome than alcoholism. Buddha was a spoiled prince before he saw the light, walked the path of wisdom and developed a big belly.

Perhaps it was Nietzsche (who may or may not be considered an elder, depending on your philosophical learnings) who said it best when he wrote the rather over used cliché, "That which does not destroy us, makes us stronger." Maybe Nietzsche was an elder because that certainly sounds like many an elder's story I've heard. The fortitude I find in many elders can only be forged from experience and suffering.

I believe it was William Blake who coined the term, "The palace of wisdom lies on the road of excess." Wisdom comes from experience. Experience comes through trial and error. Sometimes error means waking up in a place you don't know, smelling like something you don't want to, and realizing you might not have many more mornings left to wake up to. You have to travel before you know the countryside.

Several years ago I attended an Elder's conference where a bunch of us in a large room waited to be instilled with knowledge by a visiting Elder whose name I have forgotten. Several young people took out pen and paper, ready to diligently learn. This method of learning was not to be. The Elder quietly asked them to put their note pads away. "Writing something down is asking permission to forget it," he said. It made sense. A few days ago, I came across a quote in a newspaper. I think the quote was from Plato, that ancient Greek philosopher dude from twenty-five hundred years ago, who said, "Writing is the instrument of forgetfulness." Sound familiar?—Two wise individuals from primarily oral cultures. It seems great minds do think alike.

What is an Elder? How do you define one? Some say you can't be one until you are a grandfather, while others say it has to be conferred upon you by the community, not by self-identification. I've heard it said there's an inner glow that you recognize.

Perhaps a more important question is, "Who has the authority to say somebody isn't an Elder?" Let ye who is without wisdom, cast the first doubt.

GETTING TO THE ART OF THE MATTER
(Visiting Your Artistic Nature Preserve)

When Was the Last Time
You Saw a Naked Indian?

Naked Native people; you don't see a lot of them. I'm talking about their representation in television, theatre or print. Even more so, it's Native men who are remarkably absent from baring all to the world. Some time back when I was writing a play titled *alterNATIVES*, my girlfriend at the time was complaining how the media was always flaunting naked or near naked women at every possible chance, but seldom men. And when they did, it was seldom that anything remotely interesting of the man was ever shown but was only hinted at. Unlike women where you couldn't throw a rock without hitting a boob or a feminine behind. It wasn't that my girlfriend wanted to see a lot of naked men, it was more about the disproportional delineation of nudity. It was a political statement, she said … yeah, right.

Respectful of her concerns, I attempted to do my little bit to rectify that little issue in my own little way. My play *alterNATIVES* now begins with a good looking naked young Native man cartwheeling onto the stage from the bedroom.

"Now how's that for an entrance," I thought. Unfortunately, my feminist-supportive intentions were thwarted from an unexpected source—the actors. In the two productions of that play to date, the two lead actors, good looking young men with nothing to be embarrassed about, refused to do the scripted entrance. Instead, they did the cartwheel in their underwear. Both said the play was supposed to be a drama, not a comedy.

I began to think that maybe there was a logical reason for the limited amount of male Aboriginal skin out there. A year or two later, a play was produced in Toronto that called for all six of its actors (three male, three female) to be naked. I had fond recollections of a groundbreaking play from the 1970s that was one of the first in Canada to feature naked people on stage (White people though). This time around, one of the cast members was a Native man. Several weeks into the rehearsal he confessed to the director and the rest of the cast that he couldn't do the nude scenes and offered to pull out of the show. With some encouragement and creative blocking from the cast and director, he stayed in the show while maintaining his modesty. The odd thing about the show was that everyone else at various times, whether separately or together, were exceedingly naked except (noticeably) him. This made him stand out even more … so to speak.

Are Native men more shy than Native women? The only possible contradiction I can think of is Gary Farmer, Cayuga actor and media mogul. An exception to the rule perhaps. This man has appeared naked on stage and screen more times than I have at home. Anyone who's seen *Pow Wow Highway* or *Dead Man* are familiar with his cinematic backside. Add to that the various productions of Tomson Highway's play, *Drylips Oughta Move to Kapuskasing*, where he appears on stage wearing nothing but a frying pan. At the beginning of the play when the lights come up, this is the first image you see of the play and of Mr. Farmer. For good or bad, I'm sure it was many Caucasian theatre patrons' introduction to Native theatre.

The reason this has been on my mind recently is because of a documentary I've been researching for the National Film Board of Canada. The focus is Native erotica; more specifically, the reclaiming of Native sexuality. One of the avenues I want to explore deals with storytelling, since many traditional stories were bawdy and unabashedly sexual in nature. I want to juxtapose this with the way Native people are manifesting their contemporary sexuality today. Someone suggested a photo shoot might capture these elements.

I found a Native photographer who had always wanted to shoot a nude photography session for artistic reasons. He made me a deal. He was a happily married, middle-aged man with a young daughter and didn't feel comfortable going up to beautiful Native women and ask them to pose naked. He wanted me to do it. "Fine," I said, "I'll be the dirty old man." I was nervous about being in this position too, but felt it was integral to making a point in the documentary. That being said, it was the easiest thing I have ever done. I casually mentioned my dilemma to a few people and since then, without even trying to locate models, I have received three or four offers from women interested in participating. One reputable and intelligent volunteer said, "And I'm sure my younger sister would be interested too."

In the play *Drylips Oughta Move to Kapuskasing*, there is a table dance/striptease performed by a woman in the cast. In the movie *Dead Man*, a lovely woman flashes her behind. There are or were two Native porn actresses working in the States. What does this mean in the larger picture? That most Native male actors and performers are afraid to take their clothes off on stage … except Gary Farmer? That Native women have no problem with nudity? To tell you the truth, I wouldn't do the cartwheel in my own play, but then again, I just don't want to embarrass all the other men.

The Inmates are Running the Asylum

I have always been suspicious of political correctness—the imposition of a set of beliefs. Supposedly correct and socially conscious ones (though the water tends to get a bit muddy there) for the betterment of society. Some have even described the more radical forms as the new fascism. You could say they fall under the category of "seemed like a good idea at the time." Put that together with the naive enthusiasm of youth, and strange things can happen in the name of that political correctness.

Such a thing has happened in a popular western university. In this far-off small university existed a theatre department, and in that theatre department existed a theatre professor. One of his responsibilities as part of the B.F.A. faculty theatre committee was to assist in deciding the following year's theatre season which would give the acting students some practical performing experience. As is often the situation in most acting classes, three quarters of the student body were female, necessitating programming of a play which largely consisted of female characters. As this professor often lamented, this meant repeated productions of plays like *Les Belles Soeurs* over the years. It seems few plays cater to such unique female casting situations. With this being said, the professor was understandably reluctant to program yet another production of *Lysistrata*, so he came up with a brilliant idea.

One of his personal favourites was a little play called *The Rez Sisters,* by Tomson Highway. Granted all the characters were Native, but seven of the eight roles were female. Curious as to the reception of the idea, he pitched it to his theatre committee. They were concerned about the political implications of such a production, but were intrigued by the idea and suggested the professor investigate further. He called a leading Native representative in the University to bounce the idea off of him. While this man of Aboriginal descent had some personal concerns about the play and felt it glorified bingo (which he considered to be just another form of on-reserve gambling), he told the professor to go ahead and gave his blessing. Next on the list was Tomson Highway, author of the play. Via email, Tomson gave more than his blessing; he congratulated the professor for daring to go against common practice. Several months earlier, Highway wrote an article for a journal rallying against artistic directors who were reluctant to produce *The Rez Sisters* and *Dry Lips Oughta Move To Kapuskasing* because they were afraid they might not be able to find enough Native actors to fill the roles. Highway believes non-traditional casting can work both ways and White people should have the option of playing Native people. The professor was encouraged.

The only concern Highway expressed was when he was informed that the professor had consulted a Native person at the University, with no background in theatre about the political viability of such a production. Highway responded with something to the effect of, "If you were going to produce *Fiddler On The Roof* would you consult your local Jew?" A good and logical point the professor found hard to defend.

Armed with a thumbs-up from the author, and a secondary thumbs up from his colleague, the professor told his students the wonderful news. He expected some positive response to his calculated and daring programming. Instead, many of the students were dismayed; some were downright uncomfortable with the idea. In the end, several individuals refused to audition for the play and the production was shut down a year before it was scheduled tom because the students did not feel comfortable performing in a non-Native production of *The Rez Sisters*. They asked the Professor if they could do *Les Belles Soeurs* instead.

Now this is the irony of the situation: most Native actors I know, and after fifteen years in Native theatre and film I know a lot, live for the opportunity to play non-Natives. I've lost track of the times a Native friend has excitedly told me, "I've got a part in a play/movie and guess what! I'm not playing an Indian!" Actors want to be hired for their talent, not their ethnicity. But that's a one way street. Most tragic of all, these poor students didn't realize that this was probably the only time in their amateur and professional careers they would get the opportunity to portray a First Nations person. You'd think they would've jumped at the chance, since a university production for educational and training reasons was conceivably their only shot at playing the "skin game," and they turned it down. Turns out they were uncomfortable with culturally appropriating those Aboriginal characters.

No doubt, sometime in their future they will gladly jump at the chance to play a child molester, a Nazi—a whole plethora of unsavoury characters—with less thought than they put into turning down this unique theatrical opportunity. As a Native person, I feel so privileged.

This also puzzled the professor. The professor inquired, "You don't want to appropriate Native women, yet you are comfortable appropriating working class French Canadian women." The answer was, "Yes, but there are no French Canadians in (this western city), and there are lots of Native people here." I've heard the French never stray very far from their poutine and bagels.

In the end, neither *The Rez Sisters* nor *Les Belles Soeurs* were produced. The final result was the programming of The Secret Rapture by English playwright David Hare, which has four female and two male roles. I have not read this particular play but have been assured by reputable sources that there are no Native characters in the play. So they should have had no problems.

Curve Lake Speech

Ahneen. Tansi. Sago. Boozhoo. Welcome to wonderful downtown Curve Lake—my home and inspiration—deep in the heart of the Kawarthas. I always tell people Curve Lake is easy to find. Just go to the centre of the universe and you're there.

1 hope you've all had a hearty meal tonight because as luck would have it, I'm your dessert. Luckily for you, I'm free-range, low fat and all you can eat. I better warn you though, in an hour you'll be hungry for me again.

My name is Drew Hayden Taylor. I was born and raised in this community, grew up just about a hundred yards in that direction. Then again, everything in Curve Lake is about a hundred yards in whatever direction. I used to go swimming at either the park or at Henry's. Baseball was over in that direction. Caught the bus for school over there. Cashed in my pop bottles to buy ice cream down that way. Went fishing at that end. Broke my uncle's window over there. There. Now you know just about everything you need to know about wonderful downtown Curve Lake. Granted it's a fairly small community; the population was only about 800 people when I lived here. But as I've been told many times, size doesn't matter. Does it, ladies?

Ask around and they'll tell you I'm Fritzie's boy—the kid that liked to read a lot. Not the worst reputation you can have in the world, because I've heard a lot worse. Don Kelly, an Ojibway speech writer for Matthew Coon Come and a stand-up comedian in Ottawa (now there's a surreal combination if I've ever heard one), says his Indian name is Runs Like A Girl. I guess nowadays mine would be something like "Writes Like A Post-modernist Aristotelian playwright from Curve Lake." To which most of you might respond, "Oh sure, like that narrows it down."

Many of you know me or my work. For those who don't, let me provide a little background for you. I'm a playwright, a journalist, a filmmaker, a scriptwriter, and, if 1 do say so myself, I make a damn good spaghetti sauce. As a writer, I have spent most of my life communicating. This is what a writer does. This is what I do. We writers manufacture ideas, give birth to stories, reinterpret reality, and practice communication. I think I can safely say it is the dream of every writer to someday … get it right. Or, at the very least, don't get it wrong.

I often refer to myself as a contemporary storyteller. I've heard other writers use the term "word warrior" or "weaver of words." Whatever the description used, it sure beats working for a living. I say that in jest because writing is extremely hard work and awesome in the effort. Trust me, there is no more frightening experience than looking at a blank computer screen with an equally blank imagination as the deadline ticks ever so near. Comes close to the experience of looking at a restless audience before opening night. That computer screen, ticking clock, and expectant faces have sent many a stronger man than me to tears. At least in other professions you can fake it. In accounting, you can fudge the numbers. If you're a Chief, you can blame it on someone else. But you can't hide in front of a blank screen or from an audience. An old axiom says that an audience can smell fear.

At the end of this terrifying yet creative journey there is a sense of accomplishment, of achievement, when what you are struggling to create is done. To look at a poster or a television program or a book and see your name upon it is a sensation which few come close to matching. You forget the pain and insecurity and say, "That wasn't so hard." I'm told childbirth is similar, but without the stretch marks. The great wit and writer Dorothy Parker once said, "I hate writing, but I love having written." Using that childbirth metaphor, "1 hate writing, but I love having written" might explain the popularity of adoption. At least it is to my mother who takes great pleasure in reminding me that I was 11lb 12oz at birth. I wish I knew why women react so bizarrely when I mention that.

But I digress. As I said before, I am a playwright. Theatre is my life. My standard joke is I am married to theatre but have many mistresses. I have been fortunate and privileged to write a number of plays for young audiences, specifically young Native audiences. If the truth be told, I spent my first eighteen years in this place and this is where my creativity and inspiration originates. I never tell this to the Artistic Directors of the non-Native theatre companies who produced my plays. They might not appreciate my cultural nepotism. In the end, it's a small distinction because, as I'm sure you would agree, most children are alike regardless of which side of Cowboys and Indians they may play. My audiences, whether Native or non-Native, usually laugh where they're supposed to. There is a universality in being young that many of us lose as we get older. Since children share a commonality, why shouldn't their entertainment and education? One and one is still two whether you're Cree, Irish or Maori.

I am a true believer in the maxim that says true drama and comedy is universal. That is why many people today still enjoy four hundred year-old Shakespeare plays or twenty-five-hundred-year-old Greek tragedies. The fact that my plays take place in an environment, with an Aboriginal context and Aboriginal characters is irrelevant. They may add a few notes of familiarity for the kids to latch onto, but in the end it's usually the story or the emotion that kids relate to. Adults too, because as the cliché goes, there is no particular Native way to boil an egg. Thus, there is no particular Native way to fall in love, to get angry, or to be lonely … all universal traits of theatre.

That is why my plays have been produced over five dozen times across this country, in the States and in Europe. Think of it this way: of those five dozen productions, maybe one dozen were produced by a Native theatre company. That means my, and practically all, Aboriginal plays are cross-cultural enough for a non-Native mainstream theatre company to spend between $50,000 and a $100,000 on each individual production. Let's face it, they don't do that unless they know they'll pull in a primarily non-Native audience.

As a Native playwright, just by sheer population representation, five-sixths of my audience have probably never been to a reserve or ever had a car with rust spots. The point here is that, Native theatre is incredibly strong and powerful in Canada, laughably more than in the States. It survives on the interest and patronage of a Caucasian theatre-going audience. Native theatre is the darling of the middle class. Believe it or not, they can relate to our stories. So next time you hear a White person say, "I saw *The Rez Sisters* and it was simply wonderful. Wonderful! It made me take up bingo," go ahead and give them a hug.

Conversely, Native kids have many of the same feelings any other child has: they are afraid of monsters, and want to stay up past their bedtime. But, I could be all wrong since I'm not involved in Native education nor do I have kids … at least any that I know of. I've seen sufficient episodes of *7th Heaven* and *Dawson's Creek* to have a vague idea of what's going on.

By a weird quirk of irony I have dabbled extensively in the world of theatre for young audiences. Completely by accident too. I can assure you, I did not wake up one morning with a burning passion within me to write plays for young Native audiences. It just doesn't happen that way. Growing up here and going to school in Lakefield, I always believed theatre was about dead White people who talked funny.

My career in theatre happened because I just wanted to tell a good story. Plays for kids that I have written such as *Girl Who Loved Her Horses, The Boy in the Treehouse* and perhaps my most well known play, *Toronto at Dreamer's Rock*, have all explored the rocky world of Native youth. For *Toronto at Dreamer's Rock*, I won the prestigious Chalmer's Playwriting Award for Best New Play for Young Audiences. Not bad for my very first play. As a bonus, the prize included a cheque for $10,000 which I almost lost in a bar that night, but that's another story. Perhaps later.

Written in 1989, *Toronto at Dreamer's Rock* is my most successful play to date. It is rapidly approaching its one millionth production this fall in Calgary. I refer to that play as my retirement fund because that simple one act play about three sixteen-year-old Odawa boys' search for identity has been produced in practically every part of Canada and in some States. It has been produced in Germany as a radio play and was published there with great success. God bless Germany and their love of all things Aboriginal. *Das is goot. Ya.*

Again it's that concept of universality being presented in a First Nations context. Three Native boys, one from four hundred years in the past, one from today, and one from a hundred years into the future, are dealing with the universal concept of identity. Who are we? Where do we fit in today's multifaceted and culturally diverse world? We've all travelled that dusty road to some degree. Rusty, Keesic and Michael are all Native (whatever that may mean), but they still ask questions about who they are and what it means to be Native. I have a sense that is a struggle you will find in most cultures.

It is always an interesting process when I sit down to write a play for young people. Many people make the mistake of thinking writing for kids is easy, downright simple in fact. People who believe or say this are obviously not people who write for children, for a child's universe is just as complex and detailed as any one of you sitting out there. I acknowledge that I am probably preaching to the converted here, but us solitary writers have to keep that in mind when creating. Granted, there is an amazing amount of a willing suspension of disbelief in children—more so than in adults—but the story still has to be logical and make sense because children learn through familiarity. Which is to say that while a child's imagination may be vast and spectacular, it is confined within the world of reality. Their imagination is liquid, the bottle reality. Without that reality, the imagination would drip away. It would be a mess, might even be lost. At the risk of sounding like I'm repeating myself, that reality has to be real and understandable. Don't for a moment think it's an easy ride. Anything as important as a child's future shouldn't be. As a theatre artist, I know there is no tougher crowd than a room full of fidgety kids. If you don't grab and hold their attention immediately, it is lost permanently and the kids will wish they were off playing video games. Kids can be your best and your worst audience.

Working with young people is a constant, ongoing experiment that should never end. There are side benefits. Many an Elder told me it's their grandchildren that kept them young. Again, this is not my area of expertise; but, I believe you can't do what I do without letting the child within you come out and play. In fact, it sometimes makes things a lot easier. Hell, I still watch *Bugs Bunny*, and at the tender age of forty, can't pass a large tree and wonder if I can make it to the top. The only difference between me and a big kid is that I'd bring a cooler with me.

You can find epiphany in the most unusual places. For instance, I found mine in the far northeast. I remember this one time I found myself in Labrador, the town of Goose Bay/Happy Valley to be specific. I was in the area as part of a larger arts festival the Board Of Education was holding in honour of John Cabot's "discovery" of Newfoundland several years back. Over three dozen artists ranging from illustrators to scientists to poets were there. Our only purpose was to visit the local and regional schools to expand children's minds. It was truly a fabulous idea. Since I was the only Native person invited, I was trotted out to show some cultural sensitivity. I was even sent up to Davis Inlet, several hours flight, for a two hour visit. It was a fascinating experience. In that small city of Goose Bay I learned something new about kids and my own personal interrelation with them. During the week there, all the artists visited several schools during their stay to maximize the potential of their visit. One day alone I visited five classes and pretty much after talking about yourself and what you do for over five hours for five days, you can get pretty bored with yourself. At least I did ... and I'm sure that will be news to my family.

Before I arrived, I had requested that I be limited to the older classes, grade eight and up, for two reasons. The first being I wasn't sure if the younger kids would understand theatre theory. Brechtian and Aristotelean drama might not combine well with Dr. Seuss or Harry Potter. Secondly, I don't really know what makes kids that young tick. I'm a single child of a single parent. Most of my previous interaction with children was limited to elbowing my way through McDonald's to get a decent toy in my McHappy meal.

So there I am, in the wilds of Labrador after being picked up at the airport by one of the coordinators. As I'm being driven to the festival office, this particular gentleman handed me my lecture schedule. At least a third of the twenty or so lectures I was scheduled to give were to kindergarten and grades one and two. Somewhere deep inside my body seized up. I reminded them of my request and they said something to the effect that I had been in such high demand, that they wanted to make the best use of my time there. I'm afraid that didn't help much.

I confessed my uncertainty about the situation and he shrugged it off saying, "Oh just play some theatre games with them. They'll have fun with that." My response was, "Okay, what are theatre games?" He gave me a shocked double take. Famed playwright doesn't know what theatre games are? What do I know about theatre games? I'd heard of them. I am a playwright. I sit in my office alone and make things up. It's kind of hard to play theatre games with my plants. Theatre games! I was screwed.

My first class of ankle biters wasn't until the next morning, so for most of the night I was scared. I tossed and turned, trying to figure out what to do. What did I know about five, six, seven year-olds other than they can swarm like bees when bored or upset. When you're in Labrador in the middle of winter and the Festival has your return plane ticket and you don't get paid until you leave, your options are very limited. It looked like I would have to do this.

Now this may not sound like much of a dilemma to you guys, but please keep in mind, I find lecturing to people who are interested in what I do, trying at the best of times. Talking to young kids was a terrifying concept. You guys do this for a living and get paid huge sums of money I'm sure, but a writer such as myself lives a solitary life. Just me, a computer and whatever imagination I can muster. You'll notice there are no lectures to cookie grabbers mentioned in that sentence. I make it a rule not to associate with people I can't go drinking with, and I understand that's frowned upon at most primary schools.

So there I am, at this primary school early the next day and it's show time (as we say in my business). I am ushered into a room with approximately twenty to twenty-five future citizens of Canada, all sitting at their thigh-high desks. It was a scene straight out of Kindergarten Cop. At least Schwarzenegger had a gun. The kids were all looking at me with curiosity and their restlessness was evident. Like they were thinking, *Who is this guy and why is he here talking to us? Doesn't he know there's playdough to be eaten?* I am introduced and manage to make it to the front of the class to start explaining who I am and what I do in as simple terms as possible. I had written a couple of episodes of two children's series for television titled *The Longhouse Tales* and *Prairie Berry Pie* and a handful of plays by that time, so I figured those writings gave me a crash course in how to relate. That feeling was rapidly evaporating. If anybody ever doubted the existence of a patron saint of public speaking, have doubts no longer, for on that day in the far off northeast, I was blessed. Out of nowhere came a voice and an idea ... or more accurately a salvation ... and I was saved. Yeeaaahhh! Earlier that year, I toyed with an idea of writing a children's story or play about a young girl who had a monster hiding in her closet. She was terrified of it. Only this monster didn't want to be a monster, he wanted to be a dentist; but all the dentist positions were filled, and the only job available at the moment was a monster position.

The problem was the monster didn't know anything about being a monster. He could do a pretty decent root canal, but he didn't know a darned thing about scaring little girls, which was supposed to be his job. He wasn't very effective as a monster. He was actually pretty pathetic. In the story (as much of it as I'd bothered to develop before getting distracted), the little girl ended up feeling sorry for him and decided to teach him how to be a good and effective monster. She learned to not be afraid of monsters and he developed a friend.

Armed with that background, I had a brainstorm. I would ask these kids for help in developing this story. I told them I didn't know much about little girls or monsters either, so I was in a bit of a pickle. If they didn't mind, would they help me write the play. Well, I have never, in my life seen a flood of hands reach for the sky, especially when I asked, "What do you think the monster would look like?" Every student had an opinion and definitely wanted to be heard. I followed up with additional questions. "What does a monster sound like?" "What should the little girl call him?" "What's the little girl's name?" For each question I asked, I got at least two or three responses *per* student. It was wonderful. The kids didn't want me to leave when the class was over.

That was the revelation I received from kids I'd been fearing and dreading. I'd never seen such active, interested, excited faces. This is probably old hat to all of you, but it was a major discovery for me. When you have the attention of a child, they are completely and totally in your universe. They give with their heart and soul. I was amazed. These kids couldn't help quickly enough, so I ended up being as excited as them. It worked in all the other classes too. My adult-elitist butt was saved and I, not just the students, had learned something too.

The point of this little anecdote is to remind myself why I, a forty-year-old man with no children, continue to write plays and television shows for children. It is because every once in a while, I tap into the child within me. I learn something. In one of my adult plays, oddly enough called *Only Drunks and Children Tell the Truth*, I wrote a line about White people trying to tap into their inner child, while Native people try to tap into their inner Elder. I may have to revise that. Each passing day brings me closer to my inner … and outer Elder, and farther from that inner child. I find myself longing for my childhood days.

Here I am in the place I spent most of those days where much of the inspiration for my writings comes from. I proudly say that I went to Mud Lake Indian Day School for grades one and two … about a hundred yards in that direction. After that auspicious beginning, I was bussed to Lakefield from grades three up till grade twelve. At an early age I made a surprising discovery. You could learn as many interesting things on the bus as you do in class. Some things are more important.

I figured I spent approximately 1,300 hours of my life either waiting for that school bus to pick me (and everybody else) up or riding in it. That's almost two straight months of existence around a stupid yellow bus. And to think, I could have spent that time eating playdough.

My very first school is now part of the village day care ... a hundred yards in that direction. The school I went to in Lakefield was torn down about twenty years ago and the intermediate school I went to is now the junior school. When did all this happen? When did I get so old? All the kids I remember playing with, teasing, hiding on, now have kids of their own. I've partied with these kids who have grown up to have kids. I have a cousin who's two days older than me and has been a grandfather for several years now. Maybe I *won't* be climbing any more trees after all. Maybe I have found my inner Elder. As proof, people seem to think I know things now. Silly people.

I find myself lecturing at my third conference on Native childhood education with my only qualification that I was once a Native child. Silly people. The first such conference was in Whistler about five years ago, the second in Saskatoon about three years ago and now one in my own backyard. As much as it frightens me, I think this officially means I am no longer one of us, I am one of them. And so are all of you. In this world of taking sides, we are all "them"—the authority, the establishment, sources of information and allowance. We have grown to be our parents.

To use a cliché, it seems yesterday when I was learning to read. I distinctly remember my mother bringing comic books home for me when I was around four or five. I loved the vivid pictures and bold designs, not to mention all these strange white people in even stranger costumes. That was an added bonus. Now I live in Downtown Toronto, with even stranger white people in even stranger costumes. But I digress. Eventually I had a whole stack of comic books when my mother and I lived in the *Old House* ... about a hundred yards in that direction. We lived there until I was about six, when we moved to a new house across from my grandparents. The house is no longer new, about 35 years old. (Notice that age thing creeping in again?) I have definitely got to stop doing these childhood conferences. They make me too reflective.

Anyway, I remember looking repeatedly through all these comic books at all the exciting images, and thinking, "I can't wait to learn to read so I can figure out what all these people are doing and saying."

Even back then, I knew what wonderful doors reading would open for me. I knew it could take me to places the pictures couldn't. How ironic that several decades later I became a writer. I haven't written a comic book yet; but hope is eternal. Then I will have come full circle. Even my beloved grandparents thought I read way too much and once urged my mother to not let me read so much. They thought it wasn't right. This is probably one of the only things I did, and still do, to openly disobey the words of my grandparents. I'm too old to retrain.

Maybe our uncomfortable relationship with reading has something to do with the fact we all come from a traditionally oral culture. Our belief systems, our stories, our histories were all passed down by word of mouth for generations. Admittedly, I do find it ironic that I and many other Native authors make our living from this thing known as literature or the written word. As a result, we are becoming less and less oral. I am reminded of the words of the novelist James Joyce who wrote, "I am forced to write in a conquerors tongue," as he reflected Britain's control of his native Ireland and their suppression of the Irish language. This can be said of the Native literary world I'm afraid to say. And it has continued onto the next logical stage. What was once an oral culture, currently dabbling with the literary world, has basically become a media universe as television, CDs and computers all run our reserves and the world. In the end, a good story will still be a good story in whatever form it takes. A child is still a child regardless of technology. So our little ones don't play with Tonka toys as much anymore, they surf the net. Instead of listening to stories around the campfire, they watch the Star Wars series. Kraft Dinner has replaced moose meat. When I was a kid, there was one universal factor in the over 600 Aboriginal communities in Canada, that being country music. It seemed nearly everybody from Eel Ground, New Brunswick to Squamish, British Columbia, could quote Hank Williams better than the Bible. Is it still true, I wonder?

Times change and so do we. In a few hundred years, we've gone from wearing buckskin to bell bottoms and now thongs. You know who you are. Deep down inside we all know who we are and what is important. To quote that classic of Native-themed musical nostalgia from Paul Revere and the Raiders, who put it best when they sang, "Though I wear a shirt and tie, I'm still a Redman deep inside." *Indian Reservation* from the late Sixties. If I can quote from that song, boy I really am getting old.

Education for our children is pretty high on the list of things we must pay attention to. Damn near the top I would say. Teaching children everything they need to know about surviving in this technologically dominant world is extremely important. The world is changing faster than we can keep up with it. It's been said you can't teach an old dog new tricks. I don't believe that and I don't think you do. Equally important, as vitally important is teaching their past and the beliefs, language and history of their people. Unless you know where you're coming from, how can you know where you're going? Your responsibility is to teach new dogs—the children—old tricks, or traditions.

Responsibility. It's an interesting word. Just a few weeks ago, I heard a Native politician, of all people, say that being Native, Aboriginal, First Nations, Indigenous or whatever the politically correct term of the day might be, is neither a right nor a privilege, but a responsibility. With obligations and duties. One is to look after our future generations and God bless anybody who dares to take that on in a formal manner. Even if it isn't your official job, it is still your blessing and your honour to hold their hand and help them count the fingers on that hand. Indeed, it is your responsibility to provide the flashlight to show the way through the darkness of the future. Anything to do with children—having them, feeding them, teaching them—is definitely more of a responsibility than a right or privilege. A right or privilege takes the onus off us and puts it onto other people. Responsibility gives us direction. We need to keep that in mind.

Boy, for somebody who says he knows nothing about Native childhood education, I sure can preach a lot, can't I? And weirder, I sound like I almost know what I'm talking about. The beauty of being a writer is you can talk about almost anything you want and people will believe you. You should hear my lecture on nuclear physics. Please take everything I say with a grain of sand … I'm making most of it up anyways. It's the trickster in me; but since the trickster is a symbol of everything we do, right as well as wrong, maybe I'm not making anything up. As we all know, truth is truly stranger than fiction and supposedly will set us free.

So we've come to the end of a long hard day, and it was your turn to be a student today. Hopefully you have learned many fine things which you will take to your communities. 1 will leave tonight knowing the three elements that make up our unique Aboriginal reality have been fully stated today. Mind, body and spirit. Workshops, dinner and me. Now that is indeed a full day. I hope I have not bored you with my humble ramblings, but if so, blame Dixie. She hired me. Like a good Ojibway man, I just do what a woman tells me to.

Before I go, I'd like to leave you with some words of wisdom I found in the Native and non-Native worlds. I believe they encapsulate everything we are here to achieve and everything we believe in. The American author and scientist Benjamin Franklin (you may have heard of him) said over two hundred years ago, "If a man empties his purse into his head, no man can take it from him. An investment in knowledge always pays the best interest." I agree. All the money spent on education is not a waste. Any money cut from education is a loss now and in the future.

Red Cloud, a proud Sioux Chief in the late 19th century, was negotiating for his people with a group of white men. Explaining their position, he said, "I am poor and naked, but I am the chief of the nation. We do not want riches but we do want to train our children right..."

We do not want riches, but we do want to train our children right, was said 130 years ago. Today, very little difference. Truth knows no calendar. Carry on your most excellent work.

This has truly been a pleasure for me and I hope it has been for you too. Thank you for coming to this lovely little spot in the world and for putting up with me. And if anybody asks, you never saw me here. Thank you. *Ch'meegwetch.*

Naked Came the Indian—Aboriginal Erotica in the 21st Century

"Indigenous Erotica is political. More than that, it's stimulating, inspiring, beautiful, sometimes explicit. It's written by Indigenous writers, painted by Indigenous painters, filmed by Indigenous film makers, photographed by Indigenous photographers, sung by Indigenous singers."

—"Erotica, Indigenous Style," Kateri Akiwenzie-Damm

As a child I remember being told Nanabush legends. Legends are often the souls of a culture. Tales of silliness, adventure, and those with moral and philosophical implications. More than once, I distinctly remember hearing stories of a more scatological or bawdy nature. Tales which had that randy trickster from Ojibway mythology chasing women and sometimes men. Through his own insatiable sexual appetites, Nanabush created some unique erotic mischief. Nanabush is often referred to as representing the best in humanity and the worst in humanity. Often, there's no better way of investigating a nation than through their amorous adventures.

In Native communities of this country, the perception and practice of sex has gone through an amazing and, at times, tragic metamorphosis in the five hundred plus years since immigration opened. Keep in mind that there were approximately 53 distinct languages and dialects, each belonging to a unique culture, at point of contact. Through no fault of our own, every one of those diverse people's perception and practice of sexuality have been affected by colonization. Only within the last generation have Native people, mostly artists, been examining Aboriginal sexuality in its past, present and future forms.

Before contact, in what I call "The Before Time," there was a healthy and practical view of sexuality. Due to weather and available resources, many cultures often had large families with generations living under a communal roof. Privacy was a foreign concept so the act of sex was no secret, and was seen as a common occurrence. As a result, childhood awareness of sexuality began at an early age. Sex was not something to be feared or hidden but was viewed as a natural part of life.

As I stated earlier, many traditional legends of the Trickster and other generic legends often had sex as a focus because, like everything in the natural world, it was entertaining, funny, and part of everyday life. Nearly every Native person who could read or has a libido, has either bought, borrowed or stole the book, *Tales From the Smoke House,* written by Herbert T. Schwarz and illustrated by Daphne Odjig. Published in the late 1960s, the book features a collection of erotic legends from various Nations. The initial response was predictable. "Wow, Indians have sex?" This book provided yet another portal from which the general public viewed Native people and their legends. No longer were our stories seen as amusing children's stories. We also had stories of teachings for all ages.

On a more practical front, direct sex education of the younger generation began, often with family members taking charge of the instruction. It was the common practice in the Iroquois culture (and many others) for a close relative, usually an aunt or uncle, to take a young boy or girl aside at the proper time to talk about the proverbial birds and bees and, more importantly, the responsibilities involved in the act of sex. It was not something to be embarrassed about, but something to be responsible with.

Sex and its effect on culture were often in the forefront of a lot of traditional art. Various works of art at Toronto's Royal Ontario Museum, Ottawa's Museum of Civilization and other such collections reflect that freedom and convey a wide selection of erotic expressions. Phallic rattles, passionate Inuit and various other carvings attest to a traditional connection with sexuality.

Oddly enough, with the advent of interest in traditional Inuit art, most of the politically incorrect carvings were forced underground. During the middle part of this century, when the Church held sway in those communities, and art dealers from the south came looking for Inuit art, both groups frowned upon the more explicit carvings. Dealers feared they might limit the resale value in the more conservative south. As a result, many sexually based carvings ended up being sold to miners, construction workers and sailors, with very little reaching the larger galleries. It seemed to the Inuit carvers there was a smaller market for erotic carvings so logically they concentrated on the more lucrative pieces.

This was one of the many influences the Church exerted over Native sexuality and other cultural practices. The meeting of these two divergent ways of life left monumental lasting scars on the Aboriginal psyche that are still in the healing process, centuries after the first incidents. Then into the Native world of open and healthy sexuality, appeared European paternalism and the Church. Priests, missionaries and other foreigners, with different beliefs and contradictory ideas, swept across the land. They came to Aboriginal communities to teach the gospels of God, dictating "Thou shalt not acknowledge thy body." It appeared as though they didn't want Native people to have sex and that they shouldn't talk about sex, let alone enjoy it. Sex wasn't for fun—but for reproduction. Sex became evil. Sex and its many representations went underground.

Perhaps realizing the message their missionaries were preaching had limited results in this immense country, they did the best thing they could. If the mountain won't come to Mohammed, then send Mohammed to the mountain. Like pneumonia following a bad cold, the residential schools came next, with their own skewed belief in the practice of sex. Sexual abuse became rampant and the counteractive philosophy of "Do as I say, not as I do" took on tragic consequences.

The residential school system was an agreement created between the Federal Government and various churches, primarily Catholic and Anglican, to share responsibility for educating the Indigenous people of this land. To save money, huge buildings were built in strategic locations across the country. Thousands of children were huddled together in planes and trains and sent, often for twelve years at a time. Ironically, this deal made in Hell sealed the fate of several generations of Native children, and like a sickness, it was also communicable.

Abuse became cyclical, passed down over generations and resulted in a damaged consciousness and wounded psyches. Several surveys report that in some Native communities, as many as six out of ten Native women have been sexually abused. Perhaps nowhere is this distortion of sexual understanding better illustrated than through the homophobia that grips many of our communities today. Once, Two-Spirited people were given places of privilege, often as Medicine people had. Their contribution to the community was honoured, not reviled.

That being said, new winds are blowing. Like a breath of fresh air, there seems to be a resurgence of interest and pride in redefining what Aboriginal sexuality is. Many argue it never really died, but went underground to places where the dominant society couldn't find and destroy it. For example, Métis writer Maria Campbell has often told me how intrinsically saucy the Cree language is. What is normally an uninteresting sentence in English comes to life in some risqué manner when translated to Cree. I've heard the same said about other Aboriginal tongues.

As with the traditional dances, songs and languages, our sexual belief system refused to die out. Legends kept it alive. As history shows, stories are very hard to kill. The tales were merely waiting for a new generation of people to explore and reclaim their sexuality. In the late 1800s, Louis Riel said, "My people will go to sleep for a hundred years and it will be the artists that will wake them up." Who better than artists to explore the issue and revitalize it. Artists from many different disciplines have heard the cultural alarm clock go off and have eagerly set out to reclaim what is ours.

Several years ago, an art exhibit called *Exposed* toured Regina, Ottawa, and Brantford. The exhibit featured erotic visual and installation art by First Nations artists from across Canada. Rosalie Favel, Norval Morrisseau, Thirza Cuthand and Daphne Odjig, to name a few, were all represented for the first show of this kind. There have been other memorable artistic explorations. Poets like Kateri Akiwenzie-Damm, Marilyn Dumont, and Greg Scofield have pushed the boundaries of erotic writing for years now.

Theatre, one of the best barometers of what's on the mind of the people, has long been critical of the sexual abuse, which plagues our society. It seemed like practically every Native play written over the last fifteen years has made reference to rape, prostitution or some form of sexual exploitation, notably *The Rez Sisters* and *Drylips Oughta Move to Kapuskasing* by Tomson Highway, *fareWel* by Ian Ross, *MoonLodge* by Margo Kane, and *Princess Pocahontas and The Blue Spots* by Monique Mojica, to name a few.

During this transition phase, different philosophies about what is or isn't appropriate tended to bump heads. Consider the concept of "cultural hypocrisy." Somewhere in Saskatoon is a grandmother who prefers to remain nameless but, suffice it to say, she frequents many pow wows and ceremonies. She's a very hip and sexy lady who has been told several times to leave Aboriginal ceremonies because she favours skirts that are knee-length, not the more respectable and required ankle length. She finds this frustrating because many Elders she's talked with had no problem with a bare ankle; it's that middle generation who've been taught to cover up and hide their bodies. Some would argue this is a fall-out from the Christian sexual myopia.

One of the more difficult aspects of researching this issue is trying to determine what can actually be classified as Native erotica in terms of today. Back in "The Before Time" there was no pop culture other than our everyday lives. Today, mainstream industries and the dominant culture have altered what was once easily identified as ours. They have even appropriated aspects of our culture into theirs, while trading back dubious examples of their own sexuality.

In theory, I tend to discount First Nation exotic dancers as legitimate expressions of Aboriginal sexuality. As long as the girl is pretty and shapely, I don't think patrons of these establishments look above the collarbone to see what nationality the dancer is, or are interested in a frank discussion of cultural issues. I could be wrong and if any dancer would like to talk me out of that opinion, I'm willing to listen.

However, male dancers are horses of a different colour. They tend to use themes and characters in their performance such as a cop, a fireman and so on. I've heard it argued that women prefer a narrative, more context, while men don't feel the need for such unnecessary details. I found one Native male dancer in Mississauga, Ontario, who entertained the ladies dressed as an Indian Brave. Granted, that's an admittedly grey area.

I found two porn films with the titles "Poca-ho-ass" and "Geranal-mo." For obvious reasons, I don't think these films are accurate or valid reclamations of our sexuality. Also, somewhere in cyberspace is a web site devoted to nude Native Americans. "We are a beautiful people" reads the promotion. I agree, although that might not be the best venue for arguing the case.

My aim, with all this research, is to produce a documentary on Native erotica for the National Film Board of Canada. There are many interesting issues to be debated on this subject; I've only revealed the proverbial tip of the iceberg. It's a complex and controversial topic. As usual, everyone will have an opinion. What do you think Aboriginal erotica is? What does reclaiming our sexuality involve?

YAY-EES AND YA-AAS

(My Mother's Way of Saying Thingamajigs and Watcha-ma-call-its)

Injins Among Us

And now for something a little different:

Several years ago, I was asked by CAM, the Centre for Aboriginal Media, to write a Public Service Announcement about racism that would air on television. They had purchased some stock footage of Indians attacking a wagon train and urged me to consider using it. I thought about it for a while, banging my head against a wall; pacing back and forth in my house, praying to every Creator I could think of, for inspiration. I don't normally take contracts like this, because for me it's difficult enough to come up with an original idea by itself; so to develop something with strings attached was even more cumbersome. Finally, I had an idea, and this is the result.

It turned out to be one of those projects that was really fun to do (I did not use their footage, though). The more I saw it, the prouder I became of it. One person told me it was one of the smartest things I ever wrote. Because of that compliment, I'm almost impossible to live with now.

INGINS AMONG US

Fade up on a young Aboriginal couple ensconced comfortably in theatre chairs, munching on popcorn and watching a conventional cowboys and Indian movie.

On the screen the couple is watching a movie with an Indian war party and cavalry fighting it out. The woman, who is disgusted by the movie, leans over to the man and whispers.

WOMAN:

Wouldn't it be nice to see one of these things be a little bit accurate?

The man smiles in agreement.
Meanwhile, on the screen the scene changes and a war party of

young warriors ride up to their Chief who is waiting on a bluff, overlooking a slow-moving wagon tram. They wait for him to speak. After surveying the vulnerable settlers, he speaks majestically to his warriors.

CHIEF:

They come, like ants to a dead dog. We will attack and take many scalps.

One inquisitive warrior raises his hand for a question.

WARRIOR #1:

Um … excuse me. But I was talking to my grandfather last night and he doesn't know anything about this scalping thing. It was news to him.

CHIEF:

Well … umm … you see …

WARRIOR #2:

Yeah, what's up with that?

Another warrior shifts uncomfortably on his horse.

WARRIOR #3:

And will someone tell me why I'm on this horse. I'm Mohawk, man, we never had horses. Can somebody get me off this thing? Do they bite? Huh? Do they?

Another warrior interrupts.

WARRIOR #4:

And has anybody else noticed it's freezing out here and we're all sitting around in buckskin loincloths?

WARRIOR #2:

Yeah, what's up with that?

CHIEF:

Many good questions you have …

WARRIOR #4:

Hey man, do you realize that your verbiage is constantly full of syntax errors. Man, what university did you go to?

CHIEF:

Hey, get off my back, I'm not even Native, I'm Italian … but I needed the work.

All the other warriors turn their horses to leave, muttering to themselves.

VARIOUS WARRIORS:

Oh well then …

I wonder if he's related to Columbus …

Help, my horse is moving …

Anybody up for some basketball, I think I saw a hoop on that last covered wagon.

Cut back to the couple on the couch.

WOMAN:

I love happy endings.

The screen fades to white as the billboard comes up to say:
SEE PEOPLE FOR WHO THEY REALLY ARE
Fade To Black.

Mr. M. Email Response

Writing articles and having them published in a variety of newspapers and magazines can lead to some very interesting responses. Of course, the very nature of what I do—publish my opinion on a variety of controversial subject matter—can lead to heated discussions, at times to strong disagreements. This is part of the fun. How boring my job would be if everyone agreed with me.

Every once in a while, I get a unique response to something I've written. A response that requires further exploration. In my third book in the Funny series and in the Assembly of First Nations paper *The Messenger*, I published an article on our recent (well ... within the last ten or fifteen years) Aboriginal obsession with golf. Growing up, no one I knew played the game. Today, everybody I know plays the game. Yet, golf has never appealed to me. I had mentioned in the article that many of the top Native actors in Canada had cut their hair and how both were a symbol of the changing face of our Native people. Someone took exception to my puzzlement at the popularity of golf and responded.

So in all fairness, I am sharing that email, along with my response.

"I have just completed reading your article in the January/February issue of the First Nations Messenger and am quite astonished at your comments. Why wouldn't you ever take up the game of golf? You afraid you might not be able to hit that small white ball? Probably ... because it takes skill to hit it straight. What do you suggest we Natives take up as a sport? Should we go back to bingo or better yet, go back to alcohol? Maybe you are trying to hang on to your alcoholism and bingo but for a Native like myself, no thanks, I'll stick with golf, and hockey, and snowmobiling and exercising and sportsmanship. You know, I don't understand why a newspaper would print idiocy like what is coming from your computer. Yes I know about the incident with the graveyard at Oka that was turned into a golf course and I was very angry about that ... but the golf courses I play on are not on graveyards.

If you want the Aboriginal feminist aspect on this you would be surprised to know that thousands of Native women have also discovered this sport that promotes sportsmanship. Maybe you should try it, Taylor. You know you sound like a person who dislikes sports because of your idiotic comments. By the way, what's wrong with cricket? Don't tell me you can't hit a bigger ball with a flat stick either. I'm very interested to read your email back to me. And … I hope that you do answer your emails … if you don't what's the use of having email if you don't answer. From: A golfer and Native at that.

Mr. M.

p.s. I have short hair too! You know the next page in the paper where your sad article was, had a huge write up on an aboriginal golfer."

I responded:

"Dear Mr. M.,

I read your email (as you can tell I do return my emails) and was quite surprised at the strength of your response. But that is the price of individuality; very few people have the same opinion. I'm glad you have a sport to embrace. I work out at the gym, bike, run, my little bit to combat the sedentary lifestyle writers have. I have a history of diabetes in my family so I am constantly on guard.

I, by no means, meant any disrespect to any golfers who read the article. I believe the technical term for what I wrote is called, and forgive me if the description is a bit complicated, "a joke." I was hired by *The Messenger* to provide (hopefully) humorous observations on Aboriginal life. I have noticed an increased predilection for the game, far more now than in my childhood, and I reported on it with a tongue-in-cheek perspective. The assertions I made in the column have been said to my golfing friends who laughed and agreed that the game takes up far too much of their time and money. But they love the game anyway. I find that funny. I'm sorry if you don't.

Contrary to your accusations, I haven't played bingo since I was a kid (and that was only three times) and to the best of my knowledge

I am not an alcoholic, (but I do admit to having a glass of wine yesterday). I'm sorry if the piece angered you but I'll let you in on a secret ... it wasn't meant to be taken seriously. The style and tone of the article was satiric observation, not objective journalism. People who read my work may not agree with my written comments but will often appreciate the different perspective I occasionally provide. I assure you I am not that phobic about golf; I couldn't care less about the game. As Mark Twain said, "A game of golf is a good walk spoiled."

I appreciate your response, however serious the tone, and hope any offense I may have caused you has been explained.

Drew Hayden Taylor
P.S. If it's any consolation, I too have short hair and always have had."